ADRIFT

To Langhan —
Hope you like
this —

[signature]

CHARLIE SHELDON

IRONTWINE
—PRESS—

Published by Iron Twine Press
www.irontwinepress.com

Cover design, book design and illustrations by Sonja L. Gerard
© 2018 by Iron Twine Press

Back cover photo by Charles Sheldon

Photo of the author at the Royal Museum by Randa Williams

Printed in the United States of America.

ISBN 978-0-9970600-8-9 (pb)

10 9 8 7 6 5 4 3 2

"I loved it! From the first page, *Adrift* swept me away to an adventure. Anchored in the hands of a great storyteller, the characters come alive on the pages making me care about them, the sea, the future and the past. I read every word. Get on board this truly fine novel!"

~ **Jane Kirkpatrick,**
best-selling author of *All She Left Behind*

"This is one compelling novel. Having spent over 40 years working on ships I can honestly say this is very well written mariners tale. It is a definite page-turner."

~ **Captain Hans W. Amador,**
Master Mariner

"From descriptions of handling a tug in heavy weather to launching a lifeboat from a burning ship, Charlie Sheldon's years at sea show through as he recounts life and love, defeat and triumph in this exciting account of a salvage off the west coast of Haida Gwaii. The detailed technical accuracy is equaled by the sensitive descriptions of lives and loves in a small community on Washington's Olympic Peninsula. All around *Adrift* is a fine and gripping tale."

~ **Alan Haig Brown,**
Canadian author and photographer.
Among his books are *Fishing for a Living*, *The Susie A*, and *The Fraser River*

"Grabs hold of you on the first page and won't let go. Sheldon writes about the temperament and power of the sea as well as anyone I've ever read. *Adrift* was a pleasure to read."

~ **John Evison,**
best-selling author of *West of Here* and *Lawn Boy*

"As a Merchant Seaman for 44 years, many of them in the brutal, cold Northwest waters and islands, and also a former shipmate of Charlie Sheldon, I can totally relate to this seeming true to life adventure. I'm just glad it didn't happen to me. A stand alone sequel to *Strong Heart*, the story flows excitingly from character to character. It is a great, fast paced sea story from the first page to the very last."

~ **Richard Sanderson,**
SIU Chief Steward, over 10,000 days at sea

"As a mariner who has spent a bit of time in the Bering Sea, North Pacific Ocean and Northwest Coast of North America I can tell you that Charlie Sheldon captures the essence of the hazards faced by mariners in those waters. His time sailing on large ships provides accuracy that any mariner can envision while reading his works. What I find most engaging is the character development and interaction. Charlie captured not only shipboard human interaction and relationships, but those we witness in everyday life. *Adrift* is a stand alone sequel to *Strong Heart* and a very good read. I recommend reading *Strong Heart* to fully appreciate the back story."

~ **Captain Steven A. Palmer,**
Master M/V *APL Saipan*

Adrift (əˈdrɪft)

— Adj, — adv

1. floating without steering or mooring; drifting
2. without purpose; aimless
3. (*informal*) off course or amiss: *the project went adrift*

"Sometimes even to live is an act of courage."

Seneca

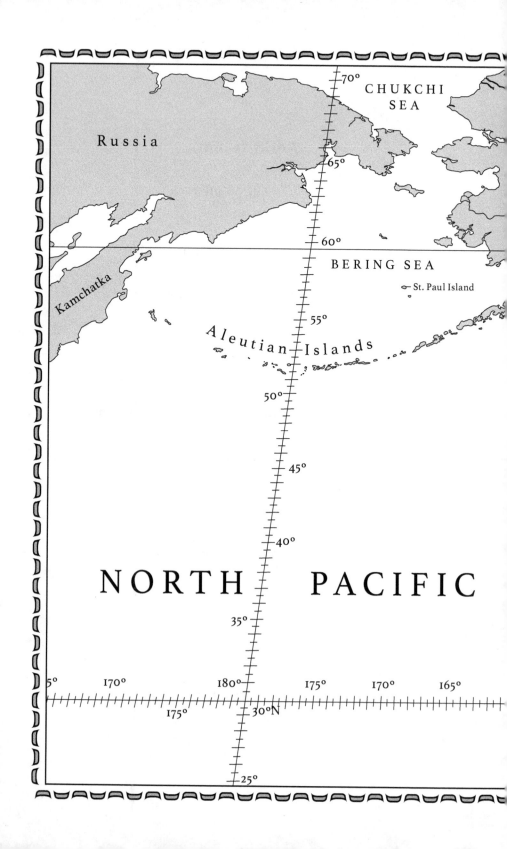

CHUKCHI
SEA

70°

Russia

65°

60°

BERING SEA

Kamchatka

St. Paul Island

55°

A l e u t i a n   Islands

50°

45°

40°

NORTH   PACIFIC

35°

5°   170°   180°   175°   170°   165°

175°   30°N

25°

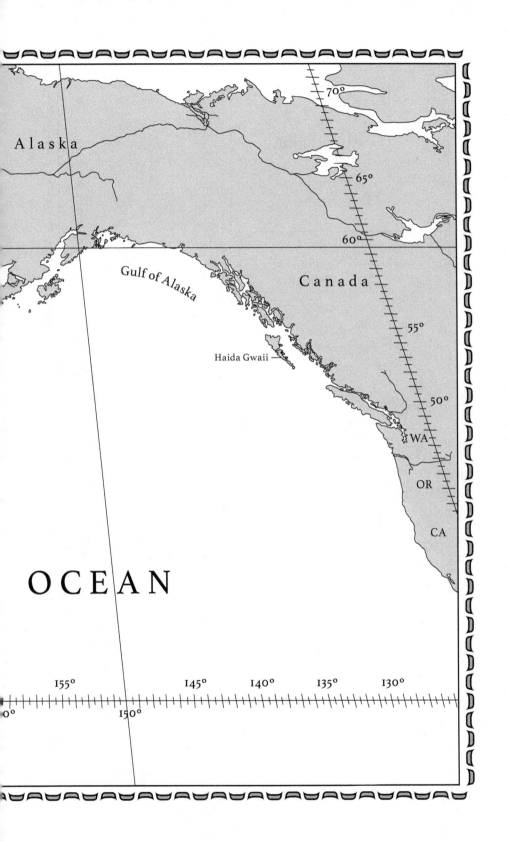

Alaska

70°

65°

60°

Gulf of Alaska

Canada

55°

Haida Gwaii

50°

WA

OR

CA

OCEAN

155°   145°   140°   135°   130°

0°   150°

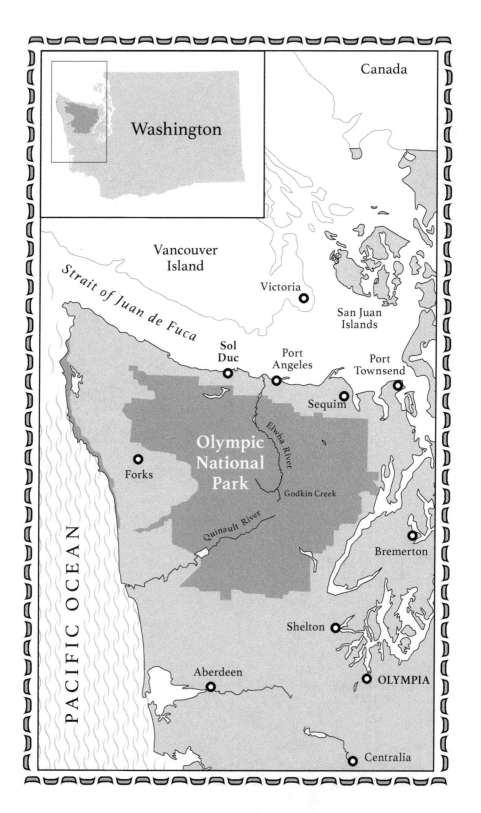

Washington

Canada

Vancouver
Island

Victoria

San Juan
Islands

Strait of Juan de Fuca

Sol
Duc

Port
Angeles

Port
Townsend

Sequim

Olympic
National
Park

Elwha River

Godkin Creek

Forks

Quinault River

Bremerton

PACIFIC OCEAN

Shelton

Aberdeen

OLYMPIA

Centralia

December 5, Sunday

Steve

The general fire alarm in the hallway outside my cabin howled, ringing, chattering. I jerked awake, sat up, grabbed my clothing, and headed for the bridge one deck above, holding the handrails, staggering up the stairs, the ship shuddering into a rising sea, rolling. When the alarm sounded I had been having my nightmare. The nightmare always came when the weather was really rough. This December night in the Gulf of Alaska, the wind blowing 70, 80 miles an hour, it was rough.

Wisps of smoke drifted in the dim wheelhouse, catching my throat. The alarm kept ringing and Anne, my third mate, stood transfixed, her hand hovering over the off switch. Wind whistled over the wheelhouse. Rain rattled against the windows. Water slid across the dark glass, beyond which I saw, faint, dark containers, spray, huge seas rising. The alarm panel against the aft bulkhead was blinking like a Christmas tree. We had an obvious short. The alarm had been tripping since we'd left Petropavlovsk a week earlier, becoming so irritating to those on watch they'd even placed a wooden matchstick beneath the toggle to keep the alarm disabled. Of course when I saw what they'd done, I'd removed it. But this smoke was real.

➤

There was a fire somewhere. Short or not, we had a fire, maybe in the wheelhouse, maybe below.

Now the bilge alarm went off.

I held on as the ship rolled. William was at the helm. I never understood how someone as tall and heavy as William could stand like a cat when the ship rolled. He stood by the wheel, looking ahead, his enormous frame braced, his wandering eye facing me. I peered at the alarm panel and jammed one of the toggles. "Check below, Anne. William, check the panels up here."

Anne ran below to check the cabin decks, one by one. It was the hour before dawn. The black night was thick with blowing rain and snow. I studied the panel. All the lights were flashing. The bilge alarm kept ringing. A huge sea boarded, filling the deck on the starboard side, foaming between the containers. I peered at the bilge display below the alarm panel. High water in number two hold forward. Wasn't that the sensor we'd replaced in Dutch Harbor a trip ago? Hadn't the first engineer checked it just last night? He'd gone forward after dinner, muttering something about the hold and sensors.

Was the smoke thicker?

William opened panels beneath the console and indicators, one by one, checking for smoke and fire. He was on his hands and knees. The phone rang from the engine room.

"Smoke in the port tunnel, captain." Carlton, nearly as old as me, the third engineer, on watch below, was matter-of-fact. "Lots of smoke."

Anne emerged from climbing the stairs, out of breath, shaking her head. All this time the general fire alarm had been sounding, a steady long blast.

"I have her," I said, holding the phone. "Go to your fire station."

Anne and William went below to join the rest of the crew

at the fire station by the engine control center on the main deck. If there was smoke in the wheelhouse where I stood, and smoke in the tunnel along the port side below the main deck, whatever was happening was serious.

"The whole alarm panel fired off up here, Carlton. Seems like a short, but there's smoke up here. How is it in the tunnel?"

"Thick smoke, captain. The chief's gone forward, in his fire suit, tanks, taking a look."

"Let me know what you find, Carlton." I spoke quietly, forcing myself to remain calm. Last thing anyone needed right now was the captain screaming, and I was known to sometimes scream.

Here we were, in terrible weather, the ship miles from land, smoke high and low. We had no idea where the fire was, or what kind of fire we had. The next few minutes were critical.

"You say, in the tunnel?" I asked. "Not in the engine room?"

An engine room fire is a sailor's worst nightmare. Another sea boarded. We'd slowed the ship at dusk the evening before, bringing her down to 42 revolutions - 10 knots - and still she was pounding and shuddering. Fighting a fire in this weather, wherever the fire was, would be almost impossible. Ahead, in the dark, rain drove against the deckhouse. Spray swept in huge swaths across the stacked containers. I could barely see forward.

"In the port tunnel, Steve." Carlton spoke calmly. He was old school. We'd come up nearly together. "Some of the lube oil canisters in the tunnel are on fire. Butch is reporting fire in the purifier room."

The purifier room was in the engine room, forward, next to the tunnel with smoke, port side. What happened to the sensors down there?

"Fire team in place, hoses rigged." Randall, my young first mate and designated fire captain, sounded steady on the phone. I heard other people, speaking beyond Randall, and they sounded steady, too. For a moment, I felt pride: my guys were calm, here. They needed to be calm.

Ahead, through the rain, I saw flames. As the ship plowed forward, the wind whipped the flames higher, rising before the stacked containers. Now, against the flame, I saw thick smoke. How long had the fire been burning up there? How long had we been steaming into the wind, fanning the flames?

I've seen three ship fires in the 40 years I've been sailing, two in the engine room. All were put out in minutes. All were terrifying. Now, on a ship longer in the teeth of her life than I was in the teeth of mine, a ship cobbled together with jury-rigs, old sensors, and air valves needing to be exercised but still often jammed shut, I was facing a fire I knew must have been burning for hours forward without anyone knowing, without any sensors going off.

Randall spoke clearly and loudly:

"Team One in place, captain. The chief went into the tunnel. The tunnel's bad. Our engine room guys cannot get into their suits because they're stored on the port side in the tunnel and the smoke's too bad. The wiper says there's flames coming out the purifier room door. Team One has hoses and will try to get the purifier fire. I have two guys in the starboard tunnel seeing what's hot over there. They haven't reported back yet."

Randall was 34, the same age as my son Jimmie, who I'd been dreaming about when the klaxon went off. Randall was exactly the high performing youngster-in-a-hurry I'd dreamed Jimmie might be, years ago. This trip I'd been hard on Randall because he suffered no lack of self-esteem, and unless he developed some depth he would never be the kind of officer he believed he already was. Randall thought he knew everything. Luckily, in the area of fire control and emergency management, he damned near did know everything. Looking at the flames forward, I knew knowing everything in this case might not be enough.

"Randall, be careful," I said. "I'm turning the ship, to get her running before the wind so the wind won't fan the flames further. Tell your guys to hang on."

I shifted to hand steering, took the wheel, and began turning to starboard. The ship rolled 40 degrees as we came crosswise to the big seas. Water poured over the deck. As we turned, the flames ahead whipped away to starboard. It took time to turn. While we turned my nightmare came before me. I was standing under a pewter sky before 11-year-old Jimmie, almost a quarter century ago, shortly after my happy, gleeful son, who once drank my words like truth, suffered his accident, becoming distant, remote. Jimmie's small frame, bulky in autumn clothing, slouched in the wheelchair next to the playground merry-go-round, head lowered. My perfect little boy, there but lost. I wanted to place an arm around those small shoulders and gather him close, safe, and warm. I wanted to fill him with promise and hope. But I was frozen, unable to move, unable to speak, just there, helpless, as the future roared at us. I struggled to speak, reach for Jimmie, offer him comfort from the dark days ahead, but what comfort could I offer? What comfort had I ever offered?

I turned the ship until the wind was coming at the stern. Big following seas now overtook us. The wind was blowing at least 70 knots. The flames and smoke sped away, forward, cloaking the forward mast and the bow. There was a lot of flame and smoke.

We had to get the purifier room fire out, then the tunnel fire, and then the fire in the hold up forward. Even running before the wind, we couldn't go on deck - we were still taking heavy water over the rail.

Randall's voice shook.

"Starboard tunnel has smoke, too, captain. The port tunnel fire is worse; now the fluids are burning. The fire in the purifier room is spreading and my guys can't work down there more than ten minutes before sucking their tanks dry. It's bad, captain."

None of the engine room crew could help with the fire because their suits and tanks had been stored in the burning tunnel. This left only fire team Number One and already they were using reserve air tanks. Randall took a deep breath. I could hear him despite all the background noise, and I knew what he was going to say even as he spoke.

"I recommend, captain, we abandon the engine room and try the Halon." The engine room space was configured so we could isolate the space, then flood the area with Halon gas. Halon pushes the oxygen out of an enclosed space, which helps force a fire out. This meant everyone had to leave the engine room. "We have guys burned already, captain."

"Do it," I said. If the Halon didn't work, it wouldn't be long before the fire rose into the deckhouse. The seas were enormous. The sky had brightened. The scene before me was grim. Huge rollers marched from behind, overtaking the ship. The wind whipped the wave crests. Flames forward flickered higher and higher. There was now heavy smoke in the wheelhouse, obviously coming up from below, creeping through the decks. The fire would reach the deckhouse in minutes.

Even if the Halon worked in the engine room, fire had spread throughout the ship, and when the generators shut down, as they eventually would, we'd lose water pressure for the hoses. The two lifeboats, and life rafts, were against the deckhouse, port and starboard side, at the mess deck level, two levels above the main deck. We'd be lucky to get clear, if we could get clear in these seas, before smoke and flames overwhelmed us. Christ, this had happened fast. The ship might remain afloat, but there was no place a person could survive while the fire raged.

I radioed the Canadian Coast Guard to report we had a ship fire. I gave them our position. We were 100 miles from the nearest land, southwest of the Queen Charlotte Islands, too far for a helicopter rescue from the mainland, if that were even possible in these conditions. Then I called Bruce, at company headquarters, the Marine Division. I woke him and gave him the bad news: we had a fire and had to abandon ship. I gave our current navigational position.

"Halon discharged, captain. Engine room sealed. Fire on the main deck and in both tunnels." Randall sounded calm.

I sounded the alarm to abandon ship. I was crying, but this time not for Jimmie.

I watched the dials and gauges as the chief began shutting down the main engine but leaving the generators going. The engine revolutions dropped to zero. In minutes, the ship would slew and begin to lose way.

"Get your boat teams to the boats now, Randall. Have people grab their survival suits and bring them, but be fast. Now. Don't even shuck your fire gear."

I coughed as the smoke grew thicker. The ship, wallowing, would track ahead for several minutes under its own momentum. I set the autopilot and left the bridge.

We were 20 souls, including the steward's department, engineers, deckhands, officers, and two Russian cargo minders. We had no time. I grabbed my wallet and personal logbook and struggled into my survival suit. The officers and engineers had cabins on the top decks and they had to climb the stairs to grab their survival suits, and I knew, as I descended, passing Jim, chief engineer, and Fred, second mate, and Anne, the third mate, not everyone would have a chance to get their suits. Those in the heavy fire coveralls and jackets would have to settle for those and pray they didn't end up in the water. Smoke swirled in the stairwell.

The two boat crews gathered in the hallway running across the ship by the mess, each group separated by a few feet. Even in the smoke and the rising heat, we fell into habit from years of drills. The lead officer called attendance, making sure everyone was present, checking that lights on survival suits worked. Then, as the last names were read, the two teams separated, one headed to the starboard side, the other to the port side.

I was assigned to the port side boat along with Fred, the second mate, all the engineers except the chief, Butch the wiper, Jamal the reefer, Harry the junior engineer, Richard the cook and the cook's helper, Raoul. The nine of us shuffled and walked in the smoke out onto the deck below the lifeboat and struggled up the steps onto the small platform where the boat hung. The lifeboat was mounted on two big davits. A small platform led onto the stern of the boat. The lifeboats were designed as closed units, able to self-right once everyone straps in. Fred held open the door and people struggled to the benches running along each side in the interior, where they grabbed canvas belts and strapped in. The big ship rolled and smoke blew into the lifeboat. Below my feet, through the grating of the platform, I saw flames licking around the main deck doorway and I could see, inside through the windows to the mess, the flickering light of fire there, igniting the fats and grease in the traps in the galley.

Everyone boarded without saying a word. Finally, I climbed in and Fred, who was the boat leader during all our drills, closed the door. I strapped into the conning seat aft and started the engine. The engine caught. The conning seat was mounted over the engine, higher than the benches along the sides where the others were strapping in. Above me was a bubble with portholes, sticking out above the covered and curved deck of the boat. Through the streaked plastic portholes I saw rain and smoke.

"Everyone strapped in?" I asked Fred.

I watched him peer forward, but it was still dark in the boat because daylight was only beginning to show. I knew Fred couldn't see the others, but he nodded to me. The ship rolled and a huge sea passed just below us. In one instant, the crest of the wave was only 10 feet below our keel, and the next, we were hanging 40 feet in the air. Looking out through a window in the steering bubble, I could see the burning ship was losing way and beginning her slew to port.

Everyone sat huddled in bulky survival suits or firefighting gear, eyes wide or shut tight. I grabbed the lever to let go the falls so our lifeboat could drop, and pulled. The boat dropped, fast. All my attention was in my ass, waiting for the slam as the next sea struck us as we dropped.

We swung away from the ship when she rolled to port and then we struck the side of the ship when she rolled to starboard. Everyone shouted at the impact. I prayed the fall lines remained free as we spun down toward the water. The lifeboat struck the face of the next sea and pulled forward, still dropping, then rose as the sea gathered, then dropped again, suddenly, as the sea passed.

"Let go," I shouted, "Now."

Mark, the first engineer, pulled the release lever for the forward falls just as Fred pulled the lever for the stern falls.

Released, the boat dropped two feet and struck the water, hard. She was free and away and the engine was running. I steered to port, away from the ship.

Fred watched me like a hawk, trying to read from my eyes and body language how we were doing, because only I could see outside, through the steering bubble.

We were swept within five feet of the rusty, rolling side of the ship, but then the little engine grabbed water and I was able to veer away. We climbed huge seas as I struggled to get around the ship into the lee where the other lifeboat should be. I clawed off to the left as giant waves passed by, until I could head downwind past the bow. The sky was becoming brighter. I started looking for the other lifeboat once we crossed the bow.

"You reach the Coast Guard, Steve?" Fred was preparing the EPIRB-the Emergency Position Indicating Radio Beacon.

"I did. We'll have to head for nearest shore, meet a tow."

"That's the Charlottes."

"I know."

I could see the ship as we crossed the bow. She lay across the wind, billowing smoke. I saw flames leaping from the containers by number two hold. The deckhouse was pouring smoke from the main deck. We had dropped free with literally seconds to spare.

The ship rolled our way and I saw the tops of the stacked containers. The other lifeboat must have dropped because the davits were empty, but the lifeboat was nowhere to be seen. Then a rain shower came down and the ship was gone.

"Inventory, second?"

Forward, two crewmen were already seasick. The lifeboat was like a cork in a stream, rolling and swinging, a motion totally unlike the long slow rolls of a ship. Vomit would gather in the bottom of the lifeboat and begin to stink, but by then we wouldn't notice because by then the boat bilges would contain feces and piss. We had no toilet. Nobody talked about this, but that's why we were supposed to bring hats - for those who refused to shit in their survival suits.

"EPIRB battery good and on. Radio battery seems good and you can try when you want. We just inventoried the water and food aboard this boat before Dutch. We've got four days of rations, but we gotta worry about the cold."

The water was warm out here in December, and the snow wasn't thick, but the air was still nearly freezing and the wind was strong. Within the lifeboat, we were protected from the wind but not the cold. The wiper and the reefer wore fire gear and all but two of the rest were in a survival suit. It would be close. If help could find us, once we got closer to land, we might be all right.

The engine throbbed. The huge seas lifted, then dropped. We were still in the lee of the ship. The seas would get worse as we moved away. I kept trying to spot the other lifeboat.

"Stay strapped in," Fred said. Harry, the junior engineer, was unstrapping his harness.

"I have to pee."

"Then pee where you are."

"Jesus."

Jamal threw up.

Perched on my raised seat above the engine, I stared ahead through the tiny windows. All I could see was water, spray, rain and snow. The seas were at least 30 feet high and came one after the other. I steered before the wind and hoped for the best. If help found us, they'd throw a line and we'd be towed for hours, if not days, behind a small tug or ship to sheltered waters, everyone in the lifeboat cold, seasick, and filthy. At least we'd be alive.

I toggled the small radio and began calling Randall in the other boat. The radio hissed. I kept calling. Our lifeboat corkscrewed and lunged. People lurched against their straps.

"Randall. First. You on? This is Boat One, vessel *Seattle Express*, radio check. Radio check...Radio check."

The radio remained silent.

"Maybe their radio's out," Fred was watching me closely.

"That can happen."

Fred sailed second mate, had for years, but he was a Master like I was and he had sailed as Master when younger, and he knew what I was feeling. I looked at my watch. It was not yet nine in the morning. I was in a lifeboat, my ship burning behind me, half, no, more than half my crew very likely crushed or drowned or burned to death and the rest now sitting on the benches below me, strapped in, relying entirely on my leadership for survival.

You couldn't drill for this, not really, just as you couldn't really drill for combat or how you were going to handle being told by your doctor you had months to live.

It felt good to be able to smile, but none of this was amusing. I knew Butch, Jamal, and the young second engineer, Carl, all felt reassured the old man was sitting there, a smile on his face, assuming I was not concerned, and therefore they should not be concerned. I was plenty concerned, but if they wanted to feel better, more power to them.

The boat already stank.

Louise

Louise woke before dawn, furious. She had known what was going on for weeks. She would dump Larry's ass except Larry owned half the business and they were already on the edge of collapse. If she threw him out now, there'd be nothing left. He slept beside her, oblivious.

It had been a while since the two of them had had anything going in the bedroom. All business, all the time - bills, breakdowns, and infrequent tows for *Warhorse*. But still, she had her pride. She was still a damn good-looking woman, if a little worn at the edges. Look at the way Travis, the cute wire splicer, had looked at her last year before he quit. He had the fire for her. Maybe she'd plan a revenge romp, she and Travis, aboard *Warhorse*, maybe in the wheelhouse.

Louise half smiled. Then she imagined Larry with the puffy bimbo he'd met that Saturday in the casino. Hell, Louise had even been there, seen in an instant what was going to happen. She didn't give a shit, not anymore, but still, it hurt. Now, though, hearing the wind, she smelled money.

She got out of bed and padded over to the big window above the shop, looked out at the harbor. The wind carried sheets of rain across the harbor, stippling the surface. That's what Louise had smelled, money. She always smelled the money, had since she was a girl following her pop around. She had a nose for this, smelling the weather, knowing when the wind might bring them work.

Christ, they needed work. They had been here before, three times in the last six years. Each time the bank bridged them over. What choice did the bank have? No bank wanted a salvage operation way out on the Olympic Peninsula, especially just a worn out house, a tin shack, rusty cranes, and an ancient salvage tug. They had three acres at the head of tiny Sol Duc harbor, next to the marina, looking over at the port dock, the one the mining company had leased. Their land might have been valuable if not so contaminated, but so long as they didn't dig beneath the surface, they could carry on, at least for a while.

When Louise's pop started the operation in the 1960s, they'd been closer than their rival salvage companies to the dangerous waters off British Columbia and Alaska. Even though old *Warhorse*, their tug, was slow, their strategic position along the Strait of Juan de Fuca meant they beat the bigger and faster tugs from Seattle and Vancouver rushing to meet foundering ships. In later years, the other tugs became faster, and fewer ships foundered. Louise and Larry were reduced to making difficult tows, sometimes cross-Pacific, babying *Warhorse* the whole way. Now even that had dried up. They had been barely hanging on. They'd been busy on a contract, scooping debris from the Elwha River as the dams were removed, but the work had ended when the rains began in October. There had been no work since, and now Larry had the gall to start an affair.

"We need a big claim." Louise spoke facing the black window.

"What?" Larry rolled over, half asleep. He'd brought *Warhorse* back from the repair yard down on Lake Union the day before, accompanied by her two brothers, Jeff and

Vince. Jeff served as engineer and Vince as assistant engineer. *Warhorse* was old, built in 1952, but built to last. The Seattle yard had billed them $23,000, money they absolutely didn't have. But Bill from the bank rolled the charges and the loan payments another month, and he'd probably have to keep rolling the charges until the cleanup work started the following spring.

The dark harbor roiled beneath the rain and wind. Larry sat up, running his eyes.

"You smell something, darlin? Money?"

Louise turned around. The room was dark, but Larry's big shoulders stood out against the headboard of the bed. He was still in damn decent shape for someone now 48. Had to be, horsing the heavy gear on that tug. Louise had liked sailing with Larry - she had papers as a first mate - but then Larry's mother had taken ill and needed care. His mother had been the bookkeeper and Louise had to take over. When she wasn't in the office, she spent her time on the road around the Sound hustling work. She had to do a lot of hustling.

Larry still looked good. "Something woke me up." Now wasn't the time to get into a fight, and besides, Louise felt something in her bones. A metal pulley rattled against a post out on their dock. "*Warhorse* all tuned up, Larry?"

"Pushed us out of the yard before they really got into the shaft coupling repair, but I think we're OK. They rebuilt the winches, the big towing bit. New wire, too."

"Yeah, that's where eight of the 23 grand went. Hell."

"We need good wire, Louise, if we hope to snag anything."

Louise was facing Larry. If she wasn't so pissed at him she'd have climbed back into bed.

She heard something on the radio they always left on. "Wait." She turned up the volume. She'd set up the receiver to scan all the distress channels, plus a couple of others companies used to send messages among themselves. Now she had picked up a transmission from Buckhorn headquarters to their big tugs down in Bremerton, west of Seattle. Louise prided herself on knowing what the competition did, and she knew the Buckhorn tugs had just hauled a decommissioned sub into the Bremerton Naval Yard where they were going to cut out the hot reactor core. The tugs were way down in the Sound, at least eight hours from Port Angeles, where they were usually based. "Listen."

The radio was scratchy but clear. "Sector Six. Open contract tow. Cast the sub after she's moored and get going. Yes, abandoned. Fire."

"There's something out there and Buckhorn's sending the big tugs." Louise was grinning.

"Sector Six is out in the Gulf of Alaska, west of the Charlottes." Larry turned on a light and examined a chart in the wall of their bedroom. "They said fire, right?"

"I heard abandoned." Louise looked more closely at the chart. "A long ways, Larry, more than 500 miles. We'll have to pass outside Vancouver Island, it's faster but more exposed."

"It'll be plenty exposed out in Sector Six."

"What do you think is out there?"

"A ship, Louise. Gotta be. Something big, for them to send their tugs. Maybe one of their ships."

"Maybe the *Express*, Larry?"

"Could be." Larry pulled on his pants. "I'll call your brothers, see if we can get their cousins, too. We'll need 10, 12 guys, if we try this. I think you're gonna have to come, too, Louise. I need another mate, someone who can help Nelson handle the tug when I take the gang aboard the ship."

"If you can get on the ship. It's been a while, Larry."

"What else can we do? You going to sit here and wait? Get Jeff's wife to monitor the chatter. Have her find out where the ship was, where the Buckhorn tugs are. You don't need to be here. Right now we got to load up on a ton of food and get going."

"You have fuel? We'll need a lot of fuel."

"She's full. Been full too long, Louise."

"Gonna be a rough trip, Larry."

"*Warhorse* is built for rough trips."

"It's not *Warhorse* I'm thinking about. It's you, my brothers and cousins. Me."

"We'll be careful. I'll make the calls. You and your brothers, get food. Is the Wal-Mart open this early? I'll call the rest of the gang, plus get some others. "

"What? Who you going to get?"

"Dark Cloud's crew. They'll come, their tug's in the yard. They have no work either."

"They're crazy." Louise didn't like Dark Cloud. He'd taken business from *Warhorse* over the years. And what was it with his name, anyway? He was about as Native American as Louise was. But he knew what he was doing on a tug and they needed people who knew what they were doing.

"I'll even call Travis, bring him."

"He's a reporter now, Larry, for the Peninsula News; has been for a year."

"Best kid splicing wire I ever saw, Louise."

Outside, the black night seemed lighter. Rain ran down the windows.

"Are we broke, Louise?" Larry, now dressed, was pulling on his boots.

"Broke as can be."

"Well, then. We want to be there first, we gotta get outa here, fast. Every hour here those big tugs are closer. They're a little faster than *Warhorse*, but not by much."

"What about the Canadian companies?" Louise knew Larry

17

carefully watched what the Canadian salvors were doing.

"They'll be nosing around, but this time of year they're usually off in Asia working over there. Risk we must take. Those Buckhorn tugs worry me. If the *Express* caught fire and was abandoned, she's a Buckhorn ship and they'll want to grab her under their contract to avoid a big claim."

"We'll be in a race, Larry." Louise knew the Buckhorn people. Their tug operation was big and they thought they were the best. The Buckhorn captains looked down their noses at Larry and his crew. To them, *Warhorse* was an ancient, useless scow. They even called Louise "Tugboat Annie" behind her back, which actually made her proud. Over the years, *Warhorse* had brought in more prizes than any other two tugs in the Pacific Northwest, and her engines were still sound, her steel good.

Larry threw clothing into a bag for the tug and called her brothers. Louise made coffee. Ten minutes later Jeff and Vince appeared.

"What is it?" Jeff looked half asleep. He was rubbing his eyes.

"Don't know. Maybe the *Express*. Up off the Charlottes."

"Jesus."

No money in the bank, broke, string nearly run out. If they steamed north 500 miles and missed the ship, or the ship was taken by the Buckhorn tugs, or if the ship sank, *Warhorse* would be out of fuel, out of money, and out of a future. If they somehow got a line on the ship before the Buckhorn tugs, claimed her, and brought her to a dock, they'd have a solid claim.

Louise knew she was going to get seasick once they got into the middle of the Strait. She always got seasick after spending months ashore. This time it had been years. They had to find the ship. Then they had to get aboard - the trickiest part, finding a way to get aboard a derelict vessel, dead in the water, almost certainly without a gangway or rope ladder down the side.

"We sure about this?" Larry asked at the front door. "All we heard was one transmission about the tugs, and the abandonment. If the captain's still aboard her we can't claim her by law."

"Larry, if she is really abandoned and is still afloat when we get there, we'll never have a head start like this again, because those tugs are usually at Port Angeles."

"Gonna be a nasty trip up there, Louise."

"Yes."

Larry donned some oilskins and headed down to the dock after calling the others to make a full crew. Louise got into her van with the brothers to get groceries.

The rain fell. The day was brightening. The wind was blowing, cold.

Travis

Travis, topside after stowing his gear down below, stood quietly aft, in the shadows. *Warhorse* eased from the dock. The sky was still dark. Lights along the shore blurred against the rain-streaked wheelhouse windows. Travis heard the fans, the clicking steering mechanism, the mutter of radios turned down low, the deep throbbing of the engine. The big tug leaned as they made their way through the channel buoys. When Travis had been awakened by the phone, his old boss Larry Hunt, Travis hadn't thought twice. As soon as Larry ended the call Travis had called Judy, his editor, left her a message, telling her he was going with *Warhorse* on a rescue mission. He knew he was being impulsive. He'd always been impulsive.

He'd probably be fired when he got back. He'd made the mistake of dating Judy's younger sister, Dale, on Judy's insistence. Last night he'd met Dale again, and explained to her, again, they were not going to be a couple, in as nice a way as he could. It wasn't nice enough. Larry's call had been a godsend, a chance to get out of town. Now, standing at the back of the wheelhouse as they left the harbor, he felt right at home. It was as if the year hadn't passed, as if he'd never gone ashore to work as a reporter.

Larry was steering. Nelson, usually first mate, adjusted the sea return on the radar. Louise, who sat in the big chair to port, feet on the rail, looked a little gray. Travis was surprised to see her aboard. She'd come ashore before Travis started with the company. The green radar scope glowed. They were passing the Port of Sol Duc dock. A long dark line of black tightly set wooden posts extended in the gloom, each covered with barnacles and seaweed.

Louise hitched herself in the chair and leaned back. The chairs were bolted to the deck. The wheelhouse was one deck above the main weather deck. *Warhorse* was a low, old-style, deep-sea tug, wide and squat, with a mostly open rear deck, huge towing winches. She carried enormous amounts of fuel and was able to pull entire ships with her huge brass wheel below, now throbbing turn by turn as they headed for the Strait. Ahead, below the curving windows overlooking the bow, Travis saw worn brass handrails, nearly white with the years, and beyond them the wide shelf running just beneath the windows. *Warhorse* still carried a traditional compass, but these days they used an electronic charting system and autopilot. The helm was no longer the huge five-foot diameter spoke wheel *Warhorse* carried when new in 1952. Instead, a small dial the size of a dinner plate stood against a console behind which sat or stood the steersman, now Jules, who had taken over from Larry.

Nelson straightened up from adjusting the radar and peered forward. Ahead stood two can buoys and then the Strait of Juan de Fuca, dark in the rain and gloom. Sol Duc lay 40 miles east of the open Pacific Ocean, but even in here, swells rose and fell.

"Is this wise?" said Nelson, half smiling. "Two days, just to get up there."

Travis, back in the gloom, knew Nelson had sailed first and second mate on big ships for years. After a divorce, he moved to Sol Duc and began to serve as relief crew on the tug. He'd taught Travis how to navigate during one long tow across the Pacific. For a few weeks, Travis had dreamed of going to school and becoming a mate.

"Wind's behind us once we get outside. Won't be so bad." Larry sounded definite.

Even in the dark wheelhouse, Travis saw Louise staring at her husband with cold eyes. Larry and Louise always spat like cats while together. She was way too old for Travis, but still, Louise was a good-looking woman. He braced his feet as the tug rose into the first swell passing the buoys.

Larry had been writing in a small notebook. Now he looked up, saw his wife staring, and looked away. He saw Travis in the corner.

"You find your bunk?" he asked.

"Yeah, I did."

Travis had taken the upper bunk in the port cabin just ahead of the engine room and workshop. He was in with Dark Cloud and Billy and Stretch. Dark Cloud had grabbed the lower bunk furthest from the door. He pulled out a small flask, drank, and then lay down, pulling a blanket over his head.

They really weren't all settled. Billy and Stretch were obviously hung over, and Travis had a small headache from drinking the night before. Dark Cloud was on a tear, and probably had been for who knows how many days. The upper bunk on the port side was the only one left when Travis came aboard.

Coming topside after claiming his bunk, Travis passed Gary and Ned frantically stowing all the groceries. Travis saw an enormous amount of food, stacks of bags and boxes.

"Well, we better get done what we can before we leave the

Strait." Larry folded the notebook. "Make sure the new wire's on right, all the fittings and seals good. When was the last time we checked the hydraulics?"

"Jeff already did," Nelson said. "First thing when he got aboard."

"We have enough survival suits?" asked Louise, staring forward.

"A dozen."

"Checked?"

"At the yard. We oughta be OK." Larry stretched. Then he grabbed a sheet of paper from the chart table and wrote names and watches, taping it to the console beside the helm. "We'll do a drill, check all the suits, today at four. Okay?"

Travis scratched his neck. The day was brightening and the rain was heavy. The big rollers in the Strait rose and fell and the tug began to wallow. There was nothing else out on the water. The radar scope was empty.

The water outside was dark gray, streaked with foam. Forward, the bow pushed huge walls of water aside, rising into coming seas. The big tug shuddered.

"Damn." Louise stood from the chair, opened the leeward door, and threw up over the wing. Larry chuckled, though he didn't look too good himself.

"Travis, if you're settled, we're gonna need double ended wire loops. There's wire down in the workshop. You get a couple guys to help you, try to splice 'em up, okay?" The workshop was located just forward of the engine room, below decks. "I mean, Travis, you're the wire man, right?" Larry started to laugh. "Your hands are gonna bleed, though, after a year spent scribbling stories about garden parties and weddings."

Larry had supported Travis's decision to leave the tug to work as a reporter, but now Travis knew Larry had missed him. Larry was no good splicing wire; not many were. For some reason Travis had the gift. He knew his hands were going to suffer.

"Two double loops?"

"Yeah. We have one short one aboard but we need more, made using three-eighths wire, 50 feet between loops. We'll need 'em to pass things to the ship, once we get aboard her."

"What's the plan?" Nelson lit a cigarette.

"Same as ever: a blind grab." Larry leaned back, reviewing his watch list. "We grab her, the boat gets half, and we share up the rest, just like always. Plus, once we reach the dock, some of us will be on the clock watching the ship pending the Coast Guard hearing. Could be weeks of pay."

"Not if we go to Sol Duc," said Nelson. "We'll need another tug to make the channel and that's Buckhorn's dock anyway. They'll watch the ship."

"Still, we get her to the channel there, hand her over, she's our claim, and a big one. Was she in danger? No question. She was burning. Unsafe and dangerous to take her? Absolutely. If we hadn't grabbed her, would she be a total loss? Probably."

"Buckhorn will argue their tugs coulda gotten the ship if we didn't."

"They'll try, but we'll have a good claim."

Louise laughed. "Little ahead of yourself, don't you think, guys? Who knows if we'll be first? We don't even know if the ship's still afloat when we reach her. Lotta wood to cut before we start arguing about the claim, and how to hand the ship off down in Sol Duc." She raised a hand to her mouth, paled, and lurched outside to be seasick again.

"Could be months, waiting for the claim," Jules muttered. He was a short man, his eyes so far apart he looked like a cow.

"Years," Nelson said.

"You guys knew the risks. I didn't shanghai you."

"No, Larry," said Nelson. "What I meant is...what's the plan for taking the ship? Assuming we find her."

"We'll find her."

Travis figured Louise and Larry were out of money and desperate. What the hell was wrong with him? The reporter job was decent, even if the pay sucked. At least he was paid, and besides, he worked in an office and got to watch the occasional beautiful woman come in for an interview or to try to sell them something. Yet here he was, headed out on this wild goose chase.

Louise came back in the wheelhouse, shivering and wiping her jaw. She looked better. Larry ignored her and kept talking.

"To start, we got to get aboard. Maybe the crew threw over a Jacobs's ladder before they abandoned ship, but I doubt it. Probably have to get aboard over the stern; the lowest place." Louise retook her chair. "We'll put five or six people on her, see if we can get one of her engines running for power, hydraulics, the winches. Probably can't, but worth a try. We'll have to run a line from the tug up through the chocks at the bow, back down to the tug, so the tug can winch the big wire aboard the ship. Then we tow her back here."

"Who's gonna go aboard?" Nelson asked.

"Me, Travis, Vince, Dark Cloud, Billy and Stretch. Rest of you guys will stay here. Nelson will be in charge. You help, Louise."

Louise said nothing. Travis knew she'd not been offshore in years.

"We better rig up some nets then, to ferry over survival suits and food and such," said Jules, wiping off the compass forward. "You could be on a dead ship a few days and the food over there will have probably gone bad."

"Just so long as there's water, we'll be OK," Larry said.

"And what about those Buckhorn tugs? If they left from the bottom of the Sound the same time we did, we only have eight hours on them, and in two days of steaming we might lose most of our lead." Nelson was looking out through the windows. "They'll really want her, Larry. If there's two of them they might try to cut off our tow, claim an accident."

"All the more reason to get up there, grab her, and tie in good." Travis looked at his soft, pale hands. He sighed.

"Well, I better get started on the wire, then."

Steve

I sensed something approaching. The lifeboat began to rise and pitch forward. Outside, impossibly far above us, I saw a dark wall of water, curling.

"Hold on," I said, surprised my voice was steady, because this sea was going to eat us alive. The lifeboat began to lift, and then the dark wall of water slammed the covered deck, clapping like thunder. The boat twisted right and began to roll. Everyone shouted as the boat went fully over. Water spewed in thin streams through cracks in the aft cabin door. We were upside down, hanging in our safety harnesses. In the dark, someone groaned, someone else prayed out loud, and water sloshed back and forth across the top of the roof, now underneath us.

"Hold on," I said. "She'll right herself. Just hold on."

I was below the others now, hanging upside down, facing dark green water outside the window. I bent forward and up to pull my head from the water, and then I puked. The engine kept running. The engine was supposed to be able to run 10 minutes when upside down, sucking air from the cabin. I looked up at everyone hanging in their harnesses, upside down, waiting, eyes wide, mouths open.

➤

Then I saw a bird in the boat. Where the hell had the bird come from? Now the bird dropped from the hanging oars down to the water pooled in the roof area. The bird disappeared beneath the water, and then popped back up, shaking itself off and flying up onto the oars again. What kind of bird did that? Water ran and sloshed and things banged. Finally the boat drunkenly swung upright.

The little bird perched on the oars hanging beneath the roof. As the lifeboat rolled, the oars swayed and clanked, but the bird remained steady, as steady as William had been while standing at the helm when Steve had come topside to face the fire. William would know what kind of bird this was; he knew a lot about the woods. But William was aboard the other lifeboat.

"Jesus," said Fred, clutching his shoulder straps. "I hope that doesn't happen too many times."

Seawater sloshed in the bottom, stinking from piss and puke.

"Well, at least now we know she'll right herself," I said. "She comes back up."

All the years I had sailed I had never been in a capsized lifeboat. In fact, I had never been in a lifeboat at all except for drills. Probably nobody here had ever been in a lifeboat away from a ship.

The little bird hopped along the oars and settled on the small ledge in the very bow, under the forward hatch.

"What kind of bird?" asked Butch, a short, skinny kid from somewhere in the Midwest, strapped in next to Fred.

"William could tell us," I said. "He can identify every bird and fish and animal from Alaska to Washington."

"This sucks. The bird's gonna die," said Mark, first engineer. Insolent and sarcastic, he was now the senior engineer aboard the lifeboat, since the chief was in the other boat. I didn't like him. He was lazy and he cut corners.

"Didn't you check those sensors last night?" I asked him. "You were headed there after dinner last night, right?" Mark looked away from me. "Did you check forward or not, Mark?"

"Yeah."

I knew he'd checked nothing. A fire had started up in number two hold and no alarms had sounded. By the time we understood what was happening, it was way too late. If Mark had checked the sensors, we probably would have been warned early enough to put the fire out.

I'd almost certainly lose my license over this. I deserved to lose my license. My ship was gone, probably burned to the keel and sunk. For all I knew, the other lifeboat had sunk too and 11 people were dead. On our boat, we were burned and scared and sick. At least the engine was running, pushing the lifeboat toward land. I knew our emergency beacon should indicate our location to rescue ships once they got close enough.

I radioed the other lifeboat every half hour, but got no response. The radio batteries were slowly dying.

Another huge sea nearly capsized us. The bird hopped back and forth, shaking its feathers dry. Two men, Butch and third engineer Carlton, had neither survival suits nor fire gear on, and they both shivered in the wet and cold. Unless they warmed up, they'd be unconscious with hypothermia by dark.

"We need to rotate the suits every hour," I said, "so nobody is more than an hour without protection."

"This sucks," said Mark. "Those assholes should have grabbed suits. Why should the rest of us suffer because they were too stupid to go get them?"

"Maybe because they didn't have time, Mark. We'll switch every hour. One man out of the straps at a time."

Changing suits would be cold and hazardous. The boat was rolling and the suits were cumbersome to get into or take off, and now they'd be wet and full of puke, piss, and eventually, shit. But once in a suit, even a wet suit, the body warmed. Looking at Butch's blue lips and sunken cheeks, I knew we had to do this.

"You take her, second," I said to Fred. I got down off the steering seat and struggled to remove my suit. Shivering, I knew the hour would be long.

"Stupid, doing this," said Mark. "The suits are different sizes; some won't fit. People's hands will be numb. They won't be able to unzip or zip up."

"Stop whining," I told him. I figured we were making about seven knots in the lifeboat, maybe more, pushed by the wind and currents. We'd left the ship five hours ago. Maybe we'd gone 35 miles. They'd have to send tugs or ships from Prince Rupert, or maybe north Vancouver Island, a long one-day journey. Butch pulled on my survival suit once I tugged it off. It took long minutes to remove my suit, then more for Butch to put it on. I still had on a thin jacket and long undershirt, giving me some protection, but I started shivering right away. Carlton had given his suit to Harry, the junior engineer. Harry was fat, wider than Carlton, and he had trouble getting into the suit. His cold hands were almost useless. The others had to help him. Once Carlton had given up his suit and strapped back into his harness, he pulled some life preservers over his shoulders.

In the storage compartment beneath the bench I found some blankets and passed them around. They were wet, but the one I hung over my shoulders slowly warmed me. Despite the wild gyrations and huge seas, the bird perched motionless in the bow, peering at us, all spirit, small gray form bristling.

Beneath the sodden blanket, I held my arms across my chest and tried not to count minutes. Mark muttered complaints as he scrawled a survival suit rotation list on a damp pad of paper.

Another huge wave slammed into the boat, and again we capsized. Water cascaded over us, the aft door bowed in under the pressure, and I heard someone's head slam against the hull. After endless minutes, the boat again turned upright.

Louise

Louise held on, braced in the top bunk. The tug was rolling. They had come to the entrance of the Strait and now they were striking northwest, parallel to the coast of Vancouver Island. The big swells from the southwest were on their beam, and the boat labored. Water ran across the aft deck when the big seas struck, but all Louise could see from the two small portholes in the cabin was either all sky or all water.

The cabin door slammed open as the tug rolled. Larry's hands appeared on the doorframe, holding on as the tug lay over to starboard. Then, when the tug rolled back, Larry fell into the cabin and fetched up against the top bunk, inches from Louise.

"The Buckhorn tugs are gonna take fuel in Port Angeles. Nelson overhead 'em on the radio. Taking fuel will add a couple hours more."

He pushed away from the bunk and braced against the small chair and table. He looked out the porthole.

"Jesus."

The tug swung over again to starboard.

"How far to Sector Six?" asked Louise. Larry would not look her in the eye.

"Nelson figures at this rate we'll reach the southern edge in

36 hours. We're 360 miles away."

Louise calculated. The Buckhorn tugs would be a good ten or more hours behind them once they took fuel. If they went 13 knots compared to *Warhorse's* 10, in 36 hours they'd pick up 108 miles on *Warhorse*. She knew they better find the ship right away.

"Gonna be close," Larry said. Now he sat on the lower bunk and braced himself as he began to pull off his boots. "Travis hasn't forgotten anything. He's already rigged up two of the choker cables. Hands are a mess, though."

"Shouldn't Jeff go over to the ship? Get the engines running?"

"Vince will be OK. Besides, Dark Cloud may be an asshole but he's one of the best engineers I know, Louise."

"He's on a tear down below. Drunk."

Larry lay on his bunk below Louise. "Yeah, but he's outa booze. In 36 hours he'll be sober and the hangover will be gone."

Louise took a breath and leaned over her edge of the bunk so she could see Larry. He still wouldn't meet her gaze.

"Larry, what are you doing?"

"Hell, Louise. I need to get my sleep."

"What do you see in her, anyway?"

"Who?"

Now Larry looked at her, eyes wide. He did the innocent victim very well.

"Come on, Larry. You and what's her name have been having a thing for three months. Hell, I was there when you met her, remember?"

"What are you talking about?" Now Larry sounded indignant. He did the "What, me?" thing pretty well, too. Louise wanted to kill him.

"Last night? After bringing the tug back? What was the reason you said you had to go out? You didn't even shower before coming to bed. I could smell her, Larry."

"Nothing's going on, Louise. You're way too jealous. Nothing."

" 'Nothing' isn't the same as, 'I'm not sleeping with her.' Are you sleeping with her, Larry?"

"No, Louise, I am not. And, come to think of it, what's between you and Travis anyway? I see how he looks at you."

"Not the same as me looking at him, Larry."

Larry turned over. He'd only met her eyes when protesting his innocence.

Louise braced as the tug rolled. Larry began to snore. She'd been on the boat long enough so she could finally look out the portholes without feeling sick. The seas were enormous, at least 25 feet high. Some were breaking at the top. The tug would shudder at the crest of the parallel sea, roll drunkenly, and then drive ahead as the sea passed. How the hell were they going to board an abandoned ship in these seas?

When they boarded, whoever was at the wheel of the tug had to be a master at boat handling, a genius. Once she had been the best there was, but years ago. Nelson would have to be at the wheel; he was skilled and had lots of recent experience. She could provide support. This was going to be hairy. Dangerous.

This whole thing was hairy and dangerous.

The sonofabitch snored like an innocent baby.

Where was a sharp knife?

Travis

Travis worked the goop into his hands, rubbing his fingers together, trying to remove the grease. The wire had been stiff, containing tiny points catching his skin. A few times he'd slipped when using the heavy fid, a tool for separating the braids of the cable. His hands were raw from all the nicks and cuts. But the chokers were done, three of them, lashed along the steel workbench. Six splices to make loops, each loop three feet wide, then collared with a steel band.

Stretch, standing beside him, lit a cigarette while waiting for his turn. Both men weaved and balanced as the tug drove ahead across the seas. Even over the sound of the engine, Travis heard water rushing across the deck topside.

"Your hands got right torn up," Stretch said. He had to speak loudly over all the noise. "Been a while, ain't it?"

"Yeah."

Travis was washing off the goop using the little sink. The water coming from the faucet was warm and discolored.

Larry appeared from forward, rubbing his eyes. Travis wondered what the time was. It seemed he'd had lunch hours ago.

"Drill, 10 minutes, at change of watch. Bring your survival suit."

➤

Travis finished drying his hands. They were still oozing blood. He opened his fingers and went forward toward the crew cabins. Four small cabins lay on each side of the tug, a passage between them. His cabin was just forward of the door to the workroom. Dark Cloud sat on a bunk, rubbing his hands through his hair. At his feet lay a survival suit. He grunted, rose, grabbed his suit, and headed topside.

Travis grabbed his own suit, which had been lying on his bunk, and followed.

The galley and mess were on the main deck, beneath the pilothouse. The booths were full, everyone gathered together with bulky survival suits at their feet or in their laps. Travis realized Louise must be up in the pilothouse, steering. Dark Cloud was pale, his eyes red. There was fresh coffee and Travis smelled something good from the kitchen.

"All right. Everyone get in their suit," said Larry.

Someone groaned. Travis removed his shoes, took his suit to the aft door, sat on the floor, and pulled the suit from its bag. The suit was bulky, the legs too long, the big, loose, heavy feet awkward. Once he got his legs into the bottom of the suit, he struggled to his feet and worked the upper half of the suit up his back. He got his arms in the sleeves, somehow worked into the shoulders, and pulled the hood over his head. He was sweating by the time the suit was fully on and zipped. He checked the little light attached near the hood. The light flashed. He blew on the whistle.

People were sprawled everywhere, hitching their way into their suits, groaning and cursing. The tug rolled and people slid. It took half an hour for all of them to get into the suits, then out again, then roll the suits and pack them back in the bags. Billy and Dark Cloud switched suits because Billy's was too large and Dark Cloud's too small.

The daylight was failing. Lights along the walkway outside

along the rail glowed in the gathering dusk. The huge seas kept passing. By now Travis was used to the motion. They all were.

"We're a third of the way up the Vancouver Island coast," said Larry, "We're 300 miles from Sector Six. We oughta be there by daylight day after tomorrow." He finished zipping his suit in its bag.

Gary emerged from the galley holding a tray of fresh hot cross buns, so hot the glaze was sticky. The tug rolled left, then right. Everyone sat in the booths with coffee or soda, devouring the buns.

"Where's the Buckhorn tugs, Larry?" asked Jeff.

He'd come up from the engine room for the drill while Vince remained below, still on watch. Jeff's glasses were on a cord around his neck. They swung as the tug rolled.

Larry finished a bun and licked his fingers. "Gonna be touch and go. Way I figure, the *Express* is in the southern end of Sector Six. We should arrive before dawn and have a few hours of daylight before those Buckhorn guys come up on us. If we aren't aboard her by then, a line attached, they'll grab her."

"Is the *Express* transmitting her position?" asked Travis. These days, all ships broadcast their position for electronic navigation.

"She's broadcasting, or was a half hour ago. Off and on, she would appear. Right down in the southeast corner of Sector Six."

"So anyone could be after her. The Canadians."

"I checked," said Larry, "And I keep checking. Their big rigs are across the Pacific. Only other outfit's in Victoria and they were over in Vancouver being worked on. Just like those Buckhorn tugs were down in Bremerton towing an old sub. We were lucky. Now, all we got to do, pray old *Warhorse* keeps running, so she can get us there. She running okay, Jeff?"

"Built to last, Larry."

"What the hell happened to your hands?" Dark Cloud was staring at Travis' hands.

"Wire." Travis turned his hands over. They looked terrible, worse than they felt.

Dark Cloud raised his head, looked around. "Where are we? Where am I?"

Travis realized Dark Cloud had been half conscious since waking up, probably still drunk. Now he was waking up.

Stretch began to laugh.

Dark Cloud looked out the porthole. It was now fully dark outside. The lights along the walkway caught the heaving shoulder of a passing sea.

"Jesus, we're at sea."

Everyone laughed.

"You were on a tear, Cloud. Don't you remember?" Ned was laughing.

"Jesus."

"Start drinking coffee, Cloud." Larry started toward the stairs to the wheelhouse. "Drink a lot. You're coming with us to the ship when we get to her."

Dark Cloud blinked. Stretch winked at Travis, whose hands were starting to throb.

"I'm going back to sleep," said Dark Cloud, grabbing his bagged suit. Everyone who was off watch headed for their bunks to grab sleep while they could.

Travis continued to sit at the booth. He was using his bagged survival suit as a brace and pillow. He grabbed himself more coffee. In the galley, Ned was cooking up a storm, singing. The tug hummed, clanked, rattled and sloshed. Inside the mess, all was warm and almost cheery. Someone had washed the floor, and the linoleum was clean and shiny.

Stretch sat down across the table from Travis, diet soda in hand.

"You crazy, Travis?"

"Whaddya mean?"

"I mean, you don't have to be here, do you? Aren't you the local reporter?"

Travis sighed. "The money sucks, Stretch. I have to be at work every day and whenever anything happens, which isn't often, I get the call. Best stories I've done for coverage, paperwise, are the accidents, but those are usually late at night and sometimes they're pretty bad. You know, like, arriving to do a story and seeing this years' homecoming queen crushed against a guardrail out on Route 101 past Lake Crescent?"

"Yeah, Travis." Stretch looked around the mess. "But this? You're crazy, man."

"Stretch, my mother's having trouble living alone. I try to help put. She really needs nursing care, and a reporter's pay and the paper's lousy medical coverage won't cover things. Maybe this will, we get this ship."

Stretch shook his head. "Like, about the time you get your social security, Travis."

Louise appeared from topside. She looked tired.

"Your hands look terrible, Travis."

She was right. They looked terrible. He knew he should put them in a hydrogen peroxide wash.

Stretch stared at Louise. He wasn't staring at her face.

"Stretch, put it back in your pants," Louise said, disgusted. "You ever think of anything else?"

"Why?"

Stretch yawned.

"Wash those hands, Travis, or you're gonna suffer," said Louise.

"Yes, mother."

Travis winked at Louise, trying to make her smile. She was a damn good-looking woman. What the hell was Larry doing to get her so pissed off at him?

"I ain't your mother, Travis."

"You could be," said Stretch.

"Shut the hell up, Stretch." Louise leaned close to Stretch, grabbed his ear, and twisted. "Why not, you go to your bunk, get some sleep? Larry's gonna take you and Travis onto the ship and you better be sharp. It's gonna be dangerous." She twisted her hand and Stretch yelped. "Understand? You go get some sleep too, Travis."

Travis found some hydrogen peroxide. He washed his hands in the galley sink with the peroxide. His hands stung. Then he followed Stretch back to their cabin. The tug was laboring. The night ahead would be long and he would be on watch in four hours.

Damn. He'd almost been able to flirt with Louise. Hadn't he seen a smile on her face, when he'd teased her? Stretch was right, though. If Louise had started young enough, she probably could be Travis's mother.

Pete

After dropping Sam off at his ex-wife Joyce's, Pete felt nothing but gloom. Raining, and cold, Christmas less than three weeks away, he still hadn't done his Christmas shopping. The truck lurched. After the fall rains, the long drive held deep, corrugated ruts. No cars could make it all the way, except at the height of the summer, during the dry season. Each jostle sent a flash of agony through his left knee.

After Pete had been shot the previous summer, he had started to see his father across the room in his father's old, tattered chair, black eyes shining, delivering testimony. "Self pity is a curse," he'd say. The visions began in the hospital, when the doctor came into Pete's room and proudly told him he was not going to lose his leg. Now his father visited not as the twisted, broken man in the wheelchair he'd been at the end but as the hot, clear spirit Pete remembered from earlier days. The vision, which had initially haunted him, now strengthened Pete's determination to recover from the accident.

Once home, groceries put away, Pete did his physical therapy. He slowly lowered himself onto a bench and strapped a small weight to his left ankle. The goal was to fully extend

➤

his leg. The bullet had gone through his lower knee, clipped off the top half of his shinbone, and nicked the kneecap.

The pain was astounding, the grinding and creaking unbelievable.

Pete lowered his chin to his chest, gripped the handholds on the bench, and lifted his foot while straightening his knee. He began to wail. Physical therapy was hardest after Sam's visits, because Pete didn't do the exercises when Sam was here, and this caused the knee to stiffen.

When the phone rang, Pete, reaching, nearly fell from the bench. Cell phones didn't work up here, so he used the landline, an older set with caller ID against a pale yellow screen. The screen read, "Buckhorn Corp." Pete knew the caller must be Roger.

"Gonna have to start ya tomorrow," Roger said.

Roger was head of security, and he hadn't been happy, Pete knew, when Buckhorn placed Pete on Roger's crew. Pete wasn't happy either, because he considered Roger a major asshole. Roger had been there when Pete was shot, way the hell back in the park, when Roger had picked a fight with the big walleyed Indian, his beautiful daughter, that pesky kid and her grandfather, and the Russian. Even now, the memory of the day he'd been shot washed over Pete: the little girl fighting, then the guns, a shot, and then he's on the ground in unspeakable pain, holding his knee, watching the blood surge between his fingers.

Roger had been injured too, and wore a sling for three weeks, but now it was as if his boss had never been hurt.

"You there, Pete?"

"Yeah. Wasn't I was starting a week from Monday?"

Pete was going to be Buckhorn's security officer down on the Sol Duc pier. The company had leased the dock and the open land behind, but ships weren't due for months, not until after Buckhorn got the mining permit. Pete dreaded the work, but a paycheck was a paycheck and he could heal and stay near Sam. At least down on the pier, in a tiny shack, he wouldn't have to listen to Roger's flat voice, or hang out among Roger's goons or the blow-dried hotshots Buckhorn flew in every now and then to survey their domain.

"Need you now, Pete. There'll be a ship tied up down there in a few days. The *Seattle Express* caught fire and was abandoned, this morning. She's Buckhorn's ship. Buckhorn's sending their tugs out to get her. They'll bring her back and tie her to the dock here. This pier's about the closest dock to where the ship is now, just off the Charlottes up north."

Pete knew nothing about ships but he knew geography. He knew the Queen Charlotte Islands were 500 miles to the north, a long way to tow a ship in December. If they put a tow on the ship in the next two days and could tow her at five knots, they'd be in the Strait of Juan de Fuca by next Sunday, a week. They could probably reach the dock the next day, Monday.

"We'll need security when they bring her in," said Roger. "Coast Guard will want her tied up and nobody aboard until the hearing. So we'll need to man the gate and have 24-hour-a-day security. You get the day shift, Pete." Pete said nothing. He wondered if the shack had some kind of heater. "The Coast Guard's making the Port set up fences, full security around the site. They want Homeland Security-compliance for the ships next spring."

Pete had planned on making a model steamboat for Sam. Even with his knee, he could still sit and bend over a table. Now the model would have to wait.

On the cluttered desk in the corner, Pete saw copies of the application forms he'd filled out the previous August, seeking work as a ranger in Olympic National Park. A park ranger position called for someone with Pete's skills, who could pack loads into the backcountry, conduct research, and help on search and rescue. But, before he'd had time to send in the forms, he'd been shot in the knee. He doubted the Park Service had interest in a ranger hardly able to walk, let alone hike. Still, he'd sent in the application. He'd heard nothing for months.

His dad's whisper echoed. Self-pity is a curse.

"Be down at the offices tomorrow morning. We'll get you signed in, then set up down there. Your knee better?"

Pete knew Roger didn't give a damn about his knee.

"It's better. I'll be there."

Pete started a fire in the wood stove. Rain thundered on the roof. Pete went back to the bench and finished his exercises. He was barely able to straighten his injured leg until fully extended.

The phone rang again. Pete's heart leapt, as always, seeing "M. Williams" on the screen. He didn't know why she called him; he worked for the enemy, after all. Apparently she felt some responsibility for what had happened to him, or maybe she was grateful for what he'd done out there. Pete's lunge at Raymond had prevented him from shooting anyone else up there. Raymond had been aching to shoot someone. Pete hadn't thought a second before leaping for the gun.

Before that trip into the back woods, before the arrival of the Russian, Sergei, Pete had hoped he and Myra might get together. But Pete worked for Buckhorn, and Myra despised the company, plus he'd been on the wrong side up in the valley when he was shot. He was surprised she spoke to him at all.

She was a tall, beautiful woman, with raven hair and a strong face. He still had a crush on her, but now he'd never let her know. The Russian was back in Russia but Pete knew where Myra's heart lay, and it wasn't with Pete.

"How's the knee?" asked Myra. She'd taken to calling him

every other week or so to check up on his injury.

"Better."

"No it's not. I saw you and Sam in town this morning, putting something in your truck. You looked in pain."

"I didn't say I didn't hurt, Myra."

"When will you start work?"

Pete knew Myra understood better than most what it meant for Pete to be unable to cruise the forest. Myra was a scientist, too. She knew Pete needed work to stay near Sam, and Buckhorn was the only choice he had.

"I just got off the phone with Roger. I'm starting tomorrow," Pete said, and then he went cold. Didn't William, Myra's father, work on a Buckhorn ship? Maybe the ship Roger said had burned and been abandoned off the Queen Charlotte Islands?

"Pete?"

Pete closed his eyes.

"Myra, Roger just told me the reason I'm working is they're sending tugs to tow the *Seattle Express* down to the pier from up off the Charlottes. He said the ship caught fire this morning and the crew abandoned her. Doesn't your dad work on a Buckhorn ship?"

"Oh my God. Did the lifeboats get away? Do you know anything else?"

"I think somewhere off the Charlottes, Myra. You'll need to call the Coast Guard or the owner, Buckhorn. I'm sorry, Myra."

"They're well-trained, Pete. My dad knows what he's doing. They'll be all right." Myra sounded like she was trying to convince herself.

"Call the Coast Guard, Myra. They should know something. I'm so sorry."

How would it feel, to hear a close family member had gone missing at sea? For all Pete knew, the crew had been lost fighting the fire, except Roger said the ship was abandoned, meaning they must have gotten word the crew had taken to the lifeboats. But this was December, a terrible month up there, and the waters off the Charlottes were among the worst in the world.

A gust of wind slammed the side of the A-frame and the whole structure shuddered. Smoke backed down the chimney and puffed into the room. Pete lurched to his feet and opened the front door. The wind rushing over the house sucked the air from the room. The smoke dissipated. Before him, Pete saw rain, trees swaying, the wind howling, water sluicing down the driveway.

Behind him were a stove, warmth, and dryness. He closed the door.

He tried to imagine being in a lifeboat, heaved and tossed among the seas, the men and women inside wet and cold, possibly burned from the fire on the ship. Among them was Myra's father, William, a towering Haida. William had an erratic wandering eye and a huge chin. William's laugh filled a room.

Until the crew was found, dead or alive, Pete knew Myra's life would be marked by a gnawing dread and a secret hope things would end well, a hope so frail just thinking the thought might render rescue impossible.

That's what he'd think. That's what he was thinking.

William

William hung on, hands gripping the shoulder straps. The engine clattered, dinging, rap-rap-rap. Water sloshed at his feet, at everyone' feet. They'd capsized twice, gone fully over, once right after leaving the ship and then once more two hours later. Each time, water burst through the aft door seal, spraying, while they all hung upside down, strapped in, eyes wide, some shouting, some praying, waiting, waiting, for the boat to come upright. Now there was piss, puke, water and debris sloshing around the bilges. The seas were huge. They'd been motoring northeast with the wind and waves, the only way they could go, blind.

It had still been nearly dark when they'd dropped from the ship and now it was dark again. William was strapped in next to the chief engineer, just forward of the engine and steering bubble. Randall, first mate, conned the lifeboat, strapped in over the engine, trying to peer out. William's hands were raw from the blisters he'd taken fighting the fire. His fire suit was soaked. Everyone was cold, shivering. William wondered whether the other lifeboat, with the captain, had been able to get away. He doubted it. They had barely gotten away themselves.

The engine stopped. Smoke rose. The lifeboat slewed.

➤

"Hell." Jim, the chief, began to loosen his straps to check the engine. William saw a sheen of oil on the water in the bottom of the boat. A sea lifted the boat high, then passed. One of the Russian cargo handlers threw up.

"Where are we?" Jim asked. Anne, the third mate, strapped in forward and across from William, had to shout over the sound of the wind, the breaking seas.

"Just before the captain sent us below to fire stations I had checked our position. We were 105 miles from the south end of the Charlottes. We've been steaming northeast with this wind 11 hours. We must be pretty close to the Charlottes by now."

William had been cold, but now he felt a deep chill. The Charlottes were Haida Gwaii, where he had been born, where he had lived as a boy. The western coast stretched 150 miles, north to south, exposed to all the Pacific had to offer, a roadless, trackless wilderness of mountains, rocks, cliffs, strong currents, death. They were now fully adrift, engine dead, pushed by the wind, every second blown closer to a deadly coast, helpless.

Jim looked up at Randall and then at the engine. He shook his head.

William pictured that trackless coast somewhere ahead, stark, cold, waiting.

Help us, grandmother.

Myra

made tea. My hands were shaking. I'd called Pete because I owed him. We all did. He'd saved us, in August, from being shot, up there, and I had promised myself to stay in touch, check on his injury, never expecting to hear bad news from him about my own family. My father sailed on the *Seattle Express*.

I called Buckhorn and got the "office is closed" message. Outside, the sky was already dark, the rain heavy. I called the Coast Guard's Port Angeles Station. Word usually travelled pretty fast when something like a ship fire happened, even way up north, but the guy on duty either didn't know or wouldn't say.

I kept trying to picture dad, out on the open sea. If they abandoned ship, he must be in one of the ship's enclosed, self-righting lifeboats. They were safe, weren't they? But early December, for God's sake—the worst possible time to be out there.

How was I going to wait this out? I don't wait very well. At work I've forced myself to sit calmly, patiently, listening to whatever idiocy those Buckhorn people spout. Despite what I tell people about the erbium mine being a bad deal,

➤

Buckhorn's winning. The same folks who wanted the casino now wanted Buckhorn's ridiculous heritage center and business deal—anything to create jobs. A few of the tribal elders, the real traditionalists, wanted nothing to do with Buckhorn's offer. They could see the snake oil but they were in the minority. And the tribe really needed jobs.

My dad's not young; we'll be celebrating his 60th birthday in a year. I'm not saying he's getting old, but I think he's passed some kind of threshold, because he seems more at peace and is finally accepting he no longer has the strength and stamina of an 18-year-old. But now, to be adrift in a lifeboat?

What happened out there? Did the crew perish in the fire? Did everyone drown when the lifeboats fell into the sea? Dad told terrible stories about accidents occurring even when they tested the lifeboats at the dock.

If what Pete had said was true, they'd abandoned the ship 12 hours ago. Way north, not far from Haida Gwaii, dad's homeland. What a terrible way to return home.

I better call my mother; she'll want to know. No, I should call Tom and Sarah first, tell them.

I walked over to the corner of my living room. The five-foot-long carved staff dad's grandmother presented to him when I was 12 and we'd gone up to Haida Gwaii to see her rested against the wall. Carved by my dad's great-great-great grandfather and well over 150 years old, the wood was dark. On top was an elegant carved raven, peering at a fish below. Dad gave me the staff when I'd graduated from Northwest Indian College up on the Lummi Reservation, saying the staff would bring me luck. Now he needed luck, not me.

I held the old wood, felt the coolness, the smoothness. I raised the staff and pictured my great-grandmother. I asked her spirit to watch over my dad.

The phone rang.

"Myra, it's Tom. Did you hear?"

Tom Olsen is dad's oldest friend, maybe his only true friend. Tom had become a grandfather in an instant when Sarah, barely 13 at the time, showed up at his door the previous spring. Now he was trying to raise her, and he needed advice more often than he admitted. My dad had fished with Tom for years. Tom then went to work for the Port of Sol Duc.

"Tom, I heard. I just now called Pete to see how he was and he'd just got off the phone with Roger, from Buckhorn, who told him the *Express* caught fire and was abandoned this morning."

"Myra, I talked to someone down in Sector Command, in Seattle. They've been monitoring the traffic up there. I don't know much, but I think it's as encouraging as it can be."

"What's encouraging about abandoning ship in December?"

"They got the call before daylight. The captain said a fire broke out and had gone into the engine room. They had to abandon ship before the fire overwhelmed the deckhouse and boat stations. They abandoned ship before dawn and it appears from a flight the Canadian Coast Guard did this morning that both lifeboats got away. The Canadian Coast Guard from North Vancouver Island is headed north and should link with the lifeboats tomorrow morning or the next day. You okay?"

"I'm worried." I held the shaft, resting my cheek against the wood.

"You eaten dinner?"

"About to start cooking. Why?"

"We're coming over. We have too much elk stew. I thought Sarah would be sick of elk by now, but no. We've got loads."

"If you can get down your driveway in this weather and then up mine, I'd love the company."

Standing vigil, I think they call this, when people gather amidst a crisis, loved ones missing or ill, and wait together.

Tom and Sarah were coming to stand vigil.

I sat down at the computer and sent Sergei a message. He deserved to know. Sergei had known my dad for years through my dad's friendship with Sergei's father, in Russia.

The living room was scattered with reports, notebooks, email print-outs, all stacked here and there according to whichever issue I was following. My offices down at the Tribal Center were famous for their clutter, and I knew if I wasn't careful my house would soon look the same. I washed some dishes. Put away clothes. Thought about Pete.

The previous summer, we'd spent time together and we liked each other, but he had a difficult family life, a small boy, and a seemingly crazy and now rich ex-wife. And he worked for Buckhorn, on the survey crew Roger ran. Pete and I found ourselves on opposite sides, but I still respected and liked him. He'd saved us, up there in the woods, and paid a terrible price. He lost his mobility, which destroyed his dream of becoming a park ranger. I tried to stay in touch without showing pity, but honestly, I'd called him out of pity.

Tom and Sarah arrived 20 minutes later. Tom was carrying a foil-covered casserole dish. Sarah followed, wearing a slicker and holding a notebook.

"He told me I have to do my homework if I wanted to come over here," Sarah said, glaring at Tom.

"Instead of what, Sarah? Sitting with Tom and me wringing your hands?"

"I guess." Sarah took off her slicker and sat on one of my two couches. Tom placed the casserole dish on the kitchen counter. I ladled some of the stew into a bowl. I was hungry.

Rain pummeled the roof.

"How's school, Sarah?"

"School sucks."

Tom rolled his eyes, shook his head, mouthed at me, "She's

doing okay."

"School totally sucks?"

"Cross country's okay. Then at least I'm not in a classroom."

I ate the stew. Tom sat opposite me, next to Sarah.

"You hear from Sergei?" Tom asked.

"He's in the middle of some kind of debate with a bunch of other Russians about glacial epochs."

"So you're in touch with him?" Tom smiled as he said this. He seemed to think Sergei and I were made for each other. What the heck did he know? Sergei was impossible. He had been impossible in August, he was worse at the conference, and then he went back to Russia. I realized, again, all men were impossible. Sarah was grinning, watching me. I felt myself redden. Then Sarah looked serious.

"William will be all right, Myra." Sarah spoke just like an adult sometimes. "He's big and tough and he's been on the water his whole life, and he's as light on his big feet as a cat. If they got off the ship all right, you'll be hearing from him soon."

I wasn't as certain as Sarah, and I could tell Tom wasn't either. Sarah looked at me with her thin, intent face. Where did this girl find her force? Wherever my dad was, he'd be helped by Sarah's will for his survival. Sarah loved my dad almost as much as I did, as much as Tom did.

"Wherever he is, Myra, we'll go up and find him," Sarah said. "Just like you and Tom-Tom and your dad found me."

Sarah had gone hiking with us the summer before, only to disappear for eight days. The helicopters and rangers searching for her gave up after seven days, but the three of us stayed. We were probably the only people in Sarah's life who had stuck around for her, and she made us her family. We'd helped her then, and now she was here to help me.

"If anyone can find him, Sarah, it's you." I was happy she'd come over with her grandfather. "I'm afraid, though, all we can do is wait."

Sarah nodded.

People began to arrive. My mother. She came inside and hugged me. Behind her, I saw two more people getting out of her car, her sister and her sister's son. I was always amazed how fast news traveled. I'd just heard about the ship, and already people from the tribe were arriving, some bringing food, some just to sit, all willing to wait with me. Another car lurched to a stop behind my mother's, and Eldon, the chair of the fish commission, emerged. Rose, his ancient mother, accompanied him. We had food and tea. People's coats were piled in the corner, the damp clothing smelling rich and thick, and the food was good. The rain beat down. Rose, 87, still spry, sat by my side and held my hand.

"William is strong, and his spirit is strong."

The wind blew around the house. I could not imagine where my dad was, whether he was alive or dead, warm or cold, whether he was still on a burning ship or in a lifeboat on the open sea.

Everyone sat and nobody spoke. We listened to the rain and the coughing and snuffling, people tapping their feet on the floor, Rose humming. Sarah had her notebook open and began drawing, while Tom cleaned the kitchen.

We sat vigil.

December 6, Monday

Pete

In the morning, Pete drove down to the Buckhorn offices in Sol Duc. The company had leased an entire building on the main street. An architect's model in the reception area showed a section of Sol Duc harbor. There was the pier the company had leased, the proposed warehouse for the mining operation, and, on the road leading down to the pier, one additional building. This would house the Human Dispersal Center, where, according to the company, scientists would gather and analyze evidence of ancient human migration patterns in the area.

Pete's knee throbbed. Roger came down the stairs, wearing a quilt jacket, followed by Raymond, his neck covered in a dark tattoo.

"I'll drive," Roger said. Raymond sucked a toothpick and rubbed his arm.

"What are you looking at," he said to Pete.

"Nothing." Pete had been watching Raymond grimace as he rubbed his arm. The previous summer, just after Pete had been shot by this asshole, Raymond has been injured, too.

Pete worked his way into the back of the four-door pick-up,

►

pushing aside a vest, assorted tools, a clipboard and pencils.

The roads had wet, icy spots. The pier lay on the west side of the small harbor. To the east, across the water, were more docks and an old fish cannery. The little port marina at the head of the harbor, between the pier and the cannery, seemed half-empty. A small creek ran alongside the road, filled with brown water.

"*Warhorse* left yesterday morning," said Roger.

Raymond took the toothpick from his mouth.

"So?"

"*Warhorse* is a salvage tug, Raymond. I bet she's after the *Express*."

Raymond began to laugh. The truck bounced over the pavement.

"Piece of shit, *Warhorse*. Louise – Tugboat Annie – she is nuts, keeping *Warhorse* going. The tug's old, Roger. She was here working when I was a kid."

The road leveled out. They drove through a bent and twisted hanging gate. Heavy, scarred timbers lined the lip of the pier, bristling with huge splinters. Enormous bollards, 100 feet apart, lined the pier. Rusty and streaked, some leaned and tilted. The land behind the pier held an empty warehouse in the middle of a wasteland of standing water, heaps of gravel and pavement, piles of twisted wire, a truck chassis leaning over, and three abandoned construction trailers, all open to the weather.

A five-foot-square shack perched on a trailer near the entrance gate. Another truck was parked next to the shack, and as they approached Pete watched the rest of Roger's security crew pile out of the cab.

Pete worked his way gingerly out of the back seat of the pickup while the others watched him. He heard water lapping against the pier. He stepped over a flapping half-burned piece of paper stuck to the pavement. Roger clapped together a pair of work gloves.

"Let's get this little building off the trailer and mounted on blocks. There are hydraulic jacks in my truck. We'll put the shack by the gate. An electrician's coming later to hook up the shack with phone, lights, power." Roger looked at Pete. "Can you drive?"

"I can drive."

Roger helped remove the hydraulic jacks from the bed of the pickup and then handed Pete the keys and some money.

"Pete, go back to town and get a bunch of coffees, those insulated cups. Some doughnuts too. Bring us back some fuel, eh?"

Pete, already cold, felt relief. He'd rather drive off in the warm truck than stand around in the cold wind watching the others work. He'd be sitting in the small shack soon enough, freezing his ass off. Maybe when they ran power they'd set things up so he could bring along a space heater. He'd need to stay warm.

Pete drove Roger's truck out the gate and over cracked pavement up the long hill to town. This had been a busy place when the timber company had a raw log yard here, but the log yard had closed years ago.

The one combined coffee shop and bakery in Sol Duc stood on the corner opposite the big building Buckhorn had rented for their operations. Pete wondered why they hadn't bought coffee before driving the half-mile down to the pier.

"Hey, Pete."

Mariana gave him a big smile from behind the counter. She seemed to always be working there whenever Pete came in. He suspected she must have a boyfriend over in Port Angeles.

"Mariana, you look way too cheerful this early in the morning."

She laughed.

"Early? I've been here since six. Feel like I've worked a full day already. What'll you have?"

"Large coffees - a dozen - and two dozen doughnuts. Make them a mix of plain, glazed, and chocolate-covered."

Pete watched Mariana pour the coffees. Aside from three Sol Duc tribal fishermen in the corner, the shop was empty. He wondered why someone like Mariana, a woman almost as beautiful as Myra, would fetch up in pokey little Sol Duc anyway. She probably had the usual tale of woe: came here as a new bride only to be abandoned by her husband. Pete wanted to laugh. He'd come up here as a new husband and his wife Joyce had abandoned him. Now Joyce was living with her new husband, Brad Withington, a lawyer, in a big house Sam called "the casbah."

"How's your leg?" asked Mariana, standing at the counter before two rigid cardboard trays, each holding six cups of coffee.

Everyone in town knew he'd been shot by Raymond, who still faced criminal charges for the shooting.

"Getting better."

Mariana went over and started loading doughnuts into a bag. The door swung open behind Pete. He felt a rush of cold air.

"Dad."

Sam stood beside him, wearing a small bill cap. This was a Monday, a school day.

"Hey, Sam. What are you doing here?"

"He's home sick."

Wincing, Pete turned and saw Joyce by the door, standing next to her new husband. Even dressed casually, Brad Withington looked like a male catalogue model.

"He's here at the coffee shop, not home sick," said Pete, winking at Sam.

"What kind of doughnuts do you have?" asked Joyce, pushing by Pete and speaking to Mariana.

"He really should be home," Brad said to Pete. "He has an infection on his ankle."

"Yes," said Joyce, turning around to look at Pete. "Didn't you notice his ankle when you had him yesterday?"

"No, Joyce. He was fine when he had his bath."

"How would you know, you never watch him."

"That was four years ago, Joyce."

Joyce bore down to make her point. For a moment, Pete almost felt sorry for Brad. "It's not safe for Sam up there, Pete. He gets an ankle infection from playing in the woods and the mud. No wonder he gets sick. Way off in the middle of nowhere, and your driveway is a joke. You've been up there two summers now and done nothing to fix things. Nothing. I think you need to have your time with him somewhere else, down here. Even at our house."

Pete had heard this before.

Sam was staring hard at the doughnuts behind the counter, and Pete saw Mariana sneak a small, plain doughnut hole to Sam.

"Plus, you're still hurt," Joyce continued. "You can hardly walk, and barely drive. If anything happened up there you'd be unable to get help. It's not safe and I have made up my mind. Sam cannot go up there. Certainly not until after the winter weather."

"Not your call, Joyce. We have joint custody."

"I'm his mother. You'll have to find a judge to change my position."

"As if I have money to take you to court. Jesus."

"I like being up there." Sam said. "I'm safer up there than the casbah."

"Sam's right," Pete said. "There are no decks at my place, 20

59

feet over the slope of the hill, like where you live."

"I've made my decision," said Joyce.

His mouth set, Sam looked at his feet while Withington glanced around the store, anywhere but where Pete, Joyce, and Sam stood.

"Just through the winter," Joyce went on, relenting. She tried to fold Sam to her side but Sam stayed away. "Your father needs to heal, honey."

"He's healing fine. Yesterday we went all the way to the back pond in the rainstorm. Saw elk."

"See? Where's your judgment, Pete? If you'd fallen, been hurt, Sam would be lost back there, alone. Christ!"

"Life isn't totally safe, Joyce," Pete said, gesturing at his bad leg. "Things happen. You can't protect them from everything bad, Joyce. And you shouldn't."

"You can try."

Joyce grabbed Sam and left, followed by Brad. As they got in their car, Pete saw Joyce speaking to her new husband, shaking her head. Mariana leaned forward on the counter.

"Let me pour you fresh coffee, Pete."

"Sorry you had to see that," he said.

"When Rick and I broke up there were no kids, thank God."

"Why stay here, then?"

"I like it here - rain, miserable black ice and all. I like the, I don't know, the spirit of this place."

"Not much social life here."

"There could be." Mariana held his gaze. Pete felt himself blushing. "Here's your fresh coffee, all hot again."

Pete took a tray and hobbled to his truck. Mariana helped him, carrying the other tray and the bag of doughnuts. The wind was blowing and Pete could see patches of blue in the sky overhead.

"Thanks, Mariana."

As he drove back to the pier, Pete pounded the steering wheel twice, hard. Christ. Joyce telling him where he could and couldn't visit with his son. An unrequited crush on Myra. Helpless to follow up on a friendly invitation from Mariana. And finally, the promise of shivering his life away in a tiny plywood guard shack. This holiday season was promising to be the worst ever.

Myra

"Thanks for stopping by last night," I called to Eldon as he passed my door on the way to his office. He's chairman of the fish commission, a council member, and my ally fighting the mining venture Buckhorn is proposing.

"Your dad, and me, we go back a long way," Eldon said, large frame and big belly filling the doorway. Years ago he had been famous around here as a runner, specializing in the mile.

"Your mother Rose is a strong spirit," I told him.

Eldon grinned. How did he lose those two front teeth, I wondered for about the hundredth time.

"Yes. I had to drag her out of your place last night, didn't I? We stayed too long."

Tom and Sarah had left at 10 the night before, my mom and her family at 11, but Rose, Eldon and the others had stayed until after midnight. I'd finally told them all to go home. When everyone had left, I cleaned up, washed the glasses, cups, and empty bowls from the rapidly eaten stew. I swept the floor. Then I'd gone to bed. I'd actually been able to sleep. Standing vigil serves a purpose.

Now in the cold light of a Monday, no longer raining but cold, I was at work. Where else would I be? If I stayed home, I would think, and brood, and wonder. The council meeting

➤

was in a week and the mining issue was up for discussion, along with the Human Dispersal Center Buckhorn wanted to build. The council had put off a decision for months, but it could no longer be tabled.

As I worked, people who had heard about the ship fire stopped by to reassure me my dad would be all right. Still, I was deeply afraid. The fire had started before sunrise the previous day, and now, a day later, nobody knew what had happened to the crew once they abandoned ship. Meanwhile, I was stuck in the office reviewing reports commissioned by Buckhorn and the local tribes.

Marcie stopped by to ask for my summary of the Buckhorn reports. Even though she'd hired me, I didn't like her much. A non-native, she was an over-the-top zealot about cultural restoration, and I felt this impaired her judgment.

"I need your summary," she said. "I wanted those reports over the weekend."

I wondered if she'd heard about my dad. Did she care? Why would she? She's married to one of the Paget brothers, and my dad and the Paget clan never got along.

I couldn't stop thinking about my father. One March, during school break, he took me out to the coast. I was nine, and he'd just stopped drinking. I remember a long drive in his rickety old truck out to La Push. We spent the night at the house of one of his friends, just the two of us, telling stories and laughing. The next morning, we began a back-packing trip, taking a trail north along the wild shore, the wind howling the entire way.

We spent two weeks out there. I was afraid, most of the time, afraid of the surf, afraid the tide would carry us away, afraid he would judge me, and afraid he would take me home.

After we set up camp for the night, he'd have me gather wood, for hours. We'd eat dinner, prepared from supplies he carried in his enormous pack: canned hash and beef stew.

He'd heat the meal in a big pot he'd hang over the fire. A tall man, he had nimble hands and graceful feet, and I was in awe of his skills as an outdoorsman - the way he built the fire and how he arranged the tripod to hang the cook pot. He taught me, in his way, never saying much, showing me, and then letting me try. Hands numb from the cold, I fumbled and failed, but he was never impatient. He would watch me try again and again, ignoring my complaints, but nodding his head in encouragement.

"Myra? Hello?"

Marcie stared at me. I shook my head.

"Sorry, Marcie."

"What's the matter? I need the report summary. The council needs their information packets tomorrow."

Marcie obviously had no idea about the ship. Never make excuses, my dad always said.

"By noontime today," I told her. "All right?"

My desk was piled high with reports, papers, books, and notes. On top were the Buckhorn reports, fancy expensive studies by one of the best environmental firms in the Pacific Northwest. The reports described how the impact of the mining operation would be minimal, almost harmless.

Beneath Buckhorn's report was one prepared by another firm for our neighboring Elwha Tribe. Their report was not nearly so positive about the proposed mining operation. Buckhorn was fighting back, trying to sell the Sol Duc Tribe on the project by promising money and jobs. Eldon reappeared at my door.

"Coffee?"

He held two big mugs. I waved him into my office. He came in and closed the door.

Eldon had been my surrogate father when I was little and my dad was either drinking or away fishing, or both. I knew

Eldon was sweet on my mom, who would have nothing to do with him, and he'd always paid attention to me, even when I was a snarling, nasty, little brat.

"How are you? Rose is worried about you."

I saw Eldon every day now. The fish commission and the tribal cultural office I worked for shared the same double-wide trailer. He handed me one of the coffees.

"Buckhorn's report is well done," I said. "They argue their project will have minimum impact on the environment, and they back it up. Now I think my own report, and the one prepared for the Elwha tribe, make a strong argument against the project. Mining will almost surely destroy important cultural sites and artifacts. But Buckhorn claims all the impacts are temporary, and they're promising all kinds of economic benefits. I think they're going to get a permit, despite our objections."

"If they're allowed to mine up the Elwha River, next thing you know they'll be in the headwaters of the Sol Duc, our river," he said.

"They mine in the Elwha watershed and this works, they'll be everywhere. They claim the stuff they're mining makes coal burn clean. How can we argue against clean coal?"

Eldon drank his coffee, a worried expression on his face. He looked sad.

"The other tribes - Suquamish, Jamestown, Elwha - they have the casinos, a string of them from Seattle all the way to here," he said. "By the time tourists reach Sol Duc, they're casinoed out. So, no casino for us. Fishing isn't good, never has been, really, and now we're thrown out of the port dock by Buckhorn, so our fleet has nowhere to tie up. Logging's died. The timber mills have died. What else is there? Marcie and the Paget clan and the chair of the council want to partner with Buckhorn, and the rest of the council will follow."

I was lucky. I had a job. A few people in town worked for the tribe, a few others at the stores here or in Port Angeles, but the real work, the solid work, the fishing and logging, seemed gone. If Buckhorn built their facility beside the port pier as they promised, there would be jobs, lots of them.

Why did this feel like death, then?

"The only thing which can stop this, Myra, is proving their mining site has archeological significance."

"I'm sure it does, Eldon."

"Being sure isn't enough, Myra. You need evidence."

We had no evidence. Outside, a shaft of sunlight glanced off the railing to the walkway between the doublewides.

"Damn, almost 11. I need to finish this summary, Eldon."

"You going to submit your report?"

"I am. But I'm pretty sure Marcie will discount my points, arguing because I was born here, I'm biased."

"How can being born here make you biased? Doesn't being born here make you more knowledgeable?"

Eldon held my eye.

"I'm worried about my father, Eldon. He's out there somewhere, on the sea. I'm thinking about him, not Marcie."

"Have faith, Myra. His spirit is strong."

A gust of wind shook the trailer.

Louise

"Sea's laying down."

Louise had been able to bring her coffee all the way up to the bridge without spilling any. The sky was still half-dark, even after eight in the morning. Nelson sat in the chair and Stretch manned the wheel. Billy followed Louise on to the bridge, ready to spell Stretch.

"Yeah," said Nelson. "The wind started to die when we came on this morning."

They were two-thirds the way up the west coast of Vancouver Island, well offshore. The seas were huge but not breaking. The tug rode them well.

"Any chatter?" asked Louise.

"The tugs behind us are pissed," said Nelson. "Heard 'em about 6 a.m., talking on channel 16 before they went to sideband. I think they're eight hours behind us."

"They've made some distance, then."

"Of course." Nelson eased out of the chair. He stretched and Louise heard his back crack. "They're faster than we are. And they're coming as hard as they can."

"Any word from the lifeboats?"

➤

"None."

"A lot better out there this morning," Louise said. She looked out at low clouds and snow flurries, but saw patches of blue sky overhead. "Where's the ship?"

Nelson adjusted the ECDIS to a much wider range. On the screen, Louise saw the symbol for a ship, far ahead of them. "Just sitting there, isn't she?"

"Yeah, but still afloat," said Nelson.

Off to the northeast, near the Charlottes, Louise saw the symbol of another ship.

"Canadian Coast Guard, right?"

"Yeah, the search ship. No reports."

To the south of *Warhorse*, Louise could see the symbols for Buckhorn's tugs, heading their way.

Nelson adjusted the ECDIS again to 20-mile range. Now the ocean appeared empty, except for *Warhorse* in the middle.

When Stretch grabbed his coat to head below, he scowled at Louise. His ear was still red from where she'd grabbed him. Nelson picked up his coffee cup and followed Stretch. Billy took over the wheel.

If this weather cleared, the wind would back to the northwest and then they'd be heading right into it. This would slow them down. The Buckhorn tugs would be slowed, too, but not as much. This was going to be very, very close. They still had over 200 miles to go.

Louise saw ice on the tops of the rails forward.

Jeff appeared. His forearms were black with grease.

"How's she running, Jeff?"

"Oh, she runs. Always runs."

"What are those engines, 60 years old?" she asked.

Jeff grabbed some paper towels and began wiping his arms.

"Older. Cleveland Diesels, big ones. Made back when we knew how to make great machinery built to last. Those diesels have lasted."

"What's Ned made for breakfast?"

"Whaddya think, Louise? What's he ever make?"

"When I was out here, he made scrambled eggs and pancakes."

"Yep." Jeff stood next to Louise, bracing against the forward rail. Spray flew back against the windows as the bow surged over the seas. The spray kept the windows clean but there was ice growing at the corners. To the east, Louise saw a glow. Dawn was breaking.

Jeff stretched, then faced Louise.

"Pop woulda told us we're crazy, doing this."

"I know. I can hear him." Louise finished her coffee.

"Are we crazy?"

"We're desperate, Jeff. This old tug will get there. We get a line on the *Express*, we'll be able to get her to the dock, easy. Hell, we hauled a ship maybe as big as the *Express* back to L.A. from Manila, didn't we?"

Jeff started to laugh.

"Jesus. Three times, we lost that tow." Jeff paused. "Hey, Louise, what's with you and Larry?"

"What?"

"Come on, Louise. You look at him like you're going to kill him."

Louise stared ahead. She could feel Jeff's gaze. He read people better than anyone she'd ever known.

"I'm not gonna kill him, Jeff."

"What, then?"

"He's messing around with some dumpy cupcake he met at the casino a few months ago. You were there that night."

"You mean Suzette?" he said. "Banker Bill's girlfriend? She's an attorney."

"She's a waitress at the casino, Jeff."

"Wait. Strawberry blonde? A little thick? Wide mouth?"

Louise remembered the wide mouth. "Whatever, Jeff. He's got something going there, I know it."

"Come on, Louise. You've always been way too jealous. Suzette's not a waitress. If Larry's seeing her, there's a reason."

She began to get pissed. Of course Jeff would defend Larry. Men were a tribe.

Louise could see it, Larry going to visit this so-called attorney. There was probably a couch in the office.

The tug rolled and her coffee cup fell from its perch, rattling across the deck. Billy picked up the cup. The handle had broken off.

Louise scowled. Her favorite cup, now useless.

December 7, Tuesday

Travis

"Get up, Travis. We're there. Dark Cloud, Stretch - get ready."

Larry turned on the light, but even then, the cabin remained half-dark. Travis looked down at his hands. They ached.

Dark Cloud peered at his watch.

"Not even six in the morning," he said. "Won't be light for two hours."

"We need eyes. Dress warmly."

Larry flashed the light a few times, until he was sure they were awake, and then he left.

Travis dropped from his bunk and began to dress. He knew he would be cold topside. The night before, they'd worked until 10, assembling gear for transfer to the ship: a cargo net holding survival suits; another, food; and a third, gear, rope, and medical supplies. Travis had brought the cable chokers topside from the workroom and lashed them just aft of the deckhouse, forward of the big winch. The deck and rails had been layered in ice an inch thick. The air had been bitter cold.

Up in the mess, the lights were bright. Travis smelled freshly- baked bread.

▶

"The ship's 10 miles ahead. Still afloat. We've had her on radar for three hours." Larry was standing by the door to the galley, holding on as the tug rolled. Louise was sitting at the end of the long booth, watching him.

"We oughta get there just about sunrise," she said.

"Where's the other tugs?" asked Billy, chewing bread.

"We got six hours, at most," said Larry, looking at his watch. "Time enough to get aboard, see if there's any machinery we can use over there to run winches and lines. Otherwise we'll run a line from *Warhorse* through the bow chocks of the ship and back to the tug. Then we'll use the tug's winch to get the towing cable to the ship."

"What's the weather?" asked Dark Cloud.

Louise shook her head.

"Gale warning, northwest, increasing. Maybe a storm warning by tonight."

Travis saw, through the windows, a sheen of ice on the tug's rail. It reflected the yellow lights hanging over the deck. A northwest gale coming after this last storm would suck icy air over the Gulf of Alaska and they'd be forced to work in freezing spray.

"Okay," said Larry. "I'm going aboard. Travis, Dark Cloud, Stretch, Vince and Billy will come with me. If we're lucky, they dropped a Jacob's ladder before abandoning."

Travis looked at his hands. The knuckles were raw.

"Louise," said Larry, "you remember how to handle this beast?" Louise looked startled. "Louise, nobody can handle this animal like you. You'd nose her anywhere, smooth as silk."

"I thought Nelson..."

"He asked me to ask you, Louise." Louise nodded, her face pale. "Look, we'll come up on her, check her out, soon as it's light. If there's no Jacob's ladder, we'll go aboard over the stern, the lowest place. Get on board, then pass over the cargo nets. There's no way we can count on there being much food over there, or any spare suits. We got radios, Vince?"

"All charged." Vince sat next to Louise. "How much do you remember, Cloud?" asked Vince.

"Been seven years."

"Yeah but you're the only one here who's ever been aboard her."

"For three years, third engineer, then second," said Dark Cloud, looking into his coffee cup. "I looked at the crew list. I know half of 'em."

"Well, I'm counting on you to know the engine room," said Larry.

"Been a while," said Dark Cloud, shaking his head.

"I want some of you guys to suit up in fire gear before we cross, the suits anyway. We don't know how much the fire's burned down. Let's rig up another net for some air tanks and masks. Pad 'em using blankets or something so they don't slam the steel sides when we haul 'em aboard." Nobody said anything. "Look, we'll get aboard, get the gear aboard, and then check out the ship. We'll stay in touch using radios. Worst case, she's totally dead, maybe taking water, no food, no nothing. Best case, we get a line on her and get her to a dock in a few days. We got enough food?"

Ned, standing in the doorway to the galley, nodded.

"You won't starve."

"It's the cold I'm worried about," said Vince, adding fresh coffee to his cup. "Dead ship, probably. No electricity, no power, no heat. We could freeze to death."

"You can stay warm," said Jeff, bracing himself in the stairway leading down to the engine room. "I bet the fire's not totally out, so there'll be warm places."

Travis hadn't thought about the ship being cold. They'd have to grab all the blankets they could find from whatever staterooms had not been ruined by the fire. Then they could huddle up inside the ship, as close to the engine space as possible.

"We're just gonna have to play things by ear," said Larry. "Main thing is, get the line on her in six hours or less."

"First, get everyone aboard safely," said Louise. Travis realized she had been startled to be asked to run the tug.

"I'm counting on you, darlin'."

Louise grimaced. Travis knew she was nervous. Maybe she'd once played this tug like an instrument, but that had been years ago. The tug was heavy, the seas huge, and the ship they had to approach would be rolling deeply. Louise would have to read the water, nose the tug close, then time things so the rail of the tug rose above the rail of the ship on a passing sea while keeping the tug right next to the ship. She couldn't allow the tug to hit the ship or get snagged among the rising and falling seas.

"No hesitation, when we go," said Larry. "We get in place, Louise puts us in position, we go. When we're near the ship, we'll beat the ice off our rails, throw some sand, and set things up so people can stand at the edge of the tug, holding on to the house, then step off on to the deck of the ship." Travis tried to imagine crossing to the ship. "Let's get the air tanks, the other fire equipment, wrapped and stowed," Larry went on. "You guys not crossing, help Nelson and Louise, and when we get near the ship, stand by on deck and help us cross. Everyone needs to be tied in, a safety line. Then if someone falls in, we can haul 'em out."

Travis thought longingly of his desk at the Peninsula News, the uncomfortable chair, and the ancient computer monitor. Right now, he'd be happy to report on garden shows. A big sea struck the front of the tug's house, booming. Travis grabbed a warm piece of fresh bread and headed for his cabin. He had failed to put on his long underwear.

Louise

The crew began filling another cargo net with air tanks as Louise went topside to join Nelson at the wheel.

"What the hell, Nelson? You want me steering?"

He nodded. He stepped away and Louise took the wheel. The wind was coming straight at them. It was growing light outside. The big tug shouldered ahead. Louise steered into the seas, a little left, a little right, just to feel how the tug responded.

"Bet we see a plane out here today," Nelson said. A dark cloud cover loomed overhead, but they could see some lighter areas. "I think the U.S. Coast Guard's sending one of their long range aircraft out. Looks like there's enough ceiling for them to fly."

To the east, some faint sunlight under lit the gray.

"I think you should do this, Nelson. Been a long damn time for me."

"Hell, Louise, a long damn time for me too. When was the last time *Warhorse* had to do any close work? Years ago. "

"Yeah, but you've been driving her, snagging logs off the Elwha each season."

Nelson laughed. "Logs? Come on, Louise, you haven't lost a thing. Just last week, Louise, you moved *Warhorse* around so her port side was at the pier? A prettier piece of tug handling

I've never seen."

Louise hadn't thought much of her tug handling, but Nelson's words made her feel a little better. Her skill at the wheel would be the difference between success and someone being dropped into the ocean where he'd be crushed against the ship.

"You'll be fine, Louise."

Nelson was so calming, so steady. He never got agitated, always listened, always knew what to do. If Nelson thought she would do a better job nosing up to the ship than him, he was probably right. She felt better.

She could see the ship on the radarscope dead ahead, five miles distant, big and bright.

Larry appeared, carrying two coffees. He handed one cup to Louise.

"Goddammit Larry," said Louise, angry. His faith in her was a surprise. She was still pissed about what's-her-name, the cupcake.

"You'll be fine, darlin." Louise could see that Larry felt no guilt at all. Asshole.

The dark seas rolled past. When the tug was between crests, in the trough, all Louise could see was the approaching rise of water. Then, when they crested the sea, she saw roller after roller, stretching ahead into the dawn.

She spotted a smudge ahead.

"The ship?"

"Yep," said Larry. "Still smoking."

She couldn't see the ship itself, just a dark plume. She expected the ship to be burned to the deck, charred and useless. The day grew brighter as the sun rose. The wheel felt natural in her hands, as if the tug was an extension of her arms. Others had entered the wheelhouse.

Now she could see the ship.

"How far are we from the Charlottes?" asked Billy.

"We're closer to the north end of Vancouver Island," said Nelson. "The last few days she blew and drifted northeast, but now before this northwest wind, she's coming down to the southeast. We're about the same latitude as the tip of the island but 100 miles west."

A plane growled overhead, a big stubby four-propeller Coast Guard aircraft, the Guard's distinguishing red stripe easy to see. About 1,000 feet up, just beneath the cloud cover, coming from the south, the plane flew ahead over the distant ship and started to circle.

"Shit, maybe some of the crew's still aboard," said Larry, watching the plane.

"Tug *Warhorse. Warhorse.*"

They all heard the drone of the airplane's engines through the scratchy radio transmission.

"*Warhorse* back." Larry had the mike. "Any sign of the lifeboats?"

"No sign yet. Either one. Not a word, I am sorry to say, from the cutters searching. But there's no lifeboats in their falls on the ship, either. Both falls clear. So they both got away."

"Is there anyone aboard the ship?"

"We saw no one, *Warhorse*. What are your intentions?"

"See if we can take her under tow, bring her home."

"There are two other tugs well behind you."

"Buckhorn's tugs. Yes. We know."

"Might take all three of you. Bad weather coming, tonight."

The plane circled the ship. Now Louise could see the red bottom paint when the ship rolled. The blackened deckhouse still stood. Smoke billowed from an area somewhat behind the bow. The ship lay crosswise to the seas, and as each wave passed the ship lifted and rolled. The plane circled the ship twice more, then straightened and started northeast.

"Good luck, *Warhorse*. We can search up here for a bit for the missing lifeboats before heading back to Port Angeles. Maybe we'll find them."

The plane flew off. Larry peered at the radar and adjusted the range. The two Buckhorn tugs lay 60 miles south and closing.

Louise wondered if the lifeboats would ever be found. The ship had been adrift for over two days, in terrible weather. The lifeboats could be anywhere, and most of those places were not good. The coast of the Charlottes was rocky, steep, and treacherous. A lifeboat coming ashore there would surely be destroyed and the crew killed. Dark Cloud stared toward the northeast. Louise knew he was thinking the same thing.

They came up on the ship. The *Seattle Express*, 700 feet long, dwarfed the 160-foot *Warhorse*. Black, her deckhouse originally painted white, a thin red stripe along the side of the hull, the *Express* rolled slowly in the passing seas. Almost the entire ship was now covered with soot and grime. Louise spotted the hanging falls from the lifeboat area: two lines dangling free. The deck above the main deck, where the lifeboat had been stored, was charred black. The blaze had even melted the emergency circular life raft mounted next to the lifeboat.

When they reached the *Express*, Louise throttled back and kept the tug standing 100 yards off the ship's bow. Containers on the deck were burned. Several were hanging over the ship's side. Louise wondered how many containers had been lost. Smoke billowed from a hatch. Louise was sure a fire was still burning below deck. She saw no Jacob's ladder hanging from the port side.

They slowly circled the ship. Louise saw they would have to go aboard over the stern. They slowly worked along the ship, and as they did, one of the containers slid off the stack and disappeared into the ocean.

"Louise," said Larry, "take her off the stern and a little downwind, then drift while we move the nets and get stuff positioned for transfer." He looked hard at her. "You okay?"

Louise nodded. She did not feel okay, but she would do anything to hide her fear from Larry. He was going to have to depend on her and she wanted him confident. She did not feel confident.

Once past the ship's stern, she took the tug out of gear and spun the wheel so the tug faced the stern. She could see the ship's name, streaked with rust. The ship was rolling almost predictably over the passing seas, and Louise began to feel some hope. Even though the seas were over 25 feet high, they were long and not steep, not breaking.

The time to approach the ship would be as the ship rose and rolled their way. At the height of the roll, the port rail of the ship's stern was within six feet of the water. She needed to nose the tug up against the ship just as the ship was completing its roll. When the rails of the two ships reached the same level, the men could step or leap from the tug to the ship. In theory it was simple, except both decks were slippery and icy.

"Not gonna be easy," said Nelson, watching as Billy and Stretch, now in fire coveralls, hauled one of the cargo nets forward. The others were laying out coils of lines and ropes. Louise had the tug now in the lee of the ship's stern, 50 yards away, making sure she backed the tug off as the ship drifted. At least the smoke was blowing past well to their left.

Using wooden mallets, Larry and Dark Cloud broke ice from the rail. Shards flew into the air. On the ship fierce heat had deformed some of the containers. The heat had also blown out the deckhouse windows at the level of the lifeboat stand, one deck above the main deck. Soot, rising three decks high, covered the white sides of the six-story amidships deckhouse.

The rear of the ship was mostly free of damage except for leaning containers.

The *Express* must have taken terrible seas. Containers were knocked askew, hanging. Louise tried to imagine dropping the lifeboats in such conditions. One moment the seas would rise as high as the boats, and the next moment there'd be a 40-foot drop to the water. How could you let go a boat in those conditions?

The ship's short aft deck, one level below the main deck, held the mooring winches - five huge spindles. Overhead, containers were stacked on frames, three-high. One loomed outboard on this side.

The men on the tug positioned the cargo nets, chokers, lines and ropes. Stretch, Billy and Dark Cloud struggled to push a heavy, awkward wooden structure up to the rail. They would use this as a platform for moving men and equipment over the rail and on to the other ship.

Louise would have to guide the tug in at an angle to keep the two ships close together while each man stepped across the heaving water. She'd have to be ready to back away quickly if something went wrong. "I'll be spotter," Nelson said, standing near the starboard windows. "Can you see from there?"

She nodded without speaking and spun the wheel, backing the tug. The ship drifted relentlessly. To the right, past the stern, spray raced over the seas as the wind picked up. Larry finished bracing the platform near the rail, slamming the wooden surface with his gloved hands, then turned and looked up at Louise. He waved his arm.

They were ready.

Louise put the tug in gear, forward. Larry held a radio.

"Forget that," Louise said to Nelson, who was raising his radio to his ear to listen to Larry. "Lower the window. I want Larry's hands free."

Nelson struggled to open one of the starboard windows. The window was frozen shut. He took his hot cup of coffee and splashed it against the glass, melting enough of the ice so he could slide the window down three inches. Icy air blew into the wheelhouse. Out on deck, Ned attached a line to each man who would be crossing to the *Express*.

"Come up slow, darlin,'" called Larry.

Louise nosed the tug ahead. As the larger ship tilted toward them, she could look down at its deck. Then, as the wave passed, the *Express* lifted up until its red-streaked bottom, pitted and rusted in places, filled the view from the tug's wheelhouse. As the two ships continued to rise and fall, Louise nosed closer and closer, until close enough so each time the *Express* reached its maximum list, Larry and Dark Cloud could reach across a narrow gap, striking ice from the ship's rusty rail with their wooden mallets.

The ship looked enormous, and way too close. One of the containers, the one hanging, would come too close when the ship rolled. Christ.

Larry, wearing a shoulder harness and a line extending to Vince on the bow, climbed on to the platform. Louise nosed the tug ahead. Larry prepared to jump, but as the ship rolled yet again it seemed to keep on going, until they were eye-to-eye with the first level of containers.

"Lord, a big one," Larry cried.

Louise heard him through the window. He sounded totally unconcerned. He was absolutely fearless.

The next sea was smaller, and this time Louise brought the tug right up to the ship's rail and Larry, holding the tug's mast stay, reached across to the *Express*, grabbing a steel post. He stepped down on to the ship's rail, and then dropped to the deck. Ned threw Larry the line attached to his harness as the ship rolled away. The end of the line flickered out of sight as the rail rose and rose and Larry disappeared. Louise backed the tug away.

"One down," Nelson said, taking a deep breath. "Nice work, Louise."

"Hell," she said, sweat dripping down her forehead.

Dark Cloud went next and made it look easy. He got up on the platform and grabbed the stay and leapt directly onto the ship's deck, avoiding the rail entirely. When he turned around, he smiled, his big, white teeth flashing.

Stretch, Billy, and Vince crossed shortly after.

With the window open, the inside of the wheelhouse grew colder. Louise saw the surface of the ocean had become white in the worsening weather. Travis, waiting to jump, shivered as he stood on the platform. Louise struggled to nose the tug close in to the ship, but the seas were much rougher now. As the biggest wave so far lifted the ship up, Larry shouted across the water at her.

The ship rolled toward the tug, containers filling Louise's view, and then she felt as much as heard a horrible sound. The tug's mast punctured the side of the overhead hanging container and then hung there for a moment until it pulled free, the steel screeching. Travis jumped inboard off the platform as the thick wire stay he'd been holding went slack. As the ship rolled away, Louise saw the tip of the mast embedded in the container. They'd lost their anchor and towing lights.

"Nuts," said Nelson, stepping out onto the wing and looking up. "Lost one of our antennas, too."

Larry, at the rail of the ship, pointed to his ear, then lifted his radio. Louise heard him on Channel 16.

"I need Travis, darlin. One more pass. Looks like you lost the top of the mast."

"Yeah. It's sticking out of one of the containers."

"You lose any antennas?"

"Yeah, honey. The sideband."

"Damn."

Travis stood shivering on deck. Once more, Louise brought the tug up to the edge of the *Express*. At the last moment, Travis ran up on the platform and, like Dark Cloud, leapt across to the ship's rolling deck. But when he landed, he stumbled and let out a yelp.

Without hesitating, the tug crew passed a heavy line over to the ship and used this to feed the cargo nets across. The men worked as quickly as possible, hauling urgently. Still, it took an hour to complete the transfers.

When they were done, Larry radioed Louise:

"We're okay here. Stand by and we'll see about getting the tow line attached. Don't know if the gear here is working. We don't have a lot of time."

The tug lay 70 yards away, in the lee of the larger ship. Louise watched Larry and the others move forward, climbing the stairs from the stern deck to the main deck, but then they all turned around and returned to the aft deck. The ship continued to drift.

The wind was whistling.

Travis

Travis followed the others up a rusty, worn stairway to the main deck, but he hadn't taken four steps before he realized the men ahead of him had turned around.

"We're not going this way," Larry said, a big coil of half-inch rope slung over one shoulder.

Travis had never been on a ship this big but he knew how containerships like the *Express* were configured. A deckhouse spanning the width of the ship rose amidships. The wheelhouse and bridge lay above three decks of crew quarters. Below the quarters were the galley and mess, then the control room on the main weather deck, then the engine room space extending deep into the ship. The rest of the ship was covered with stacks of containers, four or five-high. Walkways along each side of the deck gave access to the forecastle, at the ship's bow, and the stern, aft, where they were now gathered.

Despite knowing the general layout, Travis felt lost. The aft section was below stacked containers, which bridged the big mooring winches on the stern, braced ten feet overhead. The ship had to be almost 100 feet wide. Heavy, padlocked marine doors lined the bulkhead forward of the mooring winches, against which two stairways, one on each side, rose to the main deck and the passages forward to the deckhouse and the bow.

Larry grabbed a padlock on one of the doors.

"Shit. We can't get into the tunnels."

Travis had no idea what Larry was talking about. They stood as close to the bulkhead as they could, beneath one of the stairways, trying to escape the wind. Travis stood next to a square tank holding three-inch outlet fittings. There were four-foot high ventilators mounted by the bulkhead, topped with circular lids.

Larry keyed the radio.

"Nelson, we can't get forward through the tunnels - they're locked. The port side's trashed. It's nothing but burned containers. There's no way to pass. We gotta haul the gear forward on the windward side of the main deck. Tell Louise to head to the bow." Larry placed the radio in his pocket. "Haul this gear forward, out of the air and spray," Larry said to Travis and the others. "We gotta leave it here until we're hooked up, but I don't want it to freeze to the deck. Maybe we'll find some keys forward, to open these doors."

One of the heavy cargo nets had already half-frozen to the steel deck, and Travis and Billy had to haul and heave to break it free. The survival suit bags, wet from the crossing, were freezing together. The wire chokers made by Travis, which had been tied to each of the three cargo nets, trailed across the steel deck.

Larry led the men across the deck to the starboard stairway. On this side they were fully exposed to the wind. The surface of the ocean was white. Ice covered the gangway. As they climbed, Billy slipped and fell back against Stretch.

Reaching the top of the gangway, Travis gazed forward all the way to the bow.

Debris littered the deck. Inboard one container-width, the high sides of the hatch coamings made a wall. Overhead were stacked containers on frames, extending over the narrow passage on the side of the ship. The passage seemed dark because of the containers overhead. A rubber hose, threaded along the sides of the hatch coamings, was frozen solid. Ice lay up to five inches thick on deck, and the men slid as they struggled forward. Ice also covered the outer rail.

The ship rolled in the rising seas and the men staggered. Spray was everywhere. When they reached the deckhouse amidships, Travis saw, through an open watertight door, linoleum, frozen water, scattered fire hoses, dark streaked soot.

"We get up to the bow," said Larry, "we'll go into the foc'sle, find some come-alongs, use them to get the loop of the cable over the bitts."

Travis had no idea what Larry was talking about.

Stretch had an icicle hanging off his chin. They crept forward.

Further forward, approaching a gap in the stacked containers, Travis saw smoke, twisted metal, and shattered containers. The fire had warped and opened the hatch over the hold. The fire, which had apparently spread across the width of this part of the ship, had burned a fire hose station and fused together fittings and unidentifiable pieces of plastic. Thick smoke billowed from the hold below. Travis climbed a ladder three or four steps so he could see over the coaming and through the warped hatch into the hold. Roiling smoke and flickering flames boiled among the containers stacked in the hold. Unbelievably, thousands of gallons of water sloshed beneath the fire. The ship was burning, yet the hold was filled with water.

"I see water," Travis said.

Larry clambered up the side of the coaming and looked over. He spat.

"We got our work cut out for us. Come on." He headed to the forward bulkhead just behind the bow. A watertight door, dogged shut, stood just inboard of a stairway leading up to a wave break and the bow.

Larry undogged the door and led Travis, Dark Cloud, Billy and Vince into the forecastle. None of the lights worked. They had to use their flashlights. The room held tools, machinery, tanks, wood, stacks of rope and hose, and electrical cords, all hanging from bracings, all swinging as the ship rolled.

"There." Dark Cloud pointed to several 50-pound come-alongs - heavy blocks and chains. They grabbed three. Larry grabbed two five-pound shackles, thrusting them in his pants pockets. They pushed open the port side watertight door. As they left the forecastle, they could see the fire had nearly reached the bow on the port side. The thick smoke smelled of burning chemicals. The tug, downwind and ahead, looked tiny to Travis.

Breaking ice using mallets, they made their way up the port side stairway. In front of the row of containers closest to the bow loomed a tall, braced bulkhead, the breakwater. Beyond was the bow, exposed to the wind and sea, white beneath ice. The mooring winches were encased in ice, the mooring lines - two-inch braided hawsers - frozen on the spools.

Forward, at the peak of the bow, two big chocks gaped like eyes. Aft, halfway to the mooring winches, three two-foot diameter, three-foot high steel bitts stood welded to the center of the deck. Ice covered the 30-foot tall conning tower aft of the bitts but forward of the mooring spools. The tower held the bow light, foghorn, and forward mast lights.

Travis had seen ships towed before, although never under these conditions. The goal was to run a two-inch diameter steel cable, a loop spliced at the end, from the stern of the tug to the bow of the ship. The cable would be pulled through a chock, the loop wrapped around the bitts. Usually gear on the ship could pull the wire aboard from the tug, but the *Express* was a dead ship. They'd have to fairlead smaller line from the tug up through the chocks on the ship's bow and then back to the tug, so the tug winch could pull increasingly stronger, thicker lines, until finally the heavier towing wire made it onto the ship and over the bitts.

Larry untied his coil of rope. He tied the heavy shackles to each end, then called the tug on the radio.

"All right darlin, we're gonna fairlead the rope through the chocks, equal, so both ends are all the way to the water. You bring *Warhorse* right up to us and grab those ends. Have the men tie one of 'em to the first lead line and wrap the other on the secondary winch. Then start pulling."

"You better put some weight on the ends," said Louise, "The wind will hold the rope high."

"Got that covered," said Larry, checking the shackles. "You come with me, Travis. Vince, Cloud, set up the chain falls by the bitts. Stretch, Billy, stand by. No, Billy, go to the foc'sle, get a stopper line from the locker. We need a stopper, too."

Travis and Larry slid and slipped forward on the icy bow, bracing where they could. After breaking the ice off the big steel bitts, they carried the line and shackles to the very peak of the bow.

Larry handed Travis one of the shackle-tied ends of the line.

"Here, pass it down," said Larry.

Travis fed the rope through the starboard chock toward the surface of the ocean, while Larry fed the other end of the line through the port chock four feet away. Through the chock, Travis saw the rounded stern of *Warhorse* as Louise backed as close to the ship as she dared.

Travis watched Jeff grab one of the shackles, Nelson the other. Larry threw the rest of his rope through his chock. Now the rope was hanging from both chocks in equal measure, the ends now aboard the rolling tug just below the container ship's bow. On the tug, Nelson removed the shackle and tied the end of the line to a heavier line wound on the big drum holding the wire. Jeff tied the other end of line to the other big drum.

"Wait," said Larry.

He grabbed the rope, which was now stretched between the two forward chocks, and he pulled it back over the three bitts until the rope lay behind them. The rope now went from one winch of the tug, across the water up through the ship's port chock. It then circled around the three bitts, back out the starboard chock, and down to the water and the tug.

Larry, standing to the left of the port chock, raised his arm and slowly moved it in a circle. As the two boats rose and fell, the stern of the tug sometimes seemed only 10 feet from the peak of the ship's bow, then, a moment later, 100 feet distant.

Jeff, on the tug, worked the controls for the drum pulling the line. Travis watched as the winch pulled tight the half-inch line. When the line grew taut and began winding onto the tug's drum, it pulled the heavier line from the tug's big towing drum across the water to the damaged ship. Louise worked the tug back and forth, doing all she could to keep a steady tension on the line so it wouldn't snap. Jeff helped, allowing the small drum to spool back when the line took too much pressure. One step forward, two steps back.

The lead line was a one inch diameter nylon rope, braided for strength. The thicker line caused more friction on the bitts and through the chocks, causing the line to move slowly.

Louise moved the tug further away to give the line more play.

Larry studied the line as it crept around the bitts.

Travis saw an even thicker rope winding around the bitts. This heavier line was attached to the towing cable, pulling it toward the ship.

Travis was sure his ears were frozen. His nose was numb.

His fingers burned. The fishermen's rubberized insulated gloves he wore weren't up to this cold. The bow area was covered in frozen spray. The mooring winches looked like tombs. A sheen of ice covered the top of the outside rails. The weak sunlight occasionally piercing the low clouds glowed against the ice. Forward, to port and downwind 30 degrees, Travis saw the tug, now more distant, stern to the ship. The line from the big drum carried over the tug's stern and into the water, rode beneath the water for several hundred feet, and then rose toward the chocks. As the big seas rolled by, the line would tighten, then loosen, and Travis understood Louise was giving it a lot of scope to handle the differences in wave height. A clump of line caught coming into the chock, and for long moments stopped moving, until it popped free and jerked inboard and started around the bitts.

"Comin' good, darlin," said Larry into the radio. Vince, to the right of the starboard chock, swung his raised arm in a circle, the go-ahead sign.

The wind had strengthened. Travis watched the black towing wire come across from the tug, pulled by the mooring line. The towing wire grew heavier as each additional foot spooled off the drum.

Even in the howling wind, Travis could hear the line creaking under strain as the towing wire rose slowly toward the ship's chock. As the big knot holding together the mooring line and wire cable reached the chock, it became stuck. After several tense moments, the knot popped free and leapt inboard. The wire slowly snaked around the bits.

"Stop," said Larry into the radio just as Vince raised his other hand and crossed arms. "We gotta be careful now, darlin. Keep as much slack as you can until we seize off the cable and set the loop."

The looped end of the towing cable crept around the bits,

doubled up. Somehow they had to pry apart the loop and get it over the bitts. Travis could see the cable stiffen, then loosen, across each passing sea. The cable was two inches thick, but when it took tension those two inches seemed to shrink. Travis couldn't even begin to imagine the pressure.

"Hold on," Larry said, gesturing. "You guys let me get the stopper line around this wire, tie it to the cleat by the chock, to take the pressure. When the seas pass and you get slack, open the loop and work it over the bitts."

Larry tied a stopper knot around the cable and secured it to the cleat. Each time a sea passed, he was able to draw more tension, until finally the stopper line was taking the weight and pressure of the towing cable, not the loop of the cable itself.

"Now," Larry yelled, standing near the stopper knot. As a sea passed and the ship dropped, the towing cable went slack. For a moment there was little pressure on the loop of cable doubled around the bitts. Dark Cloud and Travis, using lengths of timber, forced apart the steel wire and stretched the loop of cable until it dropped down around the three bitts.

Just as they finished lowering the cable the ship rose on a huge, erratic sea. Travis leapt away from the cable, Dark Cloud following. He heard Stretch scream over the whistling wind. Travis stumbled, turning. Larry fell to the deck. As the ship rose, the stopper line parted and the wire cable snapped against the chock under full pressure. It caught Larry's leg and arm. Travis heard a snap and a thick, wet crunch. He saw Larry's lower right leg tear away.

Larry made a strange sound and his eyes opened wide, and then he fell back onto the deck, next to the cable. Blood poured from where his right foot and hand had been. Travis watched the color of Larry's face go from beet red to pale gray, then alabaster white.

Travis and Dark Cloud ran to Larry, and Travis wrapped a

length of rope around Larry's calf. Dark Cloud gripped Larry's right wrist, yelling, "I need a tourniquet."

Blood flowed everywhere, splashing against the ice and the deck. Travis could see a leg bone sticking out from the bottom of Larry's calf. As Travis tightened the rope, the blood flow slowed. Larry glanced back and forth between his arm and leg.

"What a rookie move," he said. "Tell Louise to get this ship back to Sol Duc. Let's do that, at least."

Then his eyes rolled into his head.

The ship took another roll and Larry slid left, then right, Dark Cloud and Travis by his side. They were all the way forward, just to the left of the port chock, protected from the wind.

"We got to get him secure somewhere," Dark Cloud said. "Now."

Travis and Dark Cloud pulled Larry away, dragging him through his own blood. With Stretch and Vince, they pulled Larry aft, past the wave break, to the head of the stairway leading to the main deck.

"What the hell are we gonna do?" said Billy, staring at Larry. "Is he alive?"

"We gotta get him aft," said Vince. "It should be warmer down in the engine space, if we can get there. We can keep him warm, keep those wounds from bleeding. Find disinfectant, bandaging, and a mattress. "

Travis spotted a five-foot-long, four-wheel pushcart, lashed against the forward hatch coaming.

"We could carry him on the cart," he said. "No, we can't. Not on this side. It's blocked, the fire."

Dark Cloud gave a short laugh, then pointed.

"We'll carry him through the foc'sle and move the cart across the ship. Then we can push him down the starboard side."

Vince had taken Billy back to the bow. Travis had no idea

what they were planning, but he prayed they'd be fast. He and Dark Cloud and Stretch managed to carry Larry down the slippery stairway to the main deck.

"You have a light?" asked Dark Cloud, looking doubtfully at the watertight door leading into the forecastle.

Travis looked forward over the rail. Down on the tug, Jeff and Nelson were peering aft, looking at the cable stretching back to the *Express*. The big drum on *Warhorse* spooled out more cable. Louise was increasing the slack between the tug and the ship.

The smoke grew thicker.

"This wind and the direction we're moving, we can't stay here. Let's move Larry," said Dark Cloud, looking back up the stairway. Vince appeared, followed by Billy.

"Who's gonna tell Louise?" asked Travis.

"I'll tell her," said Vince.

They moved the cart to the starboard side, then carried Larry through the dark forecastle and placed him on the cart. His good leg hung over the trailing edge of the cart. The ragged stump continued to seep blood. The end of his arm was also bleeding despite the makeshift tourniquet. Travis took off his gloves and placed them under Larry's head so it wouldn't bang on the cart surface as it shuddered and rattled over ice and debris. Larry was pale.

"Where do we put him?" asked Billy.

"In the engine room," said Vince. "It'll be warmer there than anywhere else, at least until we get a generator going."

When they finally reached the deckhouse, they lifted Larry and moved him inside, through the watertight door, placing him on a worn couch opposite a door down to the engine room.

On the starboard side, walls were buckled, doors sprung, piles of burned objects everywhere. The big insulated door to the cooler rooms hung open. Travis turned on his light.

The cooler room itself was a mess, but the insulated doors to the freezer and the stores refrigerator rooms were latched. He opened the stores room and gagged. Something had rotted. The freezer door, though, seemed tight.

"Not how I wanted to come back aboard this ship," said Dark Cloud. He was leading the way. Travis remembered Dark Cloud had worked on the *Express*. "Once we move Larry, we gotta move the gear we left back aft up here before we lose strength or get too cold, Let's check below. Travis, stay here. Keep Larry on the couch."

Larry's crushed and splintered leg bone was gray. Thick blood oozed from the stumps of his arm and leg. Travis briefly loosened the tourniquets on Larry's leg, then his arm, letting blood return to the areas of his arm and leg nearest the injuries. Were there medical supplies, alcohol and disinfectant somewhere aboard this ship?

Vince returned from the engine room.

"We'll move him lower. There's more heat down there, and a secure place for him to rest. Travis, you bring the couch cushions after we pick him up."

Vince, Dark Cloud, Billy and Stretch lifted Larry and carried him below. Travis grabbed the three big cushions and followed.

Down the stairway, the odor of fire and smoke grew stronger, but they saw no signs of fire along the starboard side. Opening a heavy watertight door, they entered the engine space. It was much warmer.

Travis expected to see a charred ruin. Instead, except for some signs of scorching on the port side, the engine room space seemed fine.

"The Halon put out the fire," said Vince. "Where do we put Larry?"

In the center of the engine room, a big open hatch looked

down on the main engine. Travis could see the big cylinder heads and catwalks for accessing different pieces of machinery.

"Where's the generators?" he asked.

Dark Cloud pointed. The generators were in two side rooms, one on each side. "I'll see if there's any air pressure to start a generator."

"Any lanterns for light down here?" asked Travis. "How do I get to the starboard tunnel? Don't we need to get our gear up here from the stern?"

"I'll show you," said Dark Cloud.

Travis saw doors and arrows pointing to tunnels and pilot stations. He had no idea, down here, which way was forward, which way astern, which side was port or starboard. All he saw were tools, doors, scraps of steel, barrels filled with unidentifiable substances, more tools, and gas tanks lashed to bulkheads.

"Let's put Larry here, in the incinerator room," said Dark Cloud, leading them into a small room on the starboard side containing a large, insulated burner. They could wedge Larry on the couch cushions between a bulkhead and the burner, which was now cool. "We'll brace him here, keep an eye on him, clean him up. If we get a generator going and heat things up, we can move him topside into a cabin."

Larry remained unconscious, his head lolling. As the ship rolled, he shifted one way, then another. Billy braced a folded towel beneath his amputated leg to hold the bone off the cushions.

Dark Cloud found a long set of bolt cutters in a tool room. He checked Larry and then handed the cutters to Billy.

"Travis, we've got to get the gear from the stern before it's totally encased in ice. Billy, Stretch, go back topside, go back to the stern, use these bolt cutters to cut the padlocks on the tunnel bulkhead door. I'll take Travis aft in the tunnel and we'll open the door."

After Billy and Stretch went topside, Dark Cloud squatted by Larry and made sure he was secure. Then he rose and led Vince and Travis to a watertight door on which was stenciled, "Starboard Tunnel." He spun the wheels to unlock the dogs and then swung the door open, slowly and carefully.

The tunnel, free of smoke, held a maze of pipe and valves. Travis saw pressure tanks, gear and tools. Dark Cloud led them through the tunnel. They came upon stacked boxes and plywood crates, nearly blocking the tunnel, just aft of one of the watertight doors.

"What the hell is this mess?" Dark Cloud slapped the plywood boxes as they climbed over them.

Toward the stern of the ship, it became much colder.

The radio sputtered, and they heard Louise's voice: "What's going on? Everything squared away?"

"Shit." Vince keyed the radio. "We got the cable secured, Louise. Now we're gonna move the gear to the deckhouse; try to get some power over here. We'll check the tow every hour, okay?"

"Everyone okay over there?"

Vince stared at the radio, then spoke.

"Louise, Larry's hurt."

"I knew it. Nelson said he thought something had happened." Travis wondered if Nelson had seen Larry's lower leg or hand drop through the chock into the sea. "Whaddya mean, hurt? When? What happened?"

"When we were setting the wire, Louise. Larry fell just when the stopper line let go. He's hurt bad."

"Vince, what the hell happened?"

"He lost his foot and his hand, Louise. We've got him now in the engine space. It's warmer there. He's braced and comfortable, tourniquets on his leg and arm. But he's lost a lot of blood and he needs to get off this ship."

The radio was quiet for a moment. Louise sounded shaky when she spoke.

"It's blowing 70 miles an hour, Vince, and we're at least 100 miles from the west coast of Vancouver Island, and not the part holding rescue facilities. It's gotta be a 150 mile helicopter trip out here. I'll call 'em."

Travis heard a loud snap through the aft door and he knew someone was using the bolt cutters. A blast of frigid air hit Dark Cloud when he opened the door. Billy and Stretch huddled around a corner, shivering, having dragged the cargo nets to the door. The nets were frozen.

"It's a lot warmer inside," said Travis.

"Drag everything into the tunnel and then get it up one flight to the cooler room forward," said Dark Cloud. "The refrigerator is useless but the freezer is still holding cold, and we can put the food there until we get one of the generators running."

"If we get one running."

"Have some faith, Stretch."

"Faith? We're stuck over here. Larry's almost been killed. We've got no heat. We'll be here for days and we could freeze to death."

"We won't freeze to death, Stretch," said Dark Cloud. "It's still warm in the engine room. I think heat from the fire in the forward part of the ship is working down the port tunnel and keeping the engine room warm. We might get hungry and thirsty, but we won't freeze to death."

"Plus," Billy said, "we're hooked up. The ship's ours. The claim's gonna be ours."

"If we can wait long enough for the claim to go through," said Stretch. He was obviously unhappy. Picturing Larry's listless body shifting in the incinerator room with each roll of the ship, Travis wasn't surprised. He wasn't happy himself.

Pete

On Pete's second day, Tuesday, he was sent for coffee again in the mid-afternoon after sitting in a guard shack all day, feeling useless, watching the others work, freezing.

Contractors arrived in big trucks loaded with coils of galvanized fencing and razor wire. What the hell were they building? A military compound?

The night before had brought a hard freeze. The snow had stopped, leaving six inches on the ground, and now the air was bitterly cold, the wind fresh and strong. All morning the work crew dug post holes using a specially-fitted Bobcat. The new fence would extend from the pier away to the base of a bluff, then parallel to the pier out toward the harbor entrance, before returning back to the other end of the pier. They were bolting additional posts onto each end of the pier itself to hold more chain-link fencing topped by razor wire extending out over the water. Nobody would be able to get over or around it. Just before he left for the coffee shop, Pete saw more trucks arriving, carrying some kind of pre-fab building.

"What's in the trucks?" Pete asked Roger as he approached the company truck. Roger stood easily, seemingly impervious to the cold.

➤

"Temporary office building."

Pete looked at the old warehouse.

"Need a place we can heat for offices and to store supplies. The warehouse there is almost useless. Nothing but bat and bird shit inside."

The amount of money being spent seemed enormous for this rundown site, but Pete knew Buckhorn had agreed to bring the place up to Homeland Security standards. This was a requirement before any ship, international or domestic, would be allowed to dock. And everyone entering or leaving the facility unaccompanied would have to carry a Transportation Worker Identification Credential, or TWIC, card. Pete didn't have one. However, the guard shack was outside the gate to the facility, so technically he wouldn't need it.

Driving up to the coffee shop, Pete found himself looking forward to seeing Mariana. Maybe today he would have the wit and brains to take her up on her invitation. Then Pete scowled. How likely was it she'd invite him again? Not very.

Pete drove slowly over the slippery, snow-covered road. Nobody on the Olympic Peninsula knew shit about driving in the snow, because it snowed so infrequently, but Pete knew. He'd grown up in northern Michigan and they had plenty of snow there. The lake effect, it was called. Storms often dropped a foot or two at a time back home.

Damn Joyce, trying to restrict his visits with Sam. But his son lived with his mother, and what did they say? Possession is nine tenths of the law?

"You're working today but late," said Mariana, looking fresh and rested. There was nobody else in the coffee shop. "Same thing?"

Pete nodded. "More, this time. A lot more. Been a cold damn day. There's a bunch of new workers there today."

"Yeah, saw 'em go through town earlier." Mariana was

already pouring coffee. "Your boy's a nice kid."

"Sam? Yeah. Curious, you know?"

"She can't just stop him from seeing you," said Mariana hesitantly. "This is a joint custody state."

"I know." Pete sat on a stool, nursing his bad knee. He sipped some coffee from one of the cups. The doughnuts looked fresh and good. Mariana saw where he was looking.

"Bad for your figure, you know," she said. Pete wanted to say, "Mariana, you could eat dozens before they damaged your figure." He blushed.

"The thing is, Mariana, I have the right to take Sam to my place and Joyce knows I have the right. But she can prevent him from leaving her house and if I want to see him, I'll have to go to court and get an order. It's a pain in the ass, expensive, and takes time."

"He wasn't very happy, yesterday."

"I'm glad you snuck him a doughnut hole."

"What's going on down there? I thought nothing was supposed to happen down there until next summer."

"A Buckhorn ship on the Russia run caught fire, was abandoned. If she's retrieved, she might be towed to the dock here. We need to set up the place to be secure."

Mariana finished pouring and loading cups. She looked out the front window. Snow lay in the parking lot and the trees were white. The wind was strong, but not roaring like the night before. "Abandoned? So, right now, probably, its crew is somewhere in a lifeboat. I can't even imagine."

Pete couldn't imagine, either.

Of course Mariana didn't invite Pete to do anything, but why would she? She'd made her effort and he'd blown her off. He was such an idiot.

Back at the pier, everyone had gathered inside the abandoned building midway down the pier, out of the wind. The trucks were parked, noses facing forward, all pointing toward a wide door hanging open. Roger stood just inside the open door, clapping his hands together.

Three of the wire installers, hardhats yellow and shiny, helped Pete carry the trays of coffee and the bags of doughnuts into the dark shed. At least they were out of the wind.

Roger sipped his coffee and blew on the lid.

"Good news and bad news."

Pete tried a doughnut. Roger was smiling, sort of.

"The *Express* is under tow, Pete."

"The big tugs got her?"

"I just got a call from the head office. She'll be here in five days, maybe four if this northwest wind keeps up, pushing them. Damn long ways. Good thing. We have enough time to get the fencing right, assemble the building, put power in, get heat and power to the guard shack. Tomorrow you go to Seattle, file for your TWIC card."

"Anyone aboard her?" Pete had been wondering about Myra, how she must be feeling, worried about her father.

"Didn't say. Just said she's under tow. Thing is, it's not our tugs. Louise - Tugboat Annie - she and *Warhorse* across the way, there, beat our tugs to the ship this morning." Roger sipped his coffee. "The two Buckhorn tugs are there, which is how we know she's under tow. They'll stand by. If *Warhorse* loses the tow, our tugs will take her." Pete saw the calculation in Roger's eyes. He wondered if the Buckhorn tugs would try to cut off the tow cable and seize the ship themselves. "They found one of the lifeboats, too. Saw its EPIRB signal and a cutter's heading for it."

Pete went cold.

"Seems both got away from the burning ship."

Pete wondered if Myra's father was among the sailors on the lifeboat that had been seen.

He shivered.

Myra

"Myra, it's Pete. Roger just told me the abandoned ship's been found. Should be at the dock in four or five days. Plus they spotted one of the lifeboats." I didn't dare hope my dad was on the lifeboat they'd recovered. Pete spoke before I could say anything. "How are you, Myra?"

I could hear machinery through the phone, men shouting in the distance. I wondered where Pete was. Were his teeth chattering?

"About as well as can be expected, I guess, Pete. Trying to work, keep my mind occupied. Was anyone on the ship?"

"I don't know. Oh, I also learned the other lifeboat got away, but it hasn't been seen."

"Thanks, Pete."

"Sure, Myra. I gotta go back to work."

Work? He should still be sitting at home, resting and recovering. Instead, based on the sounds I heard through the phone, he was at a construction site.

My desk was covered with the studies of Buckhorn's mining proposal. The company's reports were well done. They'd spared no expense. Their archeological study was the weakest, I felt, but I had strong opinions based on my personal

▶

knowledge of the area where they wanted to mine.

I sat at my desk, coffee cold, door half-closed, listening to people in the hallway, someone laughing, one of the council members arguing with one of the fish commission staff. I pictured the burned ship, out there somewhere, being dragged south to the Strait of Juan de Fuca and our little harbor.

Eldon leaned in, pushing my door open.

"You okay?" He wore a huge parka. "Lots of snow this morning. And now it's cold."

Beyond him, I heard Leroy, the new fish commission member, starting to argue with Emma, our young new fisheries biologist. Leroy was arrogant, opinionated, and thought he was smarter than everyone else.

"They found the ship, Eldon. And a lifeboat. But no word about my dad."

"I'm sure we'll learn more soon." Eldon saw the reports on my desk. "You better get to work, Myra." Eldon hated reading reports even more than I did.

"I know. I've been reading their claims about erbium. All morning I read. How the heck can this mineral somehow eliminate all the toxins in coal?"

"I don't know," said Eldon. "Sounds like black magic to me."

Leroy made some kind of declarative announcement and a moment later Emma passed by my door, head down, jaw thrust forward. Eldon sighed.

"Well, I better go counsel our new member. We don't want him to drive Emma off just yet."

We'd had trouble keeping fish commission staff. Working for the commissioners is not easy, as they have plenty of struggles – not enough fish, tight rules, competition with other tribes, recreational anglers. Sometimes the commissioners took their frustrations out on staff. Emma was new here - just out of school. She reminded me of myself a few years ago.

"Close the door when you go, okay, Eldon? I'll never get any work done if everyone pops in to ask how I am. Maybe I should tape a note on the door: 'Ship found. My dad, not yet.'"

"He'll be found," Eldon said. "He's tough."

"He's not a walrus, Eldon. He can freeze to death the same as any man."

"Trust his spirit, Myra."

I forced myself to read the reports.

Erbium is a somewhat rare mineral found in geological up thrust formations, of which there are plenty in the Olympic Mountains on our peninsula. Buckhorn had taken over a mining claim deep in the Olympic National Park, a claim grandfathered before the land was a park, and now they wanted to excavate the erbium. Their plan was to use big helicopters to airlift the ore to a ship here on the Sol Duc waterfront.

I didn't trust Buckhorn, which was founded by two Tacoma brothers, one who ran the family's produce company and the other who went to Washington and worked for a congressman. He became cozy with a lot of lobbyists there. Now he was in what he called the private sector. It was really an incestuous mix of private money, government favoritism, and schmooze. The brothers then sold the produce business and started a shipping line, using Jones Act preferences. In a span of 20 years, they built the company into a huge natural resources enterprise of which shipping was now the smallest part.

If testing proved the erbium made coal safe, Buckhorn had promised to build a manufacturing facility in Sol Doc, or nearby Port Angeles. If the erbium worked as Buckhorn believed, the company could potentially make hundreds of billions in profits.

I had to admit, their reports were well done. Eloquent, clear, simple. Great charts and visuals, lots of color. Clean precise printing. Beautiful.

Maybe we could argue for further delays and send an archeological team in there to do a survey and hope something turned up. But Eldon was right; many inside our own tiny tribe were abetting Buckhorn. All the families who had earlier pushed for a casino now supported this project, succumbing to promises of money, jobs and gifts to the tribe. Who could blame them? Not me.

I should have gone to work somewhere else, on another reservation. I get sucked into the immediate politics because I know all the people here and their issues. I could see why some wanted economic development and why others wanted to preserve our tribal heritage, no matter what the cost.

I felt alone, even in this place where everyone knew me.

Eldon reappeared, sitting down in a chair across from my desk.

"When's the permit meeting?"

I looked at the calendar.

"Next week, Eldon."

"What have you found?" Eldon asked, waving a hand over the reports.

I shook my head.

"It would be a lot easier to fight this if they wanted to build a road to get the erbium. A road would create a huge, permanent scar on the landscape. But they don't. The only spot they're going to touch is the erbium mining site, way up in the Godkin Creek valley, miles from any hiking trails where people might see the damage." I opened one of their reports and unfolded a lushly-rendered map so Eldon could see. "See? Four acres. They'll disturb a tiny area this coming season. Their plan is to fly in a machine or two to dig into the outwash, gather the erbium, and place the ore in big sacks. Helicopters will lift the sacks out and take the erbium to the harbor. No roads. No impact beyond the four acres, and they promise to restore the land. They're even going to keep the helicopters away from the trails so they don't disturb any hikers. They say the noise of the choppers will hardly be noticed, and they're probably right. Last summer when we were up there looking for Sarah, we barely noticed the noise of the search helicopter after a while."

"Those are a lot smaller than the freight helicopter Buckhorn will use, aren't they, Myra?"

"In any case, Eldon, Buckhorn's convinced enough council members to support them. The only people who are going to be really upset are the traditionalists, and they're dying off."

"You're not dying off, Myra."

I lowered my voice.

"Eldon, even Marcie, my boss, wants to see this thing happen. She's in the economic development camp. She always has been. She tried to get someone else to evaluate these reports, but I'm the official archeologist on staff." I closed the report. "I need to write my summary and recommendations for all these reports. Best I can argue is holding off on a decision until we've conducted an adequate archeological survey in the park, but we can't do a survey until spring, when the snow melts, months from now."

Marcie appeared in the doorway and frowned when she saw Eldon.

"I'll have something written by the end of the day, Marcie," I said. Eldon started to rise. Marcie stepped back to let Eldon pass back into the hallway.

"I appreciate your coming in to work today, Myra," she said. "I heard about your father."

"They found the ship. They found one of the lifeboats. I'm hopeful."

Marcie was already turning away.

I finished my summary. All I could argue against the project was occasional noise during the retrieval of the mineral and some land disturbance in a small, remote area of the park.

Last summer, I'd gone out twice to the sacred place where Buckhorn wanted to mine. I'd gone with dad, Tom, and Sarah the first time, and Sergei had come with us the second time. The first time we went into the park Tom carried an ancient atlatl, a spear thrower his grandfather had found there, definite evidence the remote valley was culturally and archeologically important. Unfortunately, the spear thrower had been lost, and then, when we found it again, destroyed by Buckhorn's people. Without the atlatl, or some kind of artifact, I had no evidence.

At home, I started a fire in the woodstove and sent Sergei a message telling him one lifeboat had been found. Tom and Sarah showed up. We were soon joined by my mother, and Eldon and Rose, all picking their way across the snow to my front door.

We sat in the warmth eating stew and saying little.

What was there to say?

I was thinking about Sergei. I'd sent him a message about the abandoned ship because my dad had been Sergei's father's friend, and Sergei's friend too, but I'd heard nothing back.

What was I expecting, anyway? I hadn't exactly encouraged him after our adventure last summer. Oh, we'd corresponded about work, science, archeological theory, but personal messages? Never. Not showing emotion must be the Koryak way.

Sarah had been watching me. She missed nothing. She knew I was lonely. I knew she was lonely, too.

Sarah whispered to me, "Have you heard from Sergei? Does he know?"

"I sent him emails, Sarah. Nothing."

Sarah nodded.

"Are you having dreams?" Sarah asked. "William will let you know."

Rose nodded in agreement.

I said nothing. I had hardly been sleeping, and whatever dreams I had were brief and scattered.

After everyone left, I practically collapsed into bed.

Then I did dream.

I was nine again, out on the coast, with my dad. The wind blew. The sky was gray and dark. We had made camp, on a shelf above the high tide line, beneath gnarled trees, out of the wind. Our fire crackled and sparks flew into the air before flickering out. My dad's place at the fire, across from me, sat empty. A pale orb, the descending sun, appeared beneath the clouds and lay just above the distant horizon.

My feet were in socks, warming before the flames. My boots steamed nearby, finally drying out. I'd wedged myself in the crook of a big dead log, my jacket padding my back. Beyond the fire and the trees, I could see rocks the size of houses and then the faint sheen of the ocean, the rough waves. The wind flew overhead, blowing smoke into my face, making my eyes water.

Where was my dad?

In my dream we were seven days away from our car, and tomorrow we'd start back, retracing our steps along the beach and over the headlands along the remote coast. It was just the two of us - we'd seen nobody the entire week. I'd learned to build a good fire, even using wet wood, and I'd seen pride on my dad's face.

Where was he?

The sun sank into the sea. A pasty pale glow across the western sky flashed deep pink for moments, and then green. Then the sky was dark.

I stared at the fire, watching the red coals flicker and drop from the burning logs. I added wood when the fire burned down.

I listened. Somewhere deep in the trees I heard an approaching animal. Grabbing a long stick lying partly in the fire, I held the burning brand overhead.

Over the sound of the crashing surf, underbrush snapped. The wind whistled.

A pair of eyes caught the light of the fire. The eyes were high above the ground. They were impossibly far apart.

The eyes stared at me. I stared back.

Steve

The engine had died at dawn, but I knew we were close to the coast. We'd been in the lifeboat 30 hours. I kept calling the Canadian Coast Guard.

The cook, forehead bleeding, wept quietly. I was damned cold. The summer before Jimmie's accident, when he was just seven, he and I went into the high country near Cascade Pass. We hiked about two hours, and he was a trooper, never complaining. When we got to the viewpoint, we had 10 minutes to soak in the panorama before clouds descended, bringing a light, chill drizzle. Within minutes, we were both shaking, deeply cold. The fog was so thick I was worried we'd lose the trail. I knew I'd been a fool, bringing Jimmie up into the mountains without proper clothing. I knew the weather could change fast up there, but I'd come unprepared and we almost paid the ultimate price.

We reached the car okay, but during the long drive home, I thought about what might have been. I think my error in judgment tipped the balance for Sharon, my ex-wife. Later that summer, she took Jimmie and left.

Richard pulled out some rations and started throwing crumbs at the bird. The bird ignored them, but later hopped over and ate. Finally, an hour passed and I got my survival

➤

suit back.

Engine dead, the lifeboat drifted.

Every hour I turned on the radio and broadcast: "WNDP Boat Number One, *Seattle Express*, adrift, seeking assistance. Battery low. Will turn on set every hour on the hour, five minutes."

In the afternoon, after 33 hours in the lifeboat, the radio came to life.

"Canadian Coast Guard Cutter *Gwaii Hanass* to WNDP Number One. We are northeast of you 10 miles from reading your EPIRB. Can you stream a line and a light for gathering a tow?"

"Any sign of the other lifeboat?" I asked, using the last of the radio power.

"Nothing. I'm sorry."

Catching the streamed line from the cutter would be difficult, boarding the cutter would be dangerous, and we would then have a full night of steaming to reach Port Hardy.

The bird pecked at more crumbs.

"Damn," said Butch. "Steve might make it."

"His name's not Steve," I said.

"He's just like you, cap'n. Never gives up."

Everyone except Mark was smiling. It was good to see some smiles.

Spirit's a funny thing. The bird pecking at crumbs - did it feel hope? It sure had spirit. I considered Jimmie. He'd lost his spirit at a young age, and had wandered ever since. But even today, 34 years old, he still had hope, even if his situation seemed hopeless to almost everyone who knew him. Every time I went to visit, he'd have a plan for when he finished his latest round of therapy. With almost no education, and after 10 years in and out of institutions, he still had hope. Maybe that bird's spirit would carry us through. And if it did, then maybe Jimmie's spirit would carry him through, too.

Louise

Louise wrestled the helm. The towing wire between *Warhorse* and *Seattle Express* disappeared into the water off the stern and then reappeared far behind when it rose to the *Express* bow. She'd been relieved when Larry had crossed to the *Express*. She wanted nothing to do with him, nothing at all. She'd been glad he'd be cold and miserable over there, doing his manly save-the-ship stuff, the stuff he loved and lived for. She'd struggled controlling the tug, getting the tow straight before the wind. What a relief when the ship tracked straight behind them. Then Vince called.

A foot? And a hand? He must have lost a lot of blood already. Probably in shock, certainly cold, no medicine, and no doctor, stranded on a tomb of a ship, he must be in hard shape.

Nelson appeared, removing his gloves.

"She's towing good. What's the matter, Louise?"

"Larry's been hurt. Vince just radioed. It's bad."

Nelson looked aft through the rear windows, looking at the wire, and, behind, the ship. While in a trough between waves, they couldn't see the *Express*, despite her size. She would loom behind them when lifted by a sea.

"How bad?"

"He lost his foot, Vince says, and a hand. Must have got

caught in the towing wire. I'm gonna call the Canadian Coast Guard. See if we can get a helicopter out here."

Nelson looked aft, shaking his head.

"Even if they could fly out here, Louise, where can a helicopter lower a basket in this wind? "

"He'll die if we leave him there, Nelson. It's four days, at least, until we get to shore."

"What's his blood type?" Nelson had sailed aboard merchant ships as chief medical officer. He knew medicine as well as anyone aboard.

"How the hell would I know?"

"Thought you might, that's all. He's gonna need blood."

"We aren't the Red Cross, Nelson."

Nelson walked up to Louise and looked her in the eye.

"Dark Cloud was a medic in the Middle East, one of the wars over there. The hospital on the *Express* should be pretty well equipped. It'll have needles, sterile bags, and bandages. Odds are damn good one of the other guys over there has O type blood."

"What?" Louise knew there was something she should know about blood types. The tug was wallowing but steady. Louise ached with tension.

"We need to set watches, Nelson. It's gonna be tiring handling her."

She was relieved when Nelson took the wheel. She called the Canadian Coast Guard, wondering while she waited when they'd see the Buckhorn tugs. They couldn't be far away. She looked at the clock above the forward window. They'd been at this for four hours, maybe five. It was late afternoon. The other tugs must be close, and she knew they'd hear her radio call. They'd discover *Warhorse* had the ship in tow and Larry was hurt.

"We got a man, lost a foot and an arm, on the *Seattle Express*.

We have her under tow. Can we get a medevac out here?"

"Where are you?"

Louise read off the lat and long.

"What's the weather out there?"

"Bad and getting worse. Larry's lost a lot of blood. They have him stable, but he's stuck on the ship and there's no heat or electricity. He needs help."

"By the time we can reach you it'll be dark," said the voice on the radio, "and even in daylight we can't retrieve anyone in these conditions, especially off a dead ship. I'm sorry. Perhaps late tomorrow, if this storm passes, we can get the bird out there then."

Tomorrow? Louise looked at the weather outside. Tomorrow might be too late. She felt responsible for Larry's condition. Surely her enmity toward him, her anger, had poisoned things, distracted him, drawn him into this accident. She'd been wishing ill for him, punishment for his lies and evasion, but she hadn't been wishing amputations. When her mother dragged them to church as a kid, she'd heard, many times, about the danger of wishing for something, especially before the Holy Spirit, because the Holy Spirit at times had a wicked sense of humor and you ended up getting more than you bargained for.

"You going to be okay, Louise?" asked Nelson, standing at the wheel. Louise realized she'd been standing motionless, holding the radio mike while the set whispered.

"Why'd you ask about blood type O, Nelson?"

"Universal donor, Louise. If one of the men over there has O blood, they can transfuse to Larry. Also, if we knew Larry had AB blood, then he could take blood from anyone."

"What, run a needle into someone's veins and the other end into Larry?"

"Gotta do something, Louise. He's lost a lot of blood."

Ned appeared in the wheelhouse. "Who's losing blood?"

"Larry got hurt, Ned, when we hooked the ship up. He lost a foot and a hand, Vince says."

"Jesus, Louise."

Nobody said anything.

Nelson handed the wheel to Ned, took the mike from Louise, and replaced it in its holder. Then he led her to the chair on the port side and sat her down. She stared ahead, mind blank.

Nelson called Vince and began giving him instructions about where the ship's medical supplies were likely to be, what supplies to look for, and how to treat Larry. Then Dark Cloud came on the radio and he and Nelson talked for a while. Louise didn't want a hung over alcoholic poking holes in her husband's arm, even if he was the only one over there had any idea what to do.

Nelson pointed ahead. Intermittently, Louise saw the Buckhorn tugs.

Now they had minders, vultures really, standing by and waiting for the tow to part. Maybe they'd even try to break the tow. No matter what, Buckhorn would shadow them all the way back to Sol Duc.

"Should we answer?" Nelson asked, as the Buckhorn tugs hailed them.

Louise got off the chair, looking ahead. "Yeah, we should. And anyone who's got a cellphone camera should be ready. If they try anything, film it. We need proof we're the ones who have this ship."

Even after all this effort, they still stood a good chance of losing the ship. If they couldn't get Larry to a hospital soon, they'd lose him, too.

Out over the water, the daylight faded quickly.

William

At mid-day Tuesday, their third day adrift, they passed a broken island and then approached a storm-wracked shore, helpless.

"The Queen Charlottes, ahead," said Randall, first mate, to William. Randall was peering through a window in the steering bubble. William, strapped in, unclipped his belt and stood by Randall, who was seated over the dead engine. All he could see was dark water, foam, gouts of spray, and then he saw the shore, jagged rocks, steep snow-covered ridges beyond.

"Hell," he said to Randall. The nine others in the lifeboat were watching them, eyes hollow. "I was born here."

"We're doomed," cried Jack, one of the sailors. He was weeping. They all heard the roar of surf. William could see nothing but surf through the streaked small window.

"Maybe not, Jack," Randall said. He peered. "Maybe there's a breach we'll be thrown through." He was pointing between two huge rocks just ahead. William saw a space between the rocks but nothing beyond. There were breaking seas, cliffs, and shoals everywhere. Snow fell, thick. Jim, the chief engineer, who had spent hours trying to get the lifeboat motor running, managed to turn it over just before they struck, and it roared, but by then it was too late.

ADRIFT

A sea seized the boat. They rolled, far. The boat rose before
the hungry rocks, but then miraculously skated between.
They struck, twice. One of the plastic windows cracked.
A jagged shard of rock pierced the hull. Aft, the propeller
sheared off, rattling. Everyone was thrown, hard. Then they
were through the breach into a tiny cove, miraculously behind
a sharp point, apparently safe. The boat was holed, but drifting
toward shore.

Nobody spoke. Somehow the boat had been thrown
through a hidden breach into calm water beyond. It seemed
they were in a tiny hidden cove. William felt the boat rise as
another huge sea, spent, crossed the breach and swelled into
the cove. He opened and closed his big hands.

He was alive. They all were. This coast was all rock, shoals,
cliffs, and inlets, barely charted, exposed, deadly. They should
all be battered and drowned, crushed in the surf. Instead
he was looking through the dim cabin toward Randall, who
was unstrapping himself from his steering station. Now he
gestured to William.

"Am I dead, then?" Heather, the steward, dark face swollen
and bruised, sitting across from William, was shaking her
big head. "Surely we are now dead." Her Honduran accent
was musical.

Randall opened the aft door to the small stern platform.
William followed Randall outside, blinking, stretching. His
huge frame was stiff, sore, battered after the days adrift in the
storm. Heavy snow mixed with rain. The cove was 100 yards
wide, 100 yards long, with islets in the middle. Remnants of
swells striking the breach sucked at the shore. Surf thundered
against the outer point. Inland, slopes rose, steep, snow
covering thick trees.

Inside the lifeboat Jim, the chief, was checking the others.
Some were bleeding.

"We're taking water," Jim announced. "We need to beach her."

The lifeboat was drifting close to the point. Jim and the others handed long boat hooks out to Randall and William.

Randall spoke to William.

"Do you know where we are? Weren't you born here?"

William found bottom with the pole and pushed. The lifeboat ghosted toward a beach. The snowflakes were huge. Trees grew right down to the water.

"This is surely Haida Gwaii, what you call the Charlottes, Randall. I left when I was a boy. We could be anywhere. This is a long, difficult coast. We are alive but now we have to survive."

The lifeboat grated against gravel and rock, leaning. Randall stared at the surroundings. The cove lay behind a point, with the breach to the north. The lifeboat had landed against the eastern shore of the point. Across the cove and the islets steep slopes rose into cloud, covered with snow, trees, ledges. The slopes rose a thousand feet or more.

"We're not going to survive here," Randall said, lowering his voice. "It's December for God's sake. We have little food, the boat's unheated, and this is an empty hostile coast."

"My Haida people have lived here for thousands of years, Randall. Even on this coast, a long time ago. They survived. So shall we."

Randall ducked back into the cabin and tried the radio. The radio was dead. When they had taken inventory once clear of the ship they'd learned they had no emergency position beacon. No radio, no beacon, no phone signals, they were marooned and alone.

They lashed the boat to trees overhanging the cove. William unscrewed the small compass from the steering station, thrust it in a pocket. The lifeboat, unheated, was foul and cramped. They had to make shelter ashore.

In the boat were a few remaining rations, water, line, some

oars, and tools. They gathered these and several knives, a fire ax, life jackets, two gaff hooks, some flares, blankets, and a plastic tarp. They unloaded everything, standing in line passing items hand to hand up a slippery slope into the trees.

They used the oars, line and branches to rig a lean-to on the only level spot on the point. William took the other sailors, Kirk, Willie, and Jack, to cut boughs. Charlie the ordinary and Heather the steward spread the boughs on the frame of the lean-to, then added the plastic tarp. More boughs went on the ground. It was a small shelter for 11 people. Jim, the chief engineer, took Charlie and Kirk to dig a latrine, a distance away, hidden.

All this time, snow fell. Anne, the young third mate, making her first trip on a commercial ship, and now cast away, built a fire pit with William. Heather gathered the rations. All the rest gathered wood. There was abundant wood, lying along the beach, lying among the trees. It was spruce and fir, wet, but firewood.

It took a long time to get a fire started. If it hadn't been for some diesel fuel from the lifeboat, which William used as a starter, they'd have died of exposure.

They huddled together, wood burning before them, wind howling overhead, sky dark with cloud, rain and snow falling.

"Over 13 years, making this run, Seattle to Petropavlosk, Kamchatka, unbelievably bad weather, and it's a damn fire does us in." Jim was next oldest, after William. He was badly burned. "A fire."

"We're not done in yet." William was next to Jim, hunkered down. The wind moaned.

"We have no cell phone signals, no beacons, no radios, nothing." Jim was crouched in back of the shelter next to Randall, on the other side of William. Randall wore a heavy fire jacket across his shoulders. Jim had lent his coveralls to

Heather, who wore light chinos.

"Where are we?" asked Jack. He lay beneath boughs. His Polish accent was thick.

"We must be on the Charlottes," Randall said. He had been pouring over the chart. William watched him. Randall had bad burns from fighting the fire. Their only chart was the Gulf of Alaska. "Haida Gwaii. At least the lifeboat came ashore at a small inlet, not the straight coast."

"None of the coast here is straight," William said.

"William, you were born here, weren't you? Do you know where we are?" Jim asked.

"I left 50 years ago, chief," William said. The heavy trees in front of the shelter waved in the wind. The fire smoked. "If we're on the west side of Graham Island, it's a total wilderness, nothing but mountains. But if we can cross the coastal range we'll be in hills and logging areas. There might be logging roads we can walk."

"Walk? Won't we be found?" asked Heather. Her nickname was Crazy Heather because she'd met, married and divorced two sailors in three years. William didn't think she was crazy. He knew both of her ex-husbands. They'd make anyone crazy. Right now she was frightened.

"William's talking worst case, right, William?" Anne asked. She was barely 23. "We'll be found." She eyed William. William stared back. He knew his wandering eye bothered some people. Anne was not one of them. Anne studied the sky. "When this clears, a chopper will fly the coast and see our lifeboat. We better be sure we keep scraping the snow off so they can see the color." She was looking at the sailors.

Randall was examining the dark sky, the snow.

"Do you know anything about this coast, William?"

"The mountains are steep, Randall. They are high. The growth is thick. Inlets along this coast go way back, curving, so you can climb a ridge and then come to water again. We don't want to have to walk for help."

"Did anyone see the other lifeboat?" Anne had hiked behind the shelter to the top of the point, gazing west at surf, huge seas, black jagged rocks, a broken coast stretching north and south, soon lost in cloud.

"I saw them heading for their station," said Randall. "I didn't see the boat in the water once we cleared the ship. God save them."

William suspected the other lifeboat had never been able to fall clear. The others - captain Steve, the engineers, and the cook - had probably been trapped on the burning ship.

Snow fell. Wind roared. Evening gathered.

"So, we wait," Jack said.

At the end of the shelter, the two Russian cargo handlers, Oleg and Mattiew, were quiet. They'd expected to accompany two cargo helicopters to Seattle and have time to chase girls. Instead, they were marooned.

Randall leaned close to Jim and spoke quietly, but William could hear.

"If nobody sees us, Jim, the search will be called off. The boat's shot. We have little food. We could be here until March. We'll have to send someone to walk for help. Otherwise we'll starve."

"Some of us have burns," said Jim. "If those get infected, it will be bad." He had a bad burn on his right wrist.

"Heather's diabetic," said Randall. William could see Heather moving boughs, trying to get comfortable. "She doesn't have much medicine."

William considered the people under the shelter. The Russians were overweight and ill-equipped for this weather. Of the sailors, Charlie and Kirk were in their 20s, but neither had ever been in the woods. Jack and

Willie were 10 years younger than William, smokers, late 40s, and Jack had a plastic knee. Jim was badly burned, as were Willie, Kirk and Randall. Heather was a city girl, from Queens, New York. Anne was a city girl, too, but she seemed fit. William had burns on the backs of his hands, but he knew why Randall was now looking at him.

"William, you're in the woods all the time. You're, er, ah.."

"What. I'm native? You think because I was born here I know how to live in the woods? Jesus, Randall."

Randall looked 12 years old with his hat over his ears. Now he was embarrassed.

"William, I've heard some of your stories about fishing the high lakes in Olympic National Park. That's the woods, isn't it? Who else among us knows a thing about this?"

"We'll see," William said. He knew they'd have to wait for days for the weather to break so someone could walk cross-country. "We will have to climb up there, see what we can see."

The heights beyond the tiny bay were white, steep, lost in cloud. It would be a long climb. The snow would be deep. Of the people under the shelter, William knew Anne would be capable of such a trek, maybe Charlie, surely Randall. It was not something he wanted to think about.

Randall looked over his crew. He spoke softly to Jim.

"We need to keep people engaged. We can only spend so much time gathering wood."

Everyone sat watching the fire.

An hour crept by. It was now dark. They tried to heat some rations for dinner. There was little food left.

The storm raged. They kept the fire going. It wasn't even five in the afternoon and already it was night. Sparks rose from the fire, winking. They were pinned to an unknown coast, hemmed in by mountains. Time crawled by. William could feel despair and hopelessness seeping into the shelter.

Charlie and Kirk were gazing, blank, at the top of the shelter. The Russians were muttering. Heather was tapping her fingers against her cheek. Anne was staring ahead. Willie and Jack started to argue.

Randall whispered to William.

"Tell us a story, William. You grew up here. Get our minds off where we are. What our prospects are. Give us some hope."

William had been to the west coast of Haida Gwaii as a child, somewhere, one summer, but now he didn't know where. He knew the west coast was wild, rarely visited, lacked roads, lacked settlements.

No searchers would be out in weather like this.

They could be missing for months.

The fire popped. The boughs overhead creaked.

Here he was, cast up on the west coast of his original home, not 50 miles from his birthplace, hunkered down before a fire. He knew how long this day, and all the days following, would be. Everyone was staring at the black night beyond the fire.

William got to his feet and lumbered to the front of the shelter. He threw some wood on the flames.

"I grew up in Massett, on the north and eastern side of Haida Gwaii, until I was sent to a mainland school for native children when I was eight. My grandmother, who lived to 104 years of age, was our storyteller during winter storms. The Haida way is to teach with stories, explain the world, and bring us through to spring. This was how we learned. With stories." The wind moaned. Charlie and Kirk looked William's way. Willie and Jack stopped arguing. Anne, at one end of the shelter, leaned back. The Russians were confused. Heather looked up, curious. "I will tell you what happened to me, my best friend Tom, my daughter Myra, a Russian named Sergei, and a strong young girl, Sarah Cooley, last summer. Where we are today, Haida Gwaii, is part of this story. So are the places we visited on our ship before she burned - Kamchatka, St. Paul Island, the Strait of Juan de Fuca. Our ship, the *Seattle Express*, is even in this story. Some of you may remember Sergei coming across on the ship last August with me."

William used a big stick to position the burning logs. The bed of coals was thick. Falling snow hissed against the heat. They would need to seek more wood in the morning. He felt snowflakes against his cheek. The surf against the outer point boomed. Beyond the fire all was darkness. Inside the shelter, 10 faces reflected fire, all facing him, listening. William remembered a half century earlier, his face one of many, listening to his revered grandmother's stories while the wind roared and snow fell. Now he was the elder, and, it seemed, the storyteller, too.

"Our ship has followed an ancient journey, stretching back to the beginning of time. Did you know this? I did not know this, not until last summer. Our situation today is desperate, uncertain, and might even appear hopeless. I learned, last summer, of other people, following this same route, who faced circumstances far more desperate and hopeless than ours here today. This is surely the place to tell this story. You will be the first to hear it. It begins, or I will choose to begin, this way. I was at my friend Tom's, with my daughter Myra, getting ready for a camping trip, last May."

William paused. Everyone watched him. The wind roared overhead. The fire hissed.

"The wind, that night, shook the house, roaring like a great animal. Rain thundered on the roof. I imagined ancient spirits, awakened and angry, searching, grasping.

"Three harsh blows struck against the front door, followed by three more, urgent."

Steve

Late in the afternoon a Canadian cutter came up on our windward side to create a lee, lowering a ladder. The climb out of the stinking lifeboat was tricky, but we all made it. We took showers, they gave us spare clothing, and we ate hot food in the crowded wardroom.

As the cutter headed toward Port Hardy, the lifeboat in tow, I learned a private salvage company had beaten Buckhorn's tugs to the ship and had *Express* under tow. For a captain like me, losing a ship under any circumstances usually means the end of the line, career-wise, but to abandon ship, and then have the ship recovered, is even worse. When we fled the *Express* I was sure the fire would consume her completely and she would sink. Instead, the fire burned out and she had remained afloat.

As a young sailor, I remember one captain telling me during a drill, "If something goes wrong, this ship is the last thing I will leave. It's big, powerful, and strong, and I won't go into a lifeboat unless there is no other choice. None."

The morning of the fire, it seemed clear to me we had no choice but to abandon ship.

Worse, half my crew, the other lifeboat, remained missing. As each day passed, the chances for their survival dimmed

▶

enormously. December in the North Pacific? They would be dead from hypothermia if still afloat in their lifeboat.

The west coast of the Queen Charlotte Islands is 150 miles of wild shore. If the other lifeboat got as far as land, it was surely battered to pieces. And, even if they did make it to shore, there is nothing but total wilderness. They wouldn't survive, not in December.

The cutter's captain allowed me to call Buckhorn headquarters from his cabin. He wanted me to have my privacy because he knew as well as anyone how difficult this call would be.

Buckhorn has a maritime division which administers and oversees its tug fleet and the few ships it owns. Bruce Costigan, based in Seattle, who runs the office, is a friend of mine - we had sailed together years ago - and he understood as well as anyone what I was going through. I called him at his home, even though it was late.

"Steve, good to hear your voice," said Bruce. I could tell from the way Bruce paused he was not alone. "Listen Steve, I'm here with Ken Weinhall, our attorney, and two people from the insurance division."

I took a breath. Why was Weinhall at Bruce's house? Obviously they were already lawyering up. I could hear someone talking in the background. I spoke as calmly as I could.

"Bruce. Listen. I know you're in the middle, here. I just want to get ashore and keep looking for the rest of my crew."

"I understand."

"Some guys got burned, Bruce, pretty badly. Everyone got off the ship."

"What happened?"

I knew Bruce was on speakerphone. Did I need a lawyer too? I was tired, bruised, and aching. Maybe I was being recorded. I was careful about what I said.

"We realized we had a fire forward about four in the morning. The weather was bad, and the sensors must have shorted out, because by the time we noticed the fire it was out of control up near the number two hold. It spread into the port tunnel, then into the engine room. We used Halon. The fire was in the tunnels and coming into the house and I abandoned ship because if I didn't, I was certain we'd be trapped on the ship. It looked to me, to all of us, the fire was growing."

"The ship was put under tow this morning by a private salvage firm. Do you know them? Sol Duc Towing?"

"I know who they are. I sailed with their mate, Nelson, a few times when he was sailing commercial. He stays in touch. He's a good sailor, but they're a pretty rag-tag outfit."

Someone else came on the phone.

"Well, they got the ship. Beat our tugs. By the time we got there that rag-tag outfit, as you call it, had her well under control. This is Ken Weinhall, Steve. I don't think we've ever met. I'm going to advise you to say nothing to anyone about the fire or its aftermath. Anyone at all. And, we'd like to talk to you as soon as you get down to Seattle. There will be an investigation, and a hearing, as you know. The company is very concerned for its staff and personnel, so hopefully we can all work through this calmly and reasonably."

How do lawyers talk this way? Ken was telling me to say nothing to anyone until he talked to me. I needed to get a lawyer of my own. Buckhorn was going to try to lay all this on me.

I've been sailing for a long time. Some would argue I should have retired five years ago, but what else can I do? The dirty little secret in the maritime industry is this: no matter how well officers are paid, pensions are almost non-existent these days, and, having little in savings, most of us have to keep working to survive.

I was certain to take the fall.

As I sat there considering my soon-to-be-ended career, I remembered Mark, first engineer, saying he was going forward to check the hold sensors. He had never done so. How, I wondered, had a whole bank of sensors gone down without any of us knowing?

Travis

Heading aft in the starboard tunnel, Travis discovered three plywood crates, four feet long, two feet wide, secured with metal straps, jammed against a bulkhead. They were among the boxes he and Dark Cloud had climbed over earlier. What were they doing out here blocking the tunnel when they should be properly lashed down in the cargo hold?

He turned on his flashlight. He could see Cyrillic lettering. He had no idea what the lettering meant. A corner of one box had broken off. Inside he saw canvas, lashed with duct tape. So the Russians use duct tape, too?

He helped the others haul supplies forward. They had to make several trips, each time stumbling over the crates. They stored the food in the refrigeration area and the survival suits and SCBA tanks in the engine room. Then they spent an hour looking for lingering fires and other dangers in the engine room. They needed flashlights. The air stank of oil. Later Travis held a light while Vince and Dark Cloud swore and struggled to start the soot-darkened emergency generator.

"We get this running," said Dark Cloud, "maybe we can get some lights and heat. Radio, too. Depends."

Vince traced the fuel lines, all the way back to a diesel

►

tank fed by the deep diesel bunker somewhere in the ship. Vince tapped the tank with the wrench, checking fuel level.

"Half full. We got plenty," he said. On his knees, Dark Cloud probed the engine. Vince held wrenches and passed him tools.

"This is gonna take time," Dark Cloud said. "Let's get Larry secure."

Dark Cloud led them to the ship's hospital, located on the second deck above the galley, right under the captain's and chief engineer's cabins. They found bandages, disinfectant, stitching, gauze pads, IV lines, needles, tape, as well as bags of saline solution. They put everything in a box and carried the box back to the engine deck. Larry was lying still, eyes half open.

"What's your blood type?" Dark Cloud asked Travis.

"I'm type O." Travis had a dim memory from high school days of first aid training and giving blood.

"Okay, good," said Dark Cloud, rummaging through the box. "Lay down here. We're gonna do a transfusion."

"You're kidding."

"No choice. Larry's lost at least two quarts of blood. Listen. I know my stuff. I was a medic in the army."

"Been a while, I bet," said Travis, wondering if Dark Cloud could steady his hands enough to find a vein. He'd seen them shaking earlier.

Dark Cloud laughed, almost a bark.

"You think I want to do this? Look, Vince will wash off your arm and then you'll just sit here and we'll get your blood into one of these IV bags. And then we'll drain your blood into Larry. Simple."

Vince, Billy and Stretch had no idea what their blood types were.

"I'm O, too," Dark Cloud said. "My native blood."

"You don't have native blood," said Vince.

"What, you never seen a blond Indian?" Dark Cloud turned serious. "My grandmother was Cree. My mother was a hippie and she married a Swede. Well, they had me on a commune and got married. But I've got Cree blood in me, type O. We'll drain Travis, then me."

Travis wasn't sure he liked the idea of being "drained." Larry lay motionless, his stumps wrapped in bloody bandages.

Dark Cloud got to work. One prick and Dark Cloud found a vein. His hands were steady as a rock, smooth and assured. The dark blood slowly filled the bag, held by Stretch. After the bag was filled, Dark Cloud found a vein in Larry's good arm and let the blood run into it.

Dark Cloud said to Travis, "Keep the light on me."

Dark Cloud pierced his own vein and his blood flowed into a second bag, which he also drained into Larry.

"Two quarts."

"Yes, Billy. And in the morning we'll drain two more. Meanwhile, Louise is trying to contact your families, see if there's a record of your blood types as well as Larry's."

Vince and Dark Cloud went back to work on the generator. By morning they had the engine running, feeding power to some of the cabins and the wheelhouse. They had light, and with some cabin radiators now working, they even had a bit of heat.

They carried Larry to a bunk four decks up from the engine room. They washed and treated his stumps, then wrapped them carefully in clean bandages. Although he was still unconscious, his color had improved.

Dark Cloud performed two more transfusions just before noon. Afterwards, Travis felt really light-headed and Dark Cloud told him to drink as much juice as he could find. Even though most of the ship's food was spoiled, the bottled juices and canned goods were still in good shape.

Billy, Stretch and Vince took turns monitoring the tow cable, the fire, and the flooded hold, night and day.

A lot of water had infiltrated the number two hold, and more was in the bilges and the shaft alley.

With the generator working, Vince was able to get electricity to the starboard running light, the mast light at the front of the ship, as well as the ship's radio. Now they could talk to *Warhorse*.

The big Buckhorn tugs shadowed them, cruising just to their side, now and then moving in closer, sometimes using a spotlight to sweep the ship.

Ahead of them, *Warhorse* rose and fell on the deep seas, relentlessly pulling the ship ahead.

Between lack of sleep, giving blood, and hauling supplies, Travis was exhausted.

He wished Ned had come across. All he wanted besides a good sleep was some of Ned's fresh-baked bread. He pictured the fresh bread, hot, dripping with butter.

"What the hell are you so happy about, Travis?"

"Thanks for getting the power back, Vince. How's Larry?"

Vince frowned and shook his head.

December 8, Wednesday

Steve

We reached Port Hardy, a small town at the north end of Vancouver Island, well sheltered from the raw Pacific Ocean, just before dawn. The Canadian Coast Guard has a station there with a small helicopter pad and airstrip. Buckhorn had chartered a bus to take the crew down south to Victoria, where they could then fly to Seattle. I planned to join a helicopter team searching for the other lifeboat, now missing for over three days.

I hate helicopters. They shake and rattle and thump. They drop unexpectedly. I don't understand how the contraptions even manage to get up in the air. When I'm in one, my stomach lives in my throat and my hands go clammy. But there I was at the helipad, wearing a flight suit and waiting for the chopper to lift off.

The weather had improved, slightly, and a few patches of blue sky showed through the clouds. The helicopter crew was four kids, none over 30. They had to be fearless, leaning out to lower baskets to winch up survivors or jumping into the sea to rescue victims. As we thundered north over the open ocean between Vancouver and the Queen Charlottes, they calmly

▶

checked lists and drank coffee.

Because of the noise, we used wired helmets to converse over the radio system.

"Where did they find the drifting ship?" I asked.

"Over 100 miles offshore," said Rex, the lead pilot. "Midway between the north end of Vancouver Island and the Charlottes."

"Why aren't you doing this search out of Prince Rupert? That's closer to the Charlottes, isn't it?" I asked.

"This machine's based in Prince Rupert, actually, but we were down here on another mission. This clearing weather won't last, so we're going directly north to search the west coast of the Charlottes right now. Haida Gwaii. That's what they're called now. We'll get fuel in Sandspit, on Haida Gwaii, first. This will be a long day."

Belted into the narrow seat, I felt bulky in my flight suit. The helicopter flew several hundred feet up, just below the low overcast. I saw waves, one after another, marching steadily east toward the coast.

Sandspit, halfway up the Queen Charlotte Islands on the western shore on Hecate Strait, is a long way over open ocean from the north end of Vancouver Island.

As we flew north, I worried about my son, Jimmie. I'd wanted to call down to Seattle, check on him and speak to his case manager, be by his side at a hearing they had scheduled, but there hadn't been time. Jimmie counted on me being there for him, and I'd been scheduled to visit after the *Express* arrived in Seattle, but now I didn't know when I'd see him. When we'd meet shrinks and therapists, Jimmie would sometimes turn on me, but other times I could tell he really needed my support. Sometimes all he could do was tick off all the reasons he was never going to have a real life.

He was smart, maybe too smart for his own good. He had

a good imagination, a fatal condition when you're trapped in a damaged body, unable to heal. He is sure life is passing him by - no girls, no career, and no friends. In what was supposed to be the final operation to fix his nerves, he took an infection and almost died. He'd become a permanent patient, living an institutionalized life, a mother unwilling to take him in and a father gone eight months of the year to earn enough to pay for his son's care.

I was glad I could look out the window and be alone with my thoughts. I felt I'd let my son down, again, as I always let him down.

Now I'd let down half my crew as well, not to mention Buckhorn, my employer. Who knows how many million dollars in cargo were lost. Maybe losing my license would come as a relief.

The helicopter took three hours to reach Sandspit. I saw nothing but gray heaving water below until the small harbor and green trees suddenly appeared. We landed, took fuel, and soon lifted off again.

The pilot took us to the south end of the Charlotte Islands' west coast, where we turned north again and started searching, 500 feet above the water.

To the west, on our left, I could see nothing but ocean, a gray heaving tumble of dark water marching against the coast to our right. Out the window, to the right, slopes rose steeper than I could believe into clouds. Inland, heavy snow had created a trackless, formless wilderness. The shore was all exposed rock and huge waves.

The broken coast was complex and varied, dotted with small islands, frequently pierced by narrow inlets and wider bays. We flew just off shore, following the main line of the coast, ranging in and out of the inlets.

I searched for anything orange, the color of the lifeboat.

I looked for debris, life rings, survival suits, any sign of the boat or my crew. We saw nothing.

After the search, we flew to Sandspit, took more fuel, then flew to Prince Rupert on the British Columbia mainland, arriving in the late evening. When I left the machine I could hardly stand.

Rex, the lead pilot, walking next to me, shook his head.

"Weather's going to be bad for at least the next four or five days. We won't be able to fly. I'm sorry."

I left Rex my cellphone number, just in case.

I stayed at a small motel and the next morning flew from Prince Rupert to Vancouver Airport and then on to Seattle.

I was worn out. My ship, abandoned. Three days at sea before rescue. A futile search. The battles yet to come: fighting for my license and reputation, fighting for Jimmie's future.

I felt old.

Pete

Pete rose before dawn, his knee swollen and throbbing. The cold tail of one big storm had passed, but another storm was coming, bringing warmer air. The snow was melting, water dripping off his roof, and rain was falling. Pete teetered out to his truck and headed down the driveway.

The drive to Kingston took almost an hour. Snow still covered much of the road, despite the rain. He made the 7:10 ferry and took the small elevator from the main car deck to the passenger area for breakfast.

Pete watched a big container ship steaming north from Seattle. Mist and fog sheathed the hills of the peninsula. He hoped the TWIC process wouldn't take too long. He was scheduled to see his lawyer before coming back.

Nearby Pete noticed three men dressed in suits. One was Brad Withington. The other two he recognized from the Buckhorn office in Sol Duc. They looked like they spent way too much time under sun lamps.

One of the Buckhorn men looked up, and, obviously recognizing Pete, gestured for him to join them. What was the guy's name? Fred? Fremont?

What the heck was Withington's relationship with these people anyway? Did the Buckhorn guys know Withington had married Pete's ex-wife?

"You're Pete, right?" Fred or Fremont asked, shaking Pete's hand. Pete then shook hands with the other guy, who was older, slick and shifty, with perfect silver hair.

Why did some people feel naked unless they had an American flag pin on their lapel? Pete was sure the two Buckhorn guys were ex-military. Pete had been in the service himself, and he could see ex-military from a mile away.

"I'm Fremont Smith," said the younger man. "This is Paxton Barnes. He's our director, corporate security. So, in a way, you work for him. Paxton, this is Pete Wise. He's been working with us for the last year and a half. Right now he's on our security detail. He works for Roger."

Pete thought Paxton could be Roger's older brother. They both had lifeless eyes. Fremont, on the other hand, oozed zeal.

"This is Brad Withington," said Fremont. "We brought him on board recently. Brad, Pete Wise."

"We've met," said Brad, looking uncomfortable.

"Brad's come on board in our legal department - new ventures. Matter of fact, next month he's relocating to our L.A. offices to help set up the business tied to our Port Angeles operation."

Withington would not look Pete in the eye. Relocation? As in, moving away? Suddenly, Pete was very glad he'd scheduled a session with his lawyer today in Seattle.

"You guys know each other?" asked Paxton.

Pete nodded.

"Brad's my son's step-father these days."

Withington turned red.

"Oops," said Paxton.

"Hey Pete," said Fremont. "You're gonna be manning the gatehouse down there, when the ship comes in, right?"

"That's what Roger tells me."

Paxton leaned toward Pete.

"They going to get all the fencing done in time?"

"Going to be close," said Pete. "According to Roger, the ship should arrive in four days, maybe a day sooner. The fencing's mostly done. Today they were going to set the footings for the new building, which is a prefab."

"Well, you're going to have some help, Pete. We're bringing in some people to help secure the site."

More goons for Roger's crew? Why? The facility was vacant, nothing going on, and when the ship was there the upland would still be vacant. Roger had told Pete the burned-out ship would be tagged and unused until the Coast Guard held some kind of hearing.

"They better get some more porta-potties down there, then," said Pete.

Pete wondered what branch of the service Paxton was from, and what his rank had been. He looked like a mercenary.

Fremont finished a doughnut, then asked, "You going in for your TWIC registration?"

Pete nodded.

"Us, too. Some other Buckhorn guys will be there, too."

Pete was confused. Was Buckhorn assembling a small army? He knew when the mining began Buckhorn would see protestors, but why all this muscle now?

Why did Brad need a TWIC card anyway, if he was leaving for LA? Brad excused himself to use the bathroom, saying he'd meet Fremont and Paxton down in their car. He wouldn't look at Pete.

Fremont slurped the last of his coffee, rose to leave.

"We appreciate your help, Pete." He shook Pete's hand. "Guess we'll see you at the TWIC facility. We should have all come together, would have saved a car."

Bullshit. None of these guys wanted the gate guard shack guy traveling with them. Pete was at the bottom of the food chain and these guys were at the top.

Relocating to Los Angeles? Were Joyce and Sam going too?

The ferry approached the Edmonds dock.

His knee still throbbing, he took the elevator down to his truck. The ferry blew its horn as it approached the slip. On shore, a freight train passed, heading north. In the car next to him, Pete watched two pretty women laughing together. One saw him looking. She waved.

Los Angeles was more than 1,000 miles away.

William

By the second day ashore, Wednesday, their supply of water packets was already almost gone. William found a small stream nearby and they took water from the stream. The storm continued, but holes appeared in the clouds overhead.

They had no way to signal anyone. William knew any searchers would give up as time passed. Willie and Jack were arguing over who was taking up more room in the shelter. Randall was reading his Bible. Jim was down at the lifeboat, tinkering. Already, the shelter and their gear were filthy. Three days of drifting had made a mess of everything, and it was getting worse. Heather and Anne were discussing William's story, suspicious the sea level had once been lower. William tried to explain once he got warm.

"Back then, where we are camped now would have been 300 feet above the ocean. The shoreline would have been lower, further down the slope. There's not much of a continental shelf here."

"I don't believe it." Heather's round head slowly shook.

"My daughter Myra told me archeologists dredged up artifacts along the east side of Haida Gwaii from waters over 60 feet deep. Back then, the ice time, Hecate Strait between Haida Gwaii and the mainland was dry."

▶

"So this little bay was dry, then," said Anne. William could see she didn't believe it.

"Do you remember the chart hanging on the wall of the officer's mess, Anne? Seattle's in the lower right corner, then the whole coast curving up to Alaska, the Aleutians, the Bering Sea, all the way to the Arctic Ocean. Then, curving down to the left, you find the east Siberia coast, Kamchatka peninsula, and Petropavlovsk at the southern end."

Anne nodded, calm. William was impressed. Anne was the youngest among them, yet now, shipwrecked, she was taking it in stride.

"There's a big shelf under the Bering Sea, north of Dutch Harbor and the Aleutian Islands. I fished up there. It's shallow and wide, hundreds of miles north to south, east to west. That's where the crab are, the fish, the money. That buried shelf, 50 to 80 meters deep, that's what my daughter Myra was talking about. That's what was exposed during the ice ages. Berengia, they now call it. The Bering land bridge."

"We're going to need more wood." Randall said, pocketing his Bible. Everyone groaned. They had already burned most of the wood near their shelter. Soon they would have to climb up the snowy, tree-covered slopes beyond.

By the time they had replenished the pile, everyone was wet again. They hung their clothes to dry. They ate. The rations were nearly gone.

A cold wind continued to blow but the sun came out. Eight inches of snow lay on the ground. William knew the storm would eventually break, but not this day.

"I hate it here," Oleg said. Mattiew hadn't spoken all morning. William tried to imagine spending months here with Oleg and Mattiew, Heather, Anne, Kirk, and the others. How could Randall still find things to scream about? Would he ever stop? They could survive on melted snow and no food

ADRIFT

for weeks, but not if they ended up killing each other.

In the mid-afternoon Anne rose and headed for the lifeboat to brush away snow. William went with her.

Snow lay thick. The wind blew, scattering smoke from the fire.

The lifeboat lay canted in the water, snow covering the roof and the painted call sign. From above it would look like a big snow covered rock. Anne held a branch with needles, a natural broom. William slipped on the slope but caught himself.

The helicopter came loudly over the headland to the south, painted red, big rotors flashing. It was flying a few hundred yards from the shore, about 500 feet high. The lifeboat was still covered with snow. Randall rushed down the slope.

"Why isn't the boat cleaned off? You should have cleaned the boat off, Anne. Idiot."

The helicopter thudded away. It had appeared, passed, and vanished from sight in 10 seconds.

After it passed they waited, standing down by the lifeboat, looking north. The helicopter's thudding rotors faded and did not return.

"The angle they had, they couldn't have seen the boat anyway," William said.

Time passed. Cold wind blew through the trees.

Their food was all gone.

In the sun the bright snow blinded. Thick snow lay on the roof of the shelter.

On the slope facing west, across the south end of the bay, William and the other sailors stamped out an SOS in the snow, letters 30 feet high, catching shadow. If a helicopter came the SOS would be seen.

Late in the day William and Charlie climbed the slope beyond the tiny bay. The footing was slippery. They had to weave among stands of trees in order to avoid ledges and

143

sharp slopes. They climbed higher and higher, often sliding and stumbling. William saw more clouds approaching, gathering another big storm. They needed a stretch of two or three days of clear weather if they wanted to trek out of here. Maybe when the next storm passed the weather would break.

They reached a ridge crest and followed it to a treeless summit. The sides of the ridge fell off, one side down to their camp, the other side to a different valley.

William guessed they were 1,000 feet high. Looking down, their enclosed bay resembled a teardrop, dotted with islets in the center. At the narrow end of the teardrop was the breach they'd passed through. The point on which the shelter lay was narrow, inlet on one side, ocean on the other. The shelter roof was rectangular under its snow. Smoke from the fire blew with the wind and dissipated.

Along the outer shore, beyond the point, William saw rocks, cliffs, white surf, surging seas, crashing rollers. To the north lay another headland, then another, then another.

To the south, more ridges, more peaks.

William turned and faced east. The ridge dropped steeply into a valley, then rose to another higher ridge, and then to another beyond, higher still. Somewhere east lay lowlands, logging roads, maybe a road leading to settlement.

"Jesus." Charlie stood next to William, wind buffeting his coat. "Someone's got to walk across those ridges?"

"I know." William said, shouting to be heard. "It's probably less than 10 miles, as the crow flies, to the nearest town. A long 10 miles, Charlie."

"Hope it isn't me doing the walking," said Charlie, looking pale. The ridges were forbidding.

William and Charlie slid and slipped down the slope back to the shelter. It was hard going. They had to be careful. William reported to Randall and the others what he'd seen.

"How long will they keep looking?" Heather asked Randall, studying William and Charlie's trail up the slope.

"It's not been a week since we abandoned ship, Heather," Randall said. "Until today the weather's been bad. Hopefully they'll fly this coast a few more times, but we need to stay alert."

"They'll stop looking. Didn't they stop looking when Sarah disappeared in that park, William?"

"They did. And they may stop here, too."

"I remember searches for fishing boats," said Jack. "They'd stop after a week or less. After a week anyone still missing is dead anyway, the cold. That helicopter was the last one." Jack looked like he was about to cry.

"What can we do?" Anne asked. "We have to wait."

William felt hopelessness settle like a cloak among them. Of all those here, only he had seen this kind of weather before. He'd been raised here. It looked hopeless but it was just winter weather.

"On days like this I remember the beautiful green slopes of the Olympics, the hot gravel bars by clear water, bright sun, gentle breezes, those days when the sky is clear. I always forget the sore feet, aching back, struggles up steep switch backed trails, the heavy sweat-soaked pack digging into my hip. And I always forget the rain. Cold, loud, incessant rain."

"Not as bad as here, I bet," said Kirk.

"Just as bad as here, Kirk. This is all one coast. Here we are, castaways in the twenty-first century, and not a working cell phone or GPS or radio or EPIRB in sight. All we have is this fire to make smoke signals. And with this wind, this far from anywhere, who'll see our smoke?"

Jack was looking where the rations had been stacked. Nothing was stacked there now.

"We're out of food."

"We just hang tight," said Randall, Bible in hand. "Pray

for help."

"We'll need a miracle," said Kirk, voice muffled by the life jacket pulled over his chin. He was buried under boughs, life jackets, and a blanket.

Randall gestured with the Bible.

"Miracles happen. Prayer works."

"Prayers won't feed us." Jack was sitting toward the back of the shelter, hunched. He had started to mumble at night in his native Polish. "Look at us. No guns, no harpoons, few knives."

Anne shifted her jacket, trying to get warm. Jack looked at William, saying,

"Maybe William knows how to set a snare? Fashion one of those spear throwers?"

William pictured himself using a spear thrower. Randall looked up from his Bible.

"Get real, Jack. William's story, ridiculous. Seeing extinct bears? Come on."

William was irritated. It was Randall who had demanded a story.

"You think it's ridiculous for a young girl to see an ancient bear?" asked William.

"Impossible," said Randall.

"Perhaps she had a vision."

"Those are ridiculous too."

"You're the person among us, you and Jim, who turn to prayer, praying to an entity you never see."

"That's different."

"How is it different? Your religion says a crucified man rose from the dead after three days. A man born of a virgin. Is seeing an extinct bear more ridiculous than a virgin birth?"

Randall looked up, eyes sharp. William knew he should shut up.

"Are you challenging my faith?" Randall was studying

William, deciding whether William might have insulted him.

"Not at all. I am just making a point. It makes you think, doesn't it? We're more helpless now than my ancestors who lived here. If they were here now they'd see us huddled by this fire with long faces and they'd laugh at us. We're alive, we're warm so long as we gather wood, and we have water. Things could be worse. None of us is dead yet. And if some of us do die, they'll make good food for the rest of us. Relax, Kirk, just kidding. Except I'm not, not really. Now, after we get wood, I'll keep on with the tale."

Louise

Nelson appeared from below. Louise wondered when he slept. He was supposed to be off right now.

Nelson looked aft through the windows in the back of the wheelhouse. "What the hell's he doing?"

Louise followed Nelson's gaze. One of the Buckhorn tugs was moving in toward the stern quarter of the *Express*.

"Hell." Louise grabbed the radio. "Buckhorn tugs. Dammit. Come in."

"Hey Annie. How you doing this fine morning? Parted off the wire yet?"

Tugboat Annie. Couldn't they call her by her real name?

"What are you doing, Rick?"

Rick and Louise had taken a MITAGS course together years earlier. He'd tried to pick her up, even though he knew she was married to Larry. He'd been a pain in the ass. He was still a pain in the ass. Buckhorn's senior tug captain was ruthless and nasty.

"You aren't thinking of putting a gang aboard the *Express*, are you?"

"Annie. How could you think such a thing?"

Just to Nelson, Louise said, "He's gonna put guys on the ship. Try to take over. Once he has his guys on her, they'll try to get us to part off, and then grab the tow."

The big red tug was approaching the stern, the same location on the ship where Larry and his people had boarded.

Using the handheld radio, Nelson called Dark Cloud.

"You see Buckhorn's tug behind you?"

"Yeah. I'm back here with Stretch and Billy. We'll fend 'em off."

Louise adjusted the tug's line and turned the wheel left.

"Listen, Rick, back off. You'll never get lines on the ship. Dark Cloud's back there. He'll throw them off."

"Our ship, Annie. Buckhorn owns her. We've got the contract to retrieve her. You stole her."

"Bullshit," said Louise. "The ship was abandoned. Drifting, nobody aboard. A free claim, Rick. We got her." The Buckhorn tug continued to approach. "The ship's ours, Rick. We have her, and we'll bring her to the dock, and our people will sit on her and secure her pending the settlement and investigation. A few weeks, at the dock, at least, our guys aboard, not yours."

"You're gonna be on our dock, for Christ's sake. We got important cargo aboard, stuff needing to come off. We've gotta start repairs."

"You know how this works, Rick. The ship's impounded, and she sits there until the Coast Guard hearing."

"Yeah, well if your people are on the ship at our dock, how are you going to get supplies and relief people aboard if you've got to go through the Buckhorn gate? Huh?" Louise lifted her finger from the radio's transmit button. "He's right, Nelson. It's gonna get real ugly if we tow this ship to Sol Duc."

She pressed the transmit button again.

"Back your tug off, Rick, right now."

"What are you gonna do, Louise?"

"Watch."

Louise turned the wheel hard to port, toward distant

Vancouver Island. After a long time the tug started tracking left.

"Back off your tug, Rick, or I'll tow this pile of useless steel to Canada. I'll get her secured at a dock on Vancouver Island, where you'll be paying thousands of dollars a day to lay up. You'll have to go through all the Canadian rules and customs."

"There's no dock on this stretch of the island can take this ship, Louise."

"You sure, Rick? I can drag this thing up to Port Alberni where there's definitely a dock can take her. Watch me. Hey, who's on the bridge on the *Express*?" Louise knew her people on the dead ship were listening to the radio.

"Me. Travis."

"Start making notes in the ship's log. Record what this asshole is trying to do. We'll use it at the hearing. Now listen, Rick," she continued. "We have this ship. She's ours. Dark Cloud's back on the stern and if I know him at all he's got the rifle from the radio room. No way are you guys getting aboard. And don't even think about trying to part off the wire tow. In fact, you guys need to get lost, both of you. Get the hell out of here or I'm taking this ship to Canada."

"You're bluffing, Annie. Bluffing about the rifle and bluffing about Canada."

"Am I?"

There was a long silence. The radio whispered. Minutes later the Buckhorn tugs turned away from the *Express*.

"They'll peel off, steam south, and then just sit there at the mouth of the Strait," said Nelson, "We'll need their help getting the *Express* to the Sol Duc dock."

"Travis, you still on over there?" Louise knew Nelson was right.

"Yeah."

"How's Larry?"

"I don't know, Louise. I think the blood transfusions

helped, but.....he's still not conscious. You need to talk to Dark Cloud. He really knows his stuff, Louise."

"How's the fire forward?"

"Hard to tell. Still a lot of smoke, so there must still be a fire somewhere."

Ned came forward from his stint aft by the towing drum.

"Everything's OK back there, Louise. Grab a cuppa coffee."

Louise handed the wheel over to Ned and went below. She knew she should monitor the towing drum, but she was tired and coffee sounded good.

Three, four days yet to go. Not enough people. Too little sleep. She had been wishing Larry dead just yesterday. Now her wish might come true.

Was any of this worth it? What good was the money without her husband?

Folly, coming out here.

December 9, Thursday

Myra

I'd given Marcie my summary of the mining reports the afternoon before, so when the phone rang early Thursday morning I figured it was Marcie calling. My heart sank.

"Hey, Myra, this is Richard from the hall. William listed you as his contact person."

I'd met Richard a few times, years before, when my dad took me to Seattle and we stopped by the union hall. I felt a bolt of dread.

"My father?"

"The lifeboat's passengers are back in Seattle, and the captain is flying down this morning. I, er, wanted to call you to let you know I'm sorry to say William wasn't among the people picked up. The other lifeboat's still missing."

"What about the ship? Any word there?"

"The ship's under tow, coming back south. From what I've heard there was no one aboard her when they found her."

"How long will they search?"

"They'll search long and hard, Myra. Trouble is, the weather's bad again, and will stay bad for a week at least. I'm sorry, Myra. We're all praying for them."

➤

"Thanks for calling, Richard. I know there's others you've called, too. How many are still missing?"

"Nine members of the crew including your father, plus two Russian passengers."

After the call, I swept the floor - anything to stop my dark thoughts.

It was already building, the arch of grief, loss, and an end. As each day passed, the arch became stronger, more durable, more real. I dreaded facing this day of work.

I was startled by a knock at the door.

When I opened the door, Sarah stood on my front step, soaked and breathing hard, dressed in nylon running gear, a hooded jacket, and rain pants.

"You gonna let me in?"

Water pooled at her feet as she stood in the living room. She shook off her hood and unzipped her jacket. Steam rose around her. I grabbed a towel. "Where did you run from, Sarah? It's still dark out. What about school?"

"Tom-Tom's. I got here in 47 minutes. See this reflective stuff on my jacket?" Tom lived at least six miles from the res, and there were some decent hills in between. "You looked pretty sad last night at the vigil. I needed to practice, so I ran over here. I was hoping you'd give me a ride to school."

I laughed. "Glad you're here. All I've been doing is sweeping the place, again and again. You'll make me late for work."

I made tea. Sarah dried herself off and then pulled on a sweatshirt and pair of sweatpants I'd provided her. She went over to the corner.

"He's gonna be all right, Myra," said Sarah, holding the staff my great-grandmother had given my dad and my dad had then given to me. Seeing her standing there, I realized my great-grandmother had been the same height as Sarah. I remembered my great-grandmother greeting dad and me in the rain, up on Haida Gwaii, when I was 12.

"I had a dream, Sarah." Sarah kept holding the staff. "I dreamt I was on the coast, me and my dad, camping like we did when I was nine. It was night and there was a fire, and a storm, and then my dad was missing. I heard some rustling, and when I looked around, I saw the eyes of a big animal lit up by the fire."

"A bear, Myra? Was it a bear?"

"It was like the huge bear we all saw up high last summer, Sarah, the one you drew and we didn't believe you, not until we all saw it up in that basin."

We sat by the woodstove as rain lashed the side of the house. Minutes passed.

"No cross country race this weekend?" I asked.

"Season ended last week." Sarah stretched, placing the staff by her chair. She handled it reverently. "I've kept running. Something to do."

"Are you looking forward to Christmas break?"

"Guess so."

Sarah looked around my living room. On the walls were two drums, some photographs, and two drawings Sarah had made last summer: one of me and the other of a spider web.

"He's gonna be found, Myra."

"I sure hope so."

"We should just go up there and find him ourselves."

"Go up where?"

Sarah opened her mouth. Then she closed it. On the wall was a long relief map of the Northwest Pacific Coast from the Olympic Peninsula all the way north to Alaska. Inset text boxes marked shipwrecks, famous sites, and the locations of major historical events. Vancouver Island stretched like an aircraft carrier north by northwest toward the Alaska panhandle, with Haida Gwaii, otherwise known as the Queen Charlotte Islands, in between.

"They could have landed anywhere along Haida Gwaii's 150-mile coast," I said. "Where would we look?" Sarah said nothing. "Besides, Sarah, who's to say they struck land? Maybe they're still out in the ocean, drifting. They could have been blown hundreds of miles away, in almost any direction. Besides, we'd need two days just to get there. It's 1,000 miles to Prince Rupert, then an overnight ferry ride."

"We could fly."

"How do you know we could fly?"

"I checked." Sarah poked the map. "We could fly direct, and be there in a couple of hours."

"If their little airport's open." I placed a hand on Sarah's shoulder. "I'd be the first one to fly up there if I knew I could help, but right now we don't know a thing. We'd be wasting our time and money. And we could get lost. Then the people up there might have to search for us, too."

"I'm in good shape, Myra. And I know how to camp, after last summer." Sarah stepped away from me. "I know how to survive."

"All we can do is pray, Sarah."

I wished I had Sarah's youthful confidence. We were helpless.

"You hear from Sergei yet?"

"No." I didn't want to talk about Sergei.

"You will."

"I've got other things on my mind, Sarah."

She went back to her chair and held the staff upright against her knees.

"So when are you going to do a prayer ceremony?" asked Sarah.

"Who have you been talking to?"

"Last night, Rose told me to ask you. Is a prayer ceremony some kind of secret?"

"It's our ancient way of finding truth."

"Maybe you should do a prayer ceremony, then. Find William's truth."

I had learned the previous summer that Sarah, as Tom's granddaughter, had a trace of native blood, maybe from my people, six generations earlier.

"Have you ever thought about going to such a ceremony yourself, Sarah?"

"I did when Rose said something last night."

"Would Tom agree to let you?"

"Yep. I already asked him."

"So, you ran all the way over here to tell me to pray for my dad?"

"Sort of." Sarah turned the carved staff slowly. "You and Tom and William waited for me when I was lost. And you found me. Maybe if you, Tom and I pray for your father, we'll find him."

I suddenly understood.

"You're here to tell me there's a sweat lodge ceremony. When?"

"Saturday afternoon."

"And you're the messenger?"

"Eldon said it was time for me to start understanding."

So that's what Sarah, Eldon, Rose and Tom had been talking about in the kitchen last night.

Steve

Greg Watson, my union rep, met me at the Seattle airport. "How are you, Steve?"

All I had was a carry-on bag. We moved quickly from the terminal to the parking garage. My right foot ached. My nose was peeling from frostbite.

"Do I need a lawyer?" I asked him.

"I think so. I mean, I'm your union rep, but I also represent all our members, including your officers. The Coast Guard's already hired an investigator and scheduled a hearing for next week. The investigator's started interviewing people."

"Even before the ship's back?"

"He started scheduling the members of your crew as soon as they got back yesterday."

Greg looked at me over the roof of his car. "Steve, you need to get real representation, quickly. Buckhorn wants to talk to you before you've got a lawyer. I know Bruce is an old friend, but he's representing the company in this one." Greg rested his arms on the roof of his car. "They're going to do everything they can to pin this on you, Steve. They're already working your officers and engineers, to place the blame on you."

"Blame for what?" I asked. "I didn't start any fire."

Greg sighed. We got in the car.

"Not the fire, Steve, as you well know. You abandoned ship, yet the ship survived. A lifeboat was lost. And then someone else gets the tow. You didn't hear this from me, but Buckhorn would have preferred the ship to burn fully and sink."

"Well, she was on her last legs."

"Now there's going to be a big investigation and the ship will get tagged. She'll be idle for months while they work out the settlement claims. I'm sure Buckhorn will blame you for abandoning her too soon. This could cost you your license."

"I have my own suspicions about the fire, Greg."

"I don't want to hear them, Steve. This could turn into a big 'he said, she said' thing, and I need to represent everyone."

At the waterfront shipping terminal, Greg dropped me off by my car. I found a note on the windshield, folded inside a plastic sandwich bag.

"Call me as soon as you get this. Critical." The note was from Bruce.

I didn't even stop at my place on Green Lake before heading north to Willow Run. I wanted to be on time and I was looking forward to seeing Jimmie.

Willow Run bills itself as a "Restorative Facility." Much of its work concerns the orthopedic repair of legs, hips and arms. But Willow Run is also a mental health facility, a place where patients come for other types of long-term treatment, although not for alcoholism or drug abuse. Though not a prison, at times prisoners are shipped there for treatment and observation. They have a wing where patients can't leave on their own.

Jimmie's case officer was Laureen Bishop. I was never sure if she was an M.D. or a counselor. She'd been Jimmie's case officer since he had come to Willow Run. I disliked her. I had always disliked her, from the time I first met her and she announced to me Jimmie would be fine if he just "sucked it up and applied himself."

"It's unfortunate you couldn't make our appointment earlier," she said after I reached her office. "This was difficult to reschedule."

The day we were scheduled to meet, I was opening the hatch of the lifeboat so we could climb aboard the Coast Guard cutter. As I watched Laureen shuffle papers, I remembered the bird flying out of the lifeboat as soon as I cracked open the hatch cover.

Looking over at Laureen's grim expression, I gathered myself.

"Let's review, shall we?" This was how she started every session. Jimmie's thick file stood on the table in front of her.

"James insisted on the spinal operation, with a full understanding of the risks, when he was 19."

Jimmie damaged his spine in a fall at age nine, and soon after, he suffered a concussion during a fall. I blamed myself. Jimmie's mother blamed me, too. From then on, he was confined to a wheelchair, on the sidelines. Severe headaches made him miserable, and he had the first stirrings of something else.

I'd been on the New York-Europe run, back when there was such a thing. I'd just started my normal four-month tour when Jimmie wore down his mother and the doctors and they agreed to try fixing his spine.

The operation hadn't improved his spine or helped him to walk. The infection coming afterwards made him worse, because it spread into his brain and festered. He'd entered Willow Run when the infection occurred, and he'd nearly died. By the time the infection was over, he was different, darker. Mentally, new barriers had been thrown in his way. He was aware and knew what he had lost. He wanted to live on his own but knew and resented he could not.

"In the last few years," said Laureen, "we've operated twice to reduce his pain and increase his mobility. I am afraid there isn't much we can do about his attitude, or state of mind."

She fixed me a cold stare and I knew what was coming. "Jimmie needs to have a home, not an institution. He's 34 years old. Even if he can't focus the way he'd like, there's work out there he can do. Of course he will need a safe and homelike place to stay."

In a way, I agreed. Willow Run cost me $6,000 a month. But who would look after him when I was at sea?

"His mother..."

"I know your ex-wife refuses to take him," Laureen said, "But he suffers here, Mr. Procida. He's wasting away. I think his pain comes as much from his sense of isolation as from his damaged nerves."

"I know. This is an unfortunate situation. I need to sail to provide the funds to support him here, as you know. So he is not doing well?"

"He was very upset when you had to change the schedule. I understand you had a problem on your ship."

"A problem? Yes."

"Try to visit him each day for a period. As you did last time."

"I plan to, but unfortunately I need to return to Seattle to help find some members of my crew, who are still missing."

Laureen frowned. "He'll be disappointed."

"Me too. Can I see him now?"

"Of course."

Willow Run had been built in the 1950s, not a barren and stark state hospital complex, but not a residential rest home either. At least Jimmie had his own room in one of the newer buildings, which he seemed to enjoy.

I got soaked walking to Jimmie's building. I hadn't even had time to get him a book. He was a voracious reader, and counted on getting books from me.

I waited for him in the "gathering area."

Ten minutes later, Jimmie appeared, body bent forward, pushing his wheelchair, head lowered. His legs were sticks, thin and wasted from so many years of no use. He wore institutional blue drawstring pants and a blue pullover top. He looked like the patient he was, his face pale and his eyes hollow.

"Dad. You came."

"Of course I came." I gave him a hug, then sat on a couch by his wheelchair. "How you doing?"

"How come you're late? You were supposed to be here Wednesday."

"Didn't they tell you?"

"Tell me what?"

"I was still at sea Wednesday. We had a fire. A bad one. We had to abandon ship."

Years before, I'd brought Jimmie to the ship a couple of times. We put him and his wheelchair into a cargo basket and hoisted him aboard using the stores crane. He visited the bridge, and went down to the engine room. At the end he started to cry.

"I'll never get to do this myself," he had said.

Big Russ, my bosun at the time, had said, "Well, you're doing this now," but this had only made him cry harder.

"A fire?"

"Yeah. A really bad fire. We had to abandon ship."

Jimmie stared at me.

"Is that a cut over your eye? Are those burns on your hands?"

I'd forgotten about them.

"Yes."

"You had to get in lifeboats?"

I told Jimmie about the fire, the lifeboat, the little bird.

"A Canadian cutter found us. Some of the crew had burns,

others had small injuries, but nobody on the lifeboat died. The other lifeboat is still missing."

Jimmie stared out the window.

"Did you bring some books, dad? I could use some new books."

"I just got off the airplane from Canada this morning, Jimmie. Came right up here. I need to go back for a few days to handle some Coast Guard stuff. Then I'll come up here and visit for a while. I'll bring you some new books. Okay?"

Jimmie brightened.

"Dad, I've been taking accounting courses. Online."

"They have computers here?"

"Yeah, some of us get to use them, if we're careful. I've been taking the course for six months. I have a test soon. If I pass the tests, I might be able to be a CPA when I get out of here."

"Great, Jimmie." Could this be true?

"Or even work from in here. You can do this work online, you know."

Jimmie grinned, looking like the boy he'd been before his accident.

"What else is new, Jimmie?"

He looked around. The big room was now empty. The chess players had left.

"Laureen is a bitch."

"I agree."

"The food's even worse than last winter. I think the cook was fired. There's a rumor he was found with one of the patients from the woman's wing."

"Well, you know about rumors, Jimmie." It was a crime Jimmy had to be here, but where else could he go? He needed care for his condition and he couldn't fend for himself. "An accountant, huh?"

Jimmie had wanted to become a lawyer, then a stock broker.

He wanted to earn money, enough to get a place of his own. Sometimes I thought things would be cheaper and better for him if I could lease him an apartment and give him food money, but he couldn't live alone. He couldn't even bathe himself, cook or shop.

"You gonna stay for dinner, dad?"

"Sure will, Jimmie. Tell me all about this accounting course. Your room in good enough shape to show your old man?"

"I even set up a study corner. Come on."

Jimmie whirled his chair and began pushing toward the hallway. I followed.

December 11, Saturday

William

The snow melted and thick clouds ran in from the southwest.

Randall took William aside, down by the lifeboat.

"Can you get out of here?"

"You're a lot fitter than I am, first. You, Anne, Charlie."

Randall looked back up the slope. Anne was watching them from her corner of the shelter. The others were out of sight, knowing Randall would soon ask them to gather firewood.

"You need to lead the trip to get help, William," said Randall. "You're the only one among us who knows this kind of country, has experience hiking and surviving in the woods. You just told us how you and the others searched for days in the back country for Sarah."

"Jim claims he's a hunter," William said.

Randall snorted. "Come on, sitting in a blind in Texas waiting for them to drive some deer down on him? We're out of food. We might be here for weeks. Months. Someone needs to walk for help, William. Heather will run out of her medicine. She will die."

William knew Randall believed that William's Haida

heritage gave him special knowledge. If Randall wanted to invest him with such power and authority, he might as well use it. He wanted to survive as much as anyone.

"If I'm going to do this," said William, "you need to help. Lighten up on these people, all right? I may have to take Anne with me, and I want her sane."

"She's useless. Dangerous," said Randall. "The others are worse."

"This situation is tough," William said. "Everyone's hungry, tired and scared. If you keep yelling at people, they'll yell back. What's the old saying: a sugar cube is better than a stick to get a horse to water? You want us all back alive, don't you? The fire wasn't your fault, you didn't make the call to abandon ship, but as the senior officer it's your responsibility to bring us all home safe."

"William, if you're going to go for help, you need to do it before you, too, lose your strength."

"I know."

"Yesterday when we got wood, half of us weren't really there. Every day it's harder and harder to do anything. We're going to have to do something soon."

Even as they talked, the sky filled with clouds. An increasing wind bent the tops of the trees.

After doing the daily chores - gathering wood, building a fire, hanging clothes to dry, clearing the boat of snow - everyone gathered in the shelter.

"Do you think the smoking mountains from your story could be the volcanoes on Kamchatka?" asked Heather. Sometimes when the *Seattle Express* approached Petropavlosk the crew could see the 20,000 foot high volcanoes in the distance, smoking.

Randall snorted. "Heather, William's telling a bedtime story. That's all."

Jack and Jim nodded.

"Kamchatka has many active volcanoes," said William. "If ancient people followed the coast along the Bering land bridge, St. Paul and St. George would have been high headlands midway along the route from Russia to Alaska." Randall and Jack shook their heads. William continued, "That is exactly what Sergei and Alec thought as soon as I reached that point in Sarah's story. I can see some of you don't believe it, too."

"It's impossible, dammit," said Randall.

"Come on, first," said Anne. "I don't see you wandering off when William starts a new chapter."

Randall glared at his third mate.

"There's logical reasons for Sarah's story," said Jack. "When she reappeared in a thunderstorm, she was just mumbling, not speaking another language. She could have learned about spear throwers and such in lots of ways: listening to tales on your hike, watching movies, reading books, the internet. She'd seen a model canoe at Tom's. She'd been canoeing in Canada, was even caught in a storm on a big lake. I mean, what other reason is there?"

The wind had picked up. Rain began to fall. The plastic across the back of the shelter flapped.

"Sergei would agree with you, Jack," said William. "He argued like you do. Where is the evidence, he would say. Alec, though, he wasn't so sure. How can you document this, anyway? Most of the landmarks in her story are now buried, gone, changed, invisible."

"Exactly," said Randall, looking satisfied.

William stretched his neck, scratched his chin. "I wonder, though. If my Haida people built a seagoing 60 - foot canoe by burning the inside of a big log and then carving it with stones 1,000 years ago, then we could have done it 15,000 years ago. They found evidence in Timor, in the Pacific, of people 42,000 years ago taking tuna, a deep-sea fish. People sailed across a 60-mile wide strait, out of sight of land, 80,000 years ago to reach Australia. Alec mentioned all these things to me during my visits with him. Ancient people must have been good sailors. Why not?"

"There's no evidence," said Randall. Jim, Kirk, Jack, and Willie all nodded in agreement.

"Wood, hide, bone. They all disappear," William said. "Underwater archeology didn't even exist as a field of study until 40 years ago."

Randall began to laugh. "I see. You dream up something and then build a case so there can't be any evidence found. Perfect."

"Not so different from building a case completely out of faith."

"That's different, William."

"Why couldn't ancient sailors read the wind, the weather, currents, water color, and the seasons? Why couldn't they read the moon, the stars? The way Sarah tells this story, these people made the journey because they needed women - wives and mothers. To get them required a long trip."

"What, months along a dangerous coast in a canoe to get a few women?" asked Jack. "How stupid."

Anne laughed out loud. "I might be new at this, Jack, but I've already seen the lengths you sailors go to find women."

"Not for wives," said Willie.

Now Heather started laughing. "When you need women you travel. Oh good gracious, do you travel," said Heather. "It's how you men are made. This is surely the case since the first humans."

William lumbered to his feet and crawled to the front of the shelter. He added wood to the fire, then turned and faced everyone.

"I see you shaking your head, first. You too, chief, Jack. But, back then, terrible animals roamed the whole earth. Huge meat-eating bears, wolves, cats like lions with 11-inch fangs. When people were few and children precious, those animals probably ruled the earth. The only sort of safe places left for people were islands and maybe some refuges surrounded by ice. Maybe the only place they could survive was at the edges, close to boats to allow them to escape. "

"Well, what did you think, William?" Anne asked. "About Sarah's story?"

"It seemed like a vision quest, Anne. Usually such quests require a person to go without food or drink for several days. Sarah went eight days without food. The journeys taken during such quests are long, rich, and detailed. Those who refuse to believe this will never understand."

Randall thumbed his Bible and rolled his eyes. Jack scowled.

A deep whoosh rose as a large swell passed through the narrow opening of the inlet. Before them, in the lagoon, two small whales rose, blowing mist. Swimming together, they circled the inlet, traveling around the islets. Gulls flocked behind, chasing fish. The whales crossed directly in front of the shelter before passing back through the inlet's breach. Everyone watched until they were gone.

"How did those whales get in here? We hit the bottom in the lifeboat," said Kirk. "Isn't it too shallow?"

"A sign," William said. Rain stippled the inlet's surface. The whales had ghosted into sight, ghosted away. Now a large raven landed on a tree close by and watched them.

"I hope it's a sign we get out of here," Willie said.

"It was just two whales, Willie," said Jack. Jim stared at the trail of bubbles left by the whales. Willie swallowed.

"Some people," said William, "can accept these events as normal and expected. Many times the person on a vision quest is aware he or she is half-awake and dreaming. What startled us about Sarah was she seemed entirely unaware she'd been lost and trapped beneath the ground. Instead, she gained consciousness in another place and time and never questioned what went before. She simply lived in the moment."

"Just as we now have to simply live in this moment," said Anne. "Let's hope we all later get to tell people what happened here, as Sarah told what happened to her."

"It's a fantasy," Randall said, clutching his Bible.

"Whatever Sarah knew," William said, "and however she came to know it, she told of a journey taken over weeks, not eight days. Whatever it was, to her it was real. That's how she told it and that's how it sounded, hearing it. Back then, when I heard it, and when I told Sergei and Alec, I thought it was a dream, or a wonderful vision. I envied her. I envy her still."

Pete

Pete got back from Seattle and the TWIC offices late Friday. The TWIC offices had been crowded, mostly new Buckhorn hires, and he wasn't out of there until after two. He'd raced across town to meet his lawyer, and then had to wait in Edmonds for two ferries before he could cross to Kingston. He'd hoped to catch Brad Withington at either the TWIC offices or on the return ferry, but Joyce's new husband was nowhere to be seen.

As soon as Pete got home, he called Joyce, supposedly to take Sam to see a movie the next day, Saturday, but really so Pete could talk to Joyce face to face about what he'd heard on the ferry.

"I'll be over at 11:30," he told Joyce. "We'll grab lunch before the movie. Then I'll bring him back."

"Not too late, Pete."

When he drove up the drive the next morning to the Withington casbah, Pete could see Sam waiting just inside the front door. His son wore a red-billed cap, bill to the side, like a rapper.

After letting Pete inside, Joyce sent Sam into the living room "so your father and I can talk."

➤

"I've been thinking," Joyce said. "This holiday we're going down to Hollywood Hills for vacation. We'll take Sam to Universal Studios and Six Flags, then meet some of Brad's family down there."

He wondered if Brad had already talked to her about his unexpected meeting with Pete on the ferry the day before.

"This holiday is my turn with Sam."

"Well, Pete, yes, but this trip came up suddenly and the package was too good to miss."

Pete said nothing. Joyce took a breath.

"In compensation, maybe Sam could stay at your place the weekend before Christmas break."

"The other day you decided Sam wasn't safe at my place."

"I was upset, and I do think it's unsafe back there, but I also want to do right by you because of this holiday glitch."

Sam appeared, wearing his coat. He was ready to go.

Pete nodded. Sam stood watching them, holding his small backpack. Pete decided this wasn't the time to get into a discussion. Something was going on, Pete had no doubt. Joyce never backtracked on one of her edicts about Sam. Yet here she was, changing her mind.

"Let's go, Sam."

"Bye, honey. Enjoy the movie." Joyce hugged Sam.

Inside the truck, the wipers squeaked as they swept back and forth.

"I can come to your place?" asked Sam.

"It seems so. Weekend after next. Just before Christmas break."

"I thought she said it was dangerous."

"She did. But because she's taking you guys south for the break, you can stay with me before."

"I don't want to go south."

"Whaddya mean? California heat? Sun out every day?

Touring the movie studios? Mom said you'll go to Six Flags. They've got more roller coasters than you can imagine."

"I'm not allowed to take roller coasters."

"You're older. Maybe they'll let you this time."

"Dad?" Sam turned toward Pete, eyes wide. "Am I moving?"

"Moving?" Pete's heart sank.

"I overhead Mom and Brad talking, when some other men came to the house Friday."

"What did you hear?"

"They'll find a house for us to live in when we go down for vacation. Brad will move first and then mom and I will go later. That's what they were talking about." Sam's lip quivered. "I like my school here. I like being near you."

"You don't like the casbah, Sam?" Pete tried his best.

"I don't like Brad, dad. Why does he have to move? Why can't I stay with you?"

"Sam, I don't know anything about this, and maybe you're wrong. Maybe they were talking about something or someone else."

Now Sam looked suspicious.

"I don't think so. Mom said to the men they needed a house with four bedrooms. I don't like the casbah. I like your grubby little place." Sam sniffled, wiping his cheeks.

"You know what movie we're going to see?"

Sam shook his head.

"Neither do I. Tell you what - we'll eat a big lunch and then go to the movieplex and pick the most scary, dangerous, evil movie we can find."

"Science fiction," Sam said.

"Yes."

Pete took Sam to the barbecue place and they loaded up on ribs and fries. Sam's face was smeared with ketchup and grease before he was half done. Pete knew Joyce would have a cow, Sam eating all this unhealthy food, but what the hell.

They saw a film about aliens, predators, a marooned space colony, and giant toothed worms. They ate popcorn drenched in butter and sat together in the middle of the first row. The movie wasn't very scary and the special effects were ridiculous. Sam laughed when the toothed worm appeared. So did Pete.

Pete took Sam home. There was still no sign of Brad's car.

"Honey, you go wash up, clean your greasy face," Joyce said, glaring at Pete. "Then I'll let you watch the rest of the cartoon movie until dinner."

Pete let Joyce lead him into the living room. She sat on the couch, and he deliberately picked a chair across from her.

"What's going on?" he asked.

"What do you mean?" Joyce blushed. She'd always been a terrible liar.

"Yesterday when I went to Seattle to get a TWIC card, I saw Brad on the ferry with a couple of Buckhorn suits." Joyce sucked in her lower lip. "When were you going to tell me you planned to move, Joyce?"

She faced Pete. "Brad has a terrific opportunity, as Buckhorn's lead attorney for their new operation up here, and he needs to be in Los Angeles at the headquarters offices this coming year. Then perhaps we'll move back to Sol Duc."

"I went to see my lawyer, Joyce. I won't let Sam be hauled away from here without a fight."

"He lives with me."

"We have joint custody."

"Still, he lives with me, his mother."

"Yes, but we have joint custody. You're going to have to get a judge to declare Sam needs to leave his school, his home town, and his father."

"Don't fight us on this, Pete. I know you're having a rough

time but don't take it out on Sam or us."

"What, you expect me to fly down to L.A. every month to see Sam?"

"We're only going down there for a year."

Pete stared at his former wife.

"And if Buckhorn's new venture doesn't pan out, what then? Knowing Brad, he had Buckhorn guarantee him a job in L.A. if the deal up here unravels." From Joyce's expression, Pete knew he was right. "You can't do this, Joyce."

"I can. We can." Joyce leaned back and frowned. "Look at you, Pete. You're badly hurt. You can hardly walk. You lost your livelihood as a surveyor and forester and now you're working as a security guard. A security guard, Pete." Pete said nothing. Her statements fell like blows. "You can't care for an active and curious young boy. You can barely care for yourself. I've seen you trying to get around, and it's an agony to watch. What if Sam was up at your cabin and you fell or hurt yourself? You're practically in the wilderness."

"Come on, Joyce. I'm only two miles off the main road."

"You know what I mean. And the schools up here, they're nothing compared to the school we can put Sam in down there. He'll get special attention, the kind of attention he needs and deserves."

"He likes Sol Duc. He has friends in his school, which is important, especially after the divorce and your remarriage. He finally has consistency. He should stay here."

"No way, Pete. You got yourself shot last summer. What sort of people are you running with? And now you're in security. Will you be carrying a gun?"

Pete had no idea.

"So you throw me a bone and let me have Sam before Christmas while you steal him away for at least a year."

Pete involuntarily rubbed his bad leg. Joyce wasn't going

to bend on this, he knew, but he was determined to hold firm.

"You better schedule a hearing fast, Joyce, if you want to do this."

"You can't afford it, Pete."

"You don't know what I can afford."

He made his way to the front door.

"Please, Pete, don't make a scene about this. Think of Sam."

"I am thinking of Sam."

"Are you? Ask yourself."

Pete hobbled to his truck in the rain and headed down the casbah's long, paved driveway. The house, lights blazing, receded behind him.

Driving home, he had a disturbing idea. He and Withington both worked for Buckhorn. Could Brad exert influence and get Pete fired? Then Joyce could argue at the hearing Pete had no income and therefore could not support Sam.

Wow.

Myra

Tom and Sarah arrived at my place around lunchtime, but I hadn't eaten and neither had Sarah or Tom. The heat in the lodge was best experienced on an empty stomach.

"You're coming?" I asked Tom. He was wearing shorts.

"William's my oldest friend. Perhaps my spirit will help find him."

"We'll need all our spirits to bring him home," I said.

In the rain, we drove to the end of a rutted road. Trucks, cars and two vans stood in a clearing. My father was not a blood member of our tribe, but his ex-wife, my mother, was, and I was a member through her. In a similar way, I was considered a member of dad's Haida community well to the north.

We followed a winding trail to the prayer site, a path few people ever took. We Sol Duc never mention this place to outsiders.

Eldon served as fire keeper, heating stones, fueling the fire using dry wood, bringing the hot stones to the lodge when asked by the prayer leader, in this case his brother, Gilbert. Gilbert worked for the state prison system, visiting the iron house to hold ceremonies in the traditional way, something once prohibited in the state of Washington. Rose was helping Eldon at the fire.

The small prayer lodge formed a modest dome beneath the trees. Made of willow shoots lashed together, the dome was covered by tarps, hides and blankets to keep out the daylight. A rusty livestock trough lay nearby, half filled.

Sarah nodded at a couple of the younger members of the tribe, kids she probably knew from school. Gilbert raised the flap at the front of the lodge as we removed our rain gear, and then we stepped into the lodge wearing shorts and T-shirts. The youths led the way, followed by me, Sarah and Tom, and finally two tribal members, Lydia and Rollin, who were close to William.

We sat on the dry ground along the inside edge of the circular lodge. The dirt had been dug away to give us a place to comfortably rest our feet, and then, in the center, beyond our feet, was a deeper pit where the hot stones would be placed. I felt chilled without my rain gear, and I could feel Sarah shivering beside me. Gilbert pulled the flap closed and the dome went dark. The curved roof lay just above our heads. We sat hip to hip in a circle. I could hear the trickle of the nearby stream, rain striking the roof of the domed lodge, and the sound of raindrops hissing on the fire outside.

Gilbert reopened the flap and gestured to Eldon, who was poking at the fire. Next to him, Rose began to sing.

Eldon extended a large elk horn into the lodge, a large round red-hot rock held in the crook of the upper antlers. He let the rock tumble into the deep pit. I could feel the heat at once. He added three more rocks, one at a time. Gilbert closed the flap. All I could see were the glowing red rocks. Heat radiated against my face and knees.

Gilbert poured a ladle of water on to the rocks and steam rose in a hissing rush. If the heat became too much for anyone, they were free to leave the lodge without shame. I gathered myself. I knew this was nothing compared to what would come in later rounds. I held my eyes open, seeing only the glow at my feet. Beside me, Sarah edged back toward the curved inside of the dome. I had told her earlier if she got too hot, she should get as close as she could to where the edge of the dome rested on the earth, for there she'd find cooler air. I knew Sarah well enough to know she would die before leaving the lodge before the four full rounds of prayers ended.

Gilbert began to pray.

The first few times I'd been in a sweat lodge I'd been angry and frustrated, convinced I was the victim of endless betrayals. Later I learned anger was one of my demons. In the dark lodge, my mind cleared, went blank, and became open to other realities. A lodge like this was where I'd learned to control my anger.

The first round seemed to go quickly. I lost track of the passage of time. Initially I could see the bright red of freshly-heated rocks, but the glow faded soon enough. Then the darkness within the lodge seemed infinite. Steam hissed and people gasped for breath. Some would lie on the earth close to the intersection of the dome and dirt floor, where the air was cooler. The strong ones never faltered, sitting cross-legged, backs straight and heads held high, despite the waves of searing heat.

Sarah never moved, her thigh pressed against mine. I heard Tom breathing hard. I knew he was made of iron and would endure. One of the kids began to gasp and cry, and the others hitched forward so he could crawl past their backs and slip out the entrance.

When he did, I caught a glimpse of the wet trees, the tip of Eldon's antler, now stuck in the ground, waiting for the next round, and, for just a moment, I felt a brief caress of cooler air. We prayed to the spirits and the earth, after which Eldon brought in six more rocks. Next we prayed to the four directions.

The entrance of a prayer lodge always faces east, the direction of the rising sun, the start of the day, the start of life. I sat at the north, where I always sat, the direction the bear held as the totem animal.

Before the third round, during the brief time the flap was open, I saw Sarah's face streaming with sweat. Her skin had turned pale but she still sat erect, her eyes wide open.

During the third round, we prayed to our relations and ancestors.

By now the lodge was sweltering. Over 16 stones lay in the pit, radiating heat. Gilbert ladled more water on the stones. Steam rose. In a hoarse, ragged voice, Rollin prayed for William's spirit. Lydia prayed for her mother, her father, and her brothers, all now dead. Lydia's prayer ended. Finally, Tom began to speak.

"I pray for the spirit of my grandfather, who lies in the earth in the Godkin Valley. I visited him last summer for the first time in 40 years to bring him peace, and I introduced him to his great–great-granddaughter, who is here next to me this day. I pray now for my oldest friend William, who was along last summer, who with Sarah and William's daughter Myra saw the great bear in the high country. William then, following his trade, went to sea, and is now lost. I pray for his spirit, wherever he is, in hopes he may come back to us."

The heat seared our lungs. Sarah spoke in a high, clear voice:

"I pray for my friend William who is near his homeland and his people. I pray he hears our calls and comes back to us, but if he has gone back to his home I pray the air is fresh and his smile is wide."

My turn came.

"I pray for my father who raised me and nourished me, and taught me all I know, and who brought me to these places when just a girl to show me truth. I pray, wherever he is, he hears my love and hope for him."

I could hear Sarah crying next to me.

My skin prickled in the rising steam. The heat scorched my nose and throat, my arms and hands, but I held my head high, my eyes open, staring into the dark.

I was dimly aware of rain hammering the top of the lodge, but my ears were filled with prayers, the hissing of the stones, and the breath and sobbing of others in the lodge.

I was in a state of agony, yet serenity, too. I heard Gilbert take deep shuddering breaths. Tom coughed lightly.

Then, ahead of me, I saw from within the barely-visible swirling steam a growing light, a kind of opening. I was on a long hill, looking down onto a plain, and this plain rolled and undulated below me, descending, endlessly, grasses and sedges lightly wavering in the wind.

Part of me knew I was sitting in the prayer lodge, but I watched and waited. On the plain, I saw patches of old snow, crystalline the way old snow gets in the spring after thawing and freezing many times. The surface of the snow was covered by animal tracks, some fresh, others old, leading away from me down the slope and onto the grasses of the plain.

Behind Sarah and me, I felt a bear, head looking over our shoulders. I could feel the presence, the heat, and the breath. He panted heavily just behind my ear. I knew his yellow eyes glowed behind me.

I stood on the snow, looking over the plain. I forgot the heat, the suffering, the pain. The drumming sound of rain on the roof was replaced by a sighing wind. High above, the cry of an eagle rose, sharp and clear.

I blinked. The bear next to me took a breath, chest rumbling.

Then, ahead of me, emerging from the dark beyond the plain, far away, I saw my father. He seemed to be searching, and I wanted to wave, to call out to him. Then he spotted me next to the bear, and he began to climb the slope. As he got closer, I could see he looked impossibly young. Tall as ever, he carried a stout stick in one hand and a heavy cape across his broad shoulders. His hair, entirely black, waved in the wind.

He climbed up the slope, but stopped at the line of snow. He looked at me, and then at the bear. Finally he spoke:

"I am here. I will be here until you find me."

The bear, still by my shoulder, lifted its head and softly growled.

Gilbert pushed open the flap, and the vision vanished. The third round of prayer had ended. Gray light flowed into the lodge. We stretched, inhaling cooler air. I looked to my left, but saw no bear, only Sarah, sitting erect, still staring ahead, eyes open. Tom sat next to her, eyes closed.

My heart raced.

The bear had been real - I was sure. This was the short face bear we had seen the summer before, and the same animal I'd seen in my dream the other night. I shivered, despite the heat inside the lodge.

After a brief respite, Eldon reappeared and extended six more rocks. Then Gilbert closed the flap.

"The last round," he said.

The lodge was hotter than ever. People said short prayers. When it was Sarah's turn I heard gibberish until I realized she was speaking in another language, an ancient language I'd heard her speak once before.

I felt at home.

I am here. I am here until you find me.

The round ended and we all stumbled from the lodge. Many plunged into the livestock trough full of water, some howling from the sudden cold. Eldon and Rose crawled into the lodge for a few minutes, just the two of them, the fire tender and his helper. They soaked in the spirits. Then we scattered the coals of the fire and all drove to my place, where we ate a large meal.

"You are strong," Gilbert said to Sarah, before turning to the young tribal members. "All of you are strong."

Gilbert included the teen who had left the lodge due to the heat. He had stayed to help Eldon and Rose at the fire.

Later, everyone gathered their casserole dishes, plates and utensils and went home. Tom and Sarah lingered.

"You spoke a different tongue, the last prayer round," I said to Sarah.

"I did?"

"I think so."

Sarah studied me. She said, "The bear between us was big, wasn't it?"

Tom looked confused. I was shocked. Had Sarah seen the bear too?

"I saw my dad," I told them. "He said, 'I am here. I am here until you find me.' He looked young, and his hair was black. He is in the spirit world and again free." Tears ran down my cheeks.

"If you saw him so, Myra, I am sorry for you," said Tom. "I'll miss him."

Sarah shook her head. "No. He is alive, and he will stay alive until you find him."

"Oh, Sarah," I said, both sad and frustrated. I was now sure my dad was in the spirit world. I knew grief would come in a day or two, yet after being in the sweat lodge I felt some peace.

How could Sarah have seen what I saw?

Travis

Travis struggled toward the bow. How many times had he made this trip in the last three days? The wind slashed rain across his face.

Every hour, they checked the tow, radioing a report back to the bridge. Each shift had one man on the bridge, one man on the main deck, and a third in the engine room watching the generator. The trouble was, there were just five of them because Larry was hurt.

On the main deck, Travis lowered his head as he walked into the wind. He should have taken the starboard tunnel. At least the ice had melted, and the rain felt almost hot after the freezing days. They must be less than a day to the Strait of Juan de Fuca.

Because they were only five, each had to work two six hour watches in a row every day, or 18 hours a day. Travis put in six hours on the bridge, monitoring the alarm system there, making sure the few lights and electronics they had kept working. Then he spent six hours in the engine space by the generator, battered by the constant clatter and bang. Now and then the generator smoked, but always it ran, their source of heat and light and communication. Now, on his third watch,

▶

six hours later, he checked the tow wire at the bow, his eyes stinging with fatigue.

At night, two of them would check the bow together, but during the day Travis went alone.

The bow rose and fell, pulled by the tug far ahead, lost in the rain and the seas. Travis dreamed of Ned's fresh bread, fresh eggs, and steaming roast chicken. But Ned was on the tug. Here, all they had were canned goods and the few groceries they'd brought. All the fresh food in the ship's cooler had spoiled. By the time they got the refrigeration back even the frozen meat had turned. The galley had been destroyed in the fire. They heated cans by nestling them close to a hot water line, and then ate directly from the cans.

The ship leaned far to starboard as a seething sea passed.

"I'm at the bow deck ladder." Travis radioed Dark Cloud. "Can you see me?"

"I see you. Be careful."

Looking aft, Travis could see the windows of the wheelhouse, behind him and up high.

He grabbed both rails on the narrow ladder and stepped over some lingering ice before climbing the steps.

The bow was washed clean and the deck glistened as water ran through the scuppers. The black tow wire, securely wrapped around the three bitts in the bow's center, led out through the port chock. Travis crept forward and checked the cable closely, making sure he kept a hand on a strut. The last thing they needed was him getting swept by an unexpected wave into the mooring winches.

"Wire's secure."

As he crouched below the rail, he noticed a strangely-shaped object stuck beneath the rail's flange, just aft of the port chock. Another wave hit the bow,

Travis realized he was seeing a boot. Something gray

emerged from the top. Oh God. There was Larry's boot, still holding his foot. Rather than being washed overboard, the boot and severed foot had somehow become caught, and then frozen into the ice coating the bow.

"You OK there?" asked a voice on the radio.

"Yeah, Cloud." Travis decided he wouldn't say anything about the boot and severed foot. But he couldn't just leave it there, either. He approached the boot and jabbed at it with his fist. It was frozen in solid. He braced himself against the rail, waited until the ship slid back off a sea, raised his foot, and kicked. He kicked again. The boot and foot fell to the deck, covered with ice. Travis grabbed it and threw it over the side, shuddering.

Returning to the deckhouse, he trudged down to the engine room to warm up. Billy would be down there, finishing his watch. Travis looked forward to the brightly-painted space, only partly darkened by soot, filled with engine sounds and jiggling dials.

Fire still smoldered somewhere in the forward part of the ship. Seawater had also flooded the duct keel and bilges, but Vince had the pumps running, slowly draining the ship.

"Tow all right?" asked Billy as he adjusted some wires. Vince, apparently a near-genius electrician, had run some wires down from the bridge through the stairwell. They wanted more of the ship's electronics up and working.

"Holding OK," said Travis. He had to shout over the noise of machinery. He lingered, avoiding his icy cabin, where he knew he'd fall asleep in seconds.

"How's Larry?" asked Billy.

Last time Travis had checked, Larry's stumps were oozing even more blood. He'd need another transfusion soon. He and Dark Cloud had been drinking all the fluids they could get, hoping they would soon be able to donate more blood.

Larry was still unconscious, and his complexion deadly pale. He needed to get to a hospital soon or he'd die. Travis and Dark Cloud were the only people aboard with type O blood.

On the way up to the wheelhouse, Travis looked in on Larry. This was the other duty they all shared—checking on Larry and changing his bandages. Three times Larry had started to come to, but after some incoherent muttering, he'd passed out again.

They'd strapped him in a bunk and secured his leg and arm on jury-rigged platforms to prevent him from being hurt by the motion of the ship. If they wanted the wounds to clot, they'd have to keep the stumps from banging anything. Even so, Travis could smell an awful stench. Larry's wounds were infected.

Larry's eyes were open. Travis had been checking Larry's leg for a few minutes before he noticed Larry watching him.

"Larry. How you feeling?"

Larry stared at Travis, then down at his leg and arm.

Larry worked his mouth, trying to speak. "Where are we?"

Travis toggled his hand-held radio. He knew Louise would hear him.

"Larry's awake, Louise." Travis braced as the ship rolled. "We're about a day from the Strait, maybe less, Larry."

"Wire's on?"

"Steady and strong. Louise and Nelson been bringing us down."

"The other tugs?"

"They left. But we're pretty sure they'll be waiting for us closer to Sol Duc."

Larry shook his head and winced.

"Don't matter. We get there, they'll take the ship, bring her to the dock, but we'll have the claim."

"Yeah, we will."

Larry moved his arm, the one missing a hand. The bandage at the end had turned dark red.

"How come I'm still alive? I shoulda lost all my blood."

"Dark Cloud's good. He stopped the bleeding and then we gave you blood. Me and Dark Cloud have type O blood. You can take our blood."

"I'm not gonna last two more days, Trav." Larry was pale, his eyes hollow. "This I know."

Louise came on the radio.

"Travis, can he talk?"

Larry blinked, hearing Louise's voice. Travis put the radio in Larry's good hand.

"Hey, darlin. Hear you been steering her good."

"Goddam you, Larry. You careless son of a bitch."

"These things happen."

"I'm pissed at you, dammit. Just take care of yourself, OK?"

"I'm in good care, Louise. Cabin of my own, even have lights and some heat. Not bad at all."

"I'm trying to get us in the Strait as fast as I can. Maybe we can transfer you, get you to a hospital."

"Louise. Listen."

"Larry..."

"No. Listen, OK? This ship's gonna be handed over to the Buckhorn tugs when we get close to Sol Duc. It'll take two tugs to get her to the dock."

"I thought we were gonna sit on the ship until the hearing's over and we get paid."

"No, they'll take the ship, chase you guys off. Try to blame you for some of the damage, too. It'll be them, not us, aboard, when she's at the dock, tagged, watching her. Should be us, but it's their ship, their dock. Still, the thing is, darlin', we took the ship, we have the tow, we have the claim. And it's gonna be a big one." Larry's voice grew reedy. "Get the bank to lend us money against the claim so you can pay everyone off."

"I'm not sure the bank will lend me money."

"They should. You gotta ask them."

"You need to rest, Larry. We can talk about this later."

"Yeah. Be good, darlin."

Larry stopped talking and put his head back, closed his eyes.

Dark Cloud appeared in the cabin doorway.

Travis looked at Dark Cloud and shook his head.

Larry opened his eyes, noticed Dark Cloud.

"Your bandages are good, Cloud. Now I need to sleep."

Larry slept, breathing softly. Bright blood spread over the leg bandages until Dark Cloud readjusted them.

"We gotta get him to help," said Travis as he handed Dark Cloud more bandages. The gray bone had dark patches. The odor was foul. Yellow pus oozed from near the edges of the wound.

"Start praying, Travis."

December 12, Sunday

Louise

*W*arhorse, *Seattle Express* in tow, entered the Strait of Juan de Fuca Sunday morning. Louise kept hearing Larry's voice, the way he had sounded, on the radio the day before.

They were on track to reach Sol Duc Harbor by mid-afternoon, when they would cast the towline and let the Buckhorn tugs take the ship. Larry wouldn't be able to get off until they were fast at the dock, hours and hours from now.

"He's not good, is he?" asked Nelson. Louise wondered if she looked as tired as Nelson did.

"No." She'd heard resignation, maybe acceptance, in Larry's voice. "It's my fault, Nelson. I was so angry at the son of a bitch I wished him ill, and look what happened."

"Not your fault."

"Yes. He did me wrong and now I've done him wrong, except 10 times worse. If I hadn't pulled the tug left just as we hooked up the cable he'd still have his leg and arm."

"Bullshit, Louise."

"Really?" She found it easier to be furious at Larry than

fearful he would die.

"What did he do, Louise?" asked Nelson, confused by her anger.

"He started screwing a bimbo he met in the casino."

"You mean Suzette? Tall? A little heavy? Big eyes?"

How did Nelson know her? He hadn't been at the casino. Did this mean Larry had been bringing his squeeze by the tug when Louise had been away hustling business?

Nelson started to laugh. Louise wanted to kill him.

Ahead, the water seemed calmer, and Louise could see the green slopes of the Olympic Peninsula. Home was almost in sight.

"Is that what you think, Louise?"

"What do you know?"

She wanted to kill Nelson, kill Larry, kill them all. Worthless bastards, all of them.

"Larry's not screwing her, Louise. He's been spending time because she's Bill's girlfriend. Bill, our banker. Larry's been working on her to persuade Bill to keep our credit."

"She's a casino waitress."

"She's a lawyer, Louise. She specializes in admiralty law. Larry was trying to get Bill to extend us credit, against any future work like this claim here." Could this be true? "Bill has a big problem, Louise. Gambling losses. Larry knew, so he had a little leverage."

Louise stared ahead. Could she have been wrong about Larry?

Vince came on the radio. In an unsteady voice, he said: "Louise, Larry's gone. I'm sorry."

William

Seals had come into the cove. It was raining and the southwest wind was strong, the clouds heavy, low. The ocean thundered. In the inlet, swells surged, hardly broken, it seemed, by the narrow and shallow breach to the left. The lifeboat ground against the rock shelf. William retied the ropes holding the boat to the shore. Across the bay, to the right of the islets, seals were gathered, barking, before thick trees on rocks at the base of the slope.

The snow lower down had melted. Rocks lay glistening and dark. Trees stood wet, dripping. Sheets of rain crossed before them in bands, moving fast. Above, high on the slopes, snow remained. Higher still lay cloud.

Heather and Charlie worked on the long gaff hooks. Each hook carried a dull blade with a hook behind. Heather sharpened one of the hooks with a file.

When Randall called for firewood, Oleg and Mattiew refused to budge. Everyone else followed Anne to find wood.

"We don't work for you," Oleg said.

"You don't," Randall said. "But you're using my blankets and life jackets for warmth, and you're wearing my fire jackets, so go get wood."

Randall stood watching most of the others walk in the rain toward the far ridges, where the wood was. William was down with Heather and Charlie, helping them but listening to Randall.

Oleg stared at Randall. Mattiew began to rise. Oleg placed a hand on his arm. Mattiew cast off the hand and rose. Oleg stayed put while Mattiew shrugged into his jacket and boots.

Mattiew wandered after the others. Randall joined William by Heather and Charlie. The rain was now falling hard. Oleg remained in the shelter.

Heather filed the pointed hook, intent. She bit her lip. Her dark skin was wet with rain.

"We will have meat," she said. Her accent had a strong, Caribbean lilt. The gaff hook was on a smooth pole eight feet long, an inch in diameter. The hook itself was steel, sharp, and now getting sharper. A second pole and hook lay on the ground.

Charlie held the pole behind Heather while she bent over, filing the hook between her knees.

William looked across the bay. The seals seemed small from this distance. Randall figured out what they were planning.

"You'll never get close to them anyway."

William took the gaff from Heather and began filing.

"Worth a try, first. We get a seal, we'll have some food."

Charlie held the pole for William. Heather was panting. Filing was hard work. The lifeboat rocked in the low swell coming through the breach.

"Probably an endangered species." Charlie said. "We'll have to pay a big fine when we get rescued."

Heather took the file from William when William tired.

"One good strike, to the heart," said William. "Once this thing's in, you won't get it out."

"We'll have two," Heather said. "Two strikes."

By the time the others returned with wood, each gaff hook

was as sharp as a razor.

Jack and Kirk had dragged back an entire small tree, long dead. Pete started to cut it into pieces using the dull axe. Others began to break the branches into smaller sections. The rain was heavy, but after six days everyone ignored it. They all knew after getting wood they could go back under the shelter and try to dry off. The seals barked and swam and ignored the sounds of chopping wood.

"We've been here following the same pattern each day," said William. "Maybe the seals showed up because they know our routine."

William was counting how many seals there were. They moved fast when they slipped into the water. William knew he'd never be able to approach close enough to strike one. He doubted anyone could. He remembered Sarah's story, how seal tasted of fish. Now he might find out.

"Going to be damn difficult to get close enough."

"I will get close enough, William," Heather said.

"You?" Jack was stacking wood. "This is a stretch for you, isn't it, sneaking up on a seal? How many seals are there in Honduras?"

"It was her idea," Charlie said.

"I will take Charlie with me," Heather said. The way she said Charlie's name, it sounded like Cholly.

"I don't know," Randall said. "You try, and scare them, they're gone."

"They weren't here before," Anne said. "Heather said she'll do it. Who else here is willing to try?" Nobody moved. Anne faced the group. "Who wants to eat seal meat anyway?"

Everyone raised a hand; they were all hungry.

"Waste of time, Heather." Randall stood by the fire.

"No." Heather lifted one of the poles. She wore a fire jacket, coveralls, hat. "As a girl, in Honduras, I hunted rats.

My brothers took me to the dump where the boys speared rats. I became better than they."

"A seal is not a rat," Randall said.

"Who else here has hunted anything?"

Heather examined each of them in turn. Jim, who had hunted deer in Texas, did not speak. William had done some hunting, but not this kind of hunting.

Heather and Charlie got outfitted. Across the inlet, the seals barked. They clustered on rocks at water's edge, impervious to the rain.

"Good luck, Heather," Anne said.

The day was warm compared to previous days. Strong gusts of wind swept past the shelter. The surf behind the point roared.

Everyone except Heather and Charlie gathered near or under the shelter. They hung clothes, built up the fire. Smoke swirled across the bay, above the seals.

Heather and Charlie, each carrying a gaff hook, headed south, toward the slopes. They did not follow the shore toward the seals. Heather led Charlie up the slope, higher and higher, until they were 400 feet above, in trees and shrubs.

"Where the hell is she going?" Jack was peering. "She's hunting seals and now she's hiking to Vancouver Island."

"How does a cow like her move so well?" Oleg asked, watching Heather.

"That cow, as you call her, is chasing your dinner. I don't see you doing anything." Anne spat.

William saw what Heather was doing. She led Charlie, the two of them largely hidden by rocks, downwind of the seals. Dark and wet, their tan fire jackets blended well against the rocks and trees.

"On with the story," Kirk said, now comfortable beneath life jackets, boughs, a blanket.

"When they return," William said.

All morning they watched.

Heather led Charlie behind and above the seals. Then, on their bellies, they crept down, tree by tree, rock by rock. At times William wondered if they were moving at all. The rain made the ground wet and cold, but Heather and Charlie kept themselves low as they stalked, body length by body length.

The seals were gathered on rocks beneath a copse of small trees and ledges. Occasionally, a seal dropped into the water. The seals were finding food, and their attention was on the water. The big bulls lay closest to the water. Behind them were the cows, yearlings and pups. Just before the trees, one mother and her large pup stretched on rocks.

It was this pair Heather attacked. She and Charlie suddenly rose, fast, from the tightly massed trees, poles high, points ahead. Together they plunged both hooks into the pup, which had tried desperately to wiggle away, chasing its mother. Both gaffs struck home. Charlie gave a high shout while Heather wrestled with her pole, fighting the writhing seal.

The other seals, in a great burst of barking and howls, fled splashing into the water. Charlie and Heather fought against the pup, which refused to die. They followed it as it tried to reach the water. They pushed and pulled the poles, trying to find the seal's heart.

The pup gave one final, violent twist and then fell still. Wind and rain gusted over the shelter.

Soaked, Heather waved at the others from across the bay. Charlie was dancing on the rocks, waving his arms. They were both black with water. Blood could be seen running over the rocks.

"Jesus." Jack watched Heather wave. "Now we'll have to cut it up, right?"

"Fresh meat." Kirk rose, pulling on his overalls, grabbing a knife.

"Food." Jim was searching for his boots.

Randall stood. He had been in the rain the entire time, watching the stalk. Now he cupped his hands around his lips.

"The steward and the ordinary. You two get the choices of meat. Nice job. I should have had more faith, Heather. From now on I'll keep my mouth shut." He turned to Anne, who had also been watching, standing. "Did you see? Amazing."

"Just a woman's work," Anne said, proud.

"Well, Charlie helped, too," Randall said.

Anne said nothing.

They butchered the seal where they killed it, letting the rain wash the blood away. Heather supervised the cutting. She was steward and knew something about cuts of meat, how a mammal was put together. The butchering was a mess. Fat slid and slipped, blood ran, meat flopped from bones under the knife. Guts swelled and spilled. Everyone working with knives was red with blood to the elbows. Much of the animal was blubber and fat, with about 20 pounds of meat. Heather cut both the meat and thick blubber into strips, which they carried back to the shelter. They placed the meat and blubber on long sticks and let it sizzle over the fire.

The fat and blubber dripped into the fire, flaring, became crisp, like bacon fat. The smell filled the shelter. Everyone breathed in, deep. The strips of fat were passed around. In his haste to eat, Jim burned his upper lip. Willie, Oleg, and Kirk refused to taste the cooked fat, and when the meat was done, they each took one bite and spat it out. They grew angry as they watched everyone else eat.

"Oh. My. God." Jack swallowed a piece of seal meat.

They ate all they could hold. They ate all the meat. The fire roared. The fat and grease dripped on their blankets and clothing and they did not care. Willie, Oleg and Kirk finally ate something, hunger overcoming taste.

William was impressed with Heather. She had taken three hours to creep down from the heights to the cove, steady, relentless, ruthless. Charlie, too, had been stoic and patient. Heather wore a huge smile. Charlie was swollen with pride. He kept describing the stalk to whoever would listen, and everyone listened the first and second time.

Late in the afternoon, the seals returned to the cove, cautious.

Heather gave herself medicine for her diabetes. Anne watched her and then caught Randall's eye, shaking her head. The medicine was almost gone. Without more medicine, Heather would go into shock and die.

William studied the black rocks and snow on the slopes. The rain and wind continued, but it was warmer. Later, when the storm passed, it would become colder, but clear. If they were going to try to get help, this would be the time.

William leaned back. Oh grandmother, the seal was good. Oh, grandmother.

Later, the fire a huge bed of coals, Heather and Charlie basked in appreciation. Everyone was sated, delighted to be sleepy and full. Only Willie, Oleg and Kirk were unhappy. William suspected they felt cheated, and would remain hungry. William knew everyone else would be hungry again, and soon. This was all the food they were going to get.

"You think, back then, in Sarah's vision, or dream, or whatever it was, people felt this good after eating seal?" Jack asked. He looked comfortable, lying on his back, hands behind his head, for once not grumbling.

"I think so." With Heather's accent it came out, "Ay theenk sooo."

"Now, the story." Jack settled back. "Keep going."

Pete

Pete, shivering inside the guard shack, noticed a flurry of activity at the pier. He knew the *Express* must be close.

Three flatbed trucks carrying huge, coiled, oil booms drove through the gate. Workers put the booms in the water off one end of the pier. A small launch appeared and started towing the booms out into the harbor until they stretched from the south end of the dock over toward the marina and the old dock where *Warhorse* usually lay.

Next, four big tank trucks came through the gate, parking near the abandoned building. Someone came out of the newly-assembled prefab office and had each driver fill out some paperwork. One of the drivers left his truck and walked over to Pete.

"You got heat in there?"

"You'd be warmer in your truck cab, I think."

"Hell." The driver stood by the gate and stretched.

"What's the deal about these trucks?" asked Pete.

"We're supposed to take on water."

Pete was confused.

"I'd have thought you were delivering water either to put out the ship's fire or to refresh the ship's supply."

The driver shook his head.

"Opposite. The ship's got oily water in the bilge which can't be pumped into the Strait. We'll put it in tanks, take the water to a separation facility all the way down in Tacoma."

The next truck to arrive had a telescoping boom and a platform at the end, used to work on utility lines. Then Roger drove up, accompanied by two vans of people, probably guards, holding paper cups of hot coffee.

Looking through the small windows of the guard shack, Pete saw *Warhorse* emerge from behind the bluff to the west, a towing cable stretched out behind. As *Warhorse* made her way slowly ahead, two big, red Buckhorn tugs followed.

Then Pete saw the *Express*, barely moving. *Warhorse* came to a stop and the towing cable sagged. People were on the bow of the *Express*. They detached the cable. Pete saw the tow wire slither off the ship, splashing heavily into water. The winch on the tug began reeling in.

The two Buckhorn tugs pushed the large ship into the narrow channel leading to the pier. Pete noticed signs of fire: the blackened base of the deckhouse, metal parts of the ship twisted from the heat, and leaning, broken containers spilling cargo. Smoke rose forward.

A small Coast Guard vessel hovered near the tugs as they worked. Pete knew pollution was a concern whenever a badly damaged ship was towed into a harbor and that's why the oil boom had been placed in the water. Two TV trucks and three other cars arrived at the gate almost simultaneously, as if they'd been traveling in convoy. Pete stopped them from entering because they didn't have TWIC cards.

"Security regulations," Pete told them. A television reporter climbed out of one car and approached his gatehouse.

"We need to get closer."

"Sorry."

"This is outrageous."

"The rules. If you don't have a TWIC card you can't get into this terminal, not without an escort."

The big tugs maneuvered the ship against the pier. The news people aimed cameras at the *Express* through the chain-link fence. Fremont Smith and Paxton Barnes, the two Buckhorn suits Pete had met on the ferry, drove up in a large sedan. Roger escorted them through the gate.

On the bow and stern of the ship, someone threw messenger lines to the pier. The line handlers pulled these, which were attached to the huge mooring lines.

The pier creaked and pilings groaned as the ship was pushed by the tugs. On the port side, opposite the pier side, a container slid free with a deafening screech. Someone shouted as the container tumbled into the harbor, breaking open. Thousands of shoes drifted.

Longshore line handlers from Port Angeles used gaff hooks to snag the heavy ends of the ship's mooring lines and then used forklifts to pull them to bollards on the pier, where the lines were secured.

By late afternoon, hundreds had gathered to look at the ship, watching from the marina or from behind the fence. Trucks arrived carrying portable lights and generators. One television reporter, a well-known blowhard, approached Roger, who stopped the reporter dead in his tracks with a cold stare. Pete saw Mariana in the crowd, and Myra. Then he saw Brad Withington, Joyce, and Sam. Sam gave Pete a small wave.

Flexible hoses were lifted to the ship by the stores crane.

"What are they doing?" a reporter asked Pete.

"Preparing to pump water from the bilges," Pete said.

"Polluted water?" asked the reporter, scribbling.

Pete shut up. He knew he'd get in trouble if Buckhorn thought he was acting like an unofficial spokesman.

The boom truck backed to the ship and lifted the boom and platform to the main deck level.

An ambulance and two police cars arrived at the gate. Pete waved them through.

On the ship, sailors carefully carried a still form, on a stretcher, covered, from inside the deckhouse. They placed the stretcher on the platform of the boom truck. Three men also stepped on to the platform, which was then carefully lowered to the ground. The ambulance backed up and the EMTs loaded the stretcher into the ambulance.

The crowd murmured.

The ambulance pulled away.

Across the water, Pete could see two figures watching from the wings of *Warhorse.*

The boom truck lifted other people off the ship. A van pulled up and they climbed aboard. Pete spotted Travis, a guy who'd been working as a reporter for the local paper, in the exhausted group.

Next, Roger's men, 10 in all, rode the boom platform up to the ship's deck. Soon afterward, supplies were being loaded aboard.

Roger asked Pete to stand by at the guardhouse. "We're short guys," he explained.

What choice did he have? He needed to keep this job.

"Sure, Roger. Spell me whenever you can."

A cold wind ruffled the surface of the harbor.

Across the way, under the tug's mast light, Pete saw Louise standing alone, watching.

William

The weather stayed bad - rain, wind, occasional snow. It was too foggy and cloudy for search helicopters, and they heard none. All they heard was surf, wind, seals barking, ravens croaking. The weather had to break before William could leave and seek help over the mountains.

The seals were wary. They now avoided the shelf where Heather and Charlie had taken the pup. The seals moved to an exposed stretch of shore with a long, open slope behind them, where they would be very difficult to approach.

Finding wood became a trial. The easy, nearby wood had long since been hauled back to the shelter. Now they had to walk over the ridge to the south to find any.

William was always startled at how much wood they could burn. They had to start rationing wood. For the past two days, they had kept the fire low, just coals, and enough branches to keep it going. They only built the heat for a few hours around dinnertime so they could be comfortable before the long night. The days passed slowly without a warm fire. They huddled close together beneath blankets, life jackets, and boughs, struggling to stay warm.

Oleg and Mattiew, at the end of the shelter, had fallen mute.

➤

They lay on their backs, staring at the plastic and boughs overhead. Mattiew had joined Oleg in refusing to go for wood.

Anne, the third mate, remained with Heather at the other end of the shelter. Now and then they talked, their soft voices rising and falling under the wind. Heather lived in Queens, New York. She had been a member of the steward's union for almost 20 years. In talking, they discovered Anne had grown up 10 blocks away.

William kept to himself, except during those times when he narrated his tale. He knew his story must come to an end as soon as the weather broke. He had decided to bring Anne with him. She did not know this. He had decided on Anne because she was in good shape, she was smart, and she had a good memory. She would be able to find her own way if it became necessary, if for example William was hurt and had to send her on. Randall was unable to get over Anne's inexperience and youth, and Anne was unwilling to kiss Randall's ass to gain favor. Because they hated each other, it would be best to leave Randall here with the others and take Anne with him. This left Heather alone with all the men, but William knew she could handle herself. She always kept the sharpened gaff hook by her side.

For breakfast this day they had nothing to eat.

"Heather, we'll need another seal soon." Jack had really liked the fresh seal meat.

"I'll bring you with me, then."

"Me? Why me?"

"It is your time to help."

Jack and Willie kept complaining, and Kirk had picked up on their attitude.

Jim, the chief engineer, was the one person on the crew aside from William who talked to Randall. The others had grown tired of Randall's shouting and self-righteous prayers. As chief engineer, Jim was ahead of Randall in the line of command, although here on the beach it was the deck officers, not the engineers, who ruled. Jim spent the time when William was not telling his story down at the lifeboat. He tinkered, trying to fix the leak and get the engine running even though the propeller had sheared off coming across the breach. William knew he was filling the time.

In the early morning, they'd search for wood, use the latrine, and gather water from the small trickle coming down the southern slope. After their chores, they had little to do.

William climbed the ridge to the small summit. He took Anne with him to see how she handled herself hiking. With the hard rain, little snow was left on the lower slopes.

The slope was gentle down low but then grew steeper. They labored up, step by step.

"Heather came up high when she hunted the seal, didn't she?" Anne said, standing waist high in the low shrubs halfway up the slope.

"She had to. Heather and Charlie had to climb this high in order to pass downwind of the seals."

William moved ahead, breaking trail. The wet brush soaked his clothing.

By the time they reached the spine of the ridge they were in two feet of wet snow. The rain came and went. William saw ridges and valleys to the east. They would have to cross at least three spines to reach the lowland east side of the island. Somewhere over there were roads, power lines, other people.

"Heather is running out of medicine." Anne was standing next to William. "She has about one week left, maybe eight days, if she stretches it."

"I know. I need to leave soon. I'd like you to come with me."

Anne turned and faced William. The wind buffeted her eyebrows.

"I might have even less hiking experience than Heather."

"You're strong. Intelligent. You don't need much food. If I can't get there, you will."

Anne studied William, then smiled, wry. "If Randall came with you then I'd be in charge here, and some of them wouldn't like me in charge, partly because I am a woman, mostly because I am on my first trip ever as a mate."

"I don't imagine King's Point spends a lot of time training you for being cast away."

The wind blew. William looked back down the slope. The shelter was a dark rectangle among the trees. Smoke swirled across the water. Further west, past the point, the three-mile inlet widened to the Pacific. All along each shore big rolls of surf curled, smothering the rocks. There was nothing in sight except water, mountains, trees and rocks, all dark, streaked, and wet.

"I'm not sure where we are, exactly, Anne. South Graham Island, I hope."

Anne stared out over the ridges, which disappeared into the mist.

"Heather needs her medicine."

"They all need food, Anne. I doubt Heather will be able to kill another seal. They're too wary now."

Anne had her hands together sleeve end to sleeve end, for warmth.

"When?"

"As soon as this weather breaks. Hopefully in two, three more days. Let's make sure we have our stuff ready."

Anne needed warmer clothing. She would have to use Kirk's coveralls; they were about the same size. Kirk would not give them up without a fight.

Anne turned and started back down the slope, saying, "We'll find help, William. I know we will."

As she picked her way down the slope, balancing by leaning back on a hand, William saw how her small form resembled Sarah's when Sarah climbed down the slopes to the river to wash bowls and spoons. William realized Anne had some of Sarah's grit. She would need it. So would William.

That evening William told them the rest of his story.

Steve

had an unlisted landline number, but they still found me on Saturday. The recovery of the ship was a big local story. People wanted to interview the captain. I lay low in my place by Green Lake. I saw how much work the place needed: repainting, new fixtures, new windows, floor refinishing.

I bought groceries, got the furnace running, and avoided the phone. Buckhorn kept calling, but I refused to pick up. I'd sailed for them for over 10 years, but now I was on the opposite side, someone they could blame for their cargo loss and ship damage. I decided to get out of town. I had no girlfriend, and my few friends were mostly sailing.

My car wasn't much, but it ran, and Sunday morning I headed north and got on one of the early Kingston ferries.

I boarded easily because not many people are heading away from the city early on a Sunday morning. The sun glistened on the ferry decks as I stood outside while the boat rumbled toward the Olympic Peninsula. My face was healing and now only thin gauze bandages covered the burns on the backs of my hands.

I couldn't stop thinking about the people on the other lifeboat: Randall, Jim, Heather, William, the other sailors,

➤

and the Russians. The last time I'd seen them, they'd been clustered in the hallway making their way through smoke to the lifeboat station.

A couple wandered by, braving a stiff breeze on the upper deck. The Olympics blazed white with snow, a wall straddling the western sky. Before them were dark hills of forest green. Nestled on shore were the buildings of Kingston. We passed the other ferry, heading back to Edmonds.

Did the other lifeboat capsize when falling from the ship? Or had it motored off like we had? Nobody had heard any radio chatter or picked up an emergency signal or seen any blips on the radar. The helicopters and planes crisscrossing the search area had found nothing.

If the cutter hadn't found us we would have all died from the cold. How could the others still be alive, eight days after we abandoned the *Express*? I drank my coffee. The couple on deck kissed, caressing each other. I envied them, their stolen day, the two of them off on a small adventure, maybe innocent, maybe not.

I drove to Sol Duc. I wanted to see the ship. The fire had been burning fiercely when we abandoned her. The fire had been raging forward, and I was sure the deckhouse was ready to go. Could we have retreated aft? Even if we'd lived, we had no heat, food or water. Maybe we could have survived in the steering gear room, below the aft deck. That's what Buckhorn would argue.

Who knows, maybe some of the crew will make the same argument, especially Mark, who had it in for me. He'd been acting strange and aggressive, almost hostile, the entire trip. And something had happened to the fire sensors.

No. This was my fault. This was the peril of command.

When I reached Sol Duc I wasn't sure how to get to the harbor, so I stopped at a coffee shop where a pretty woman behind the counter said, "What can I get you?"

"I'll have a small coffee and some directions, please."

"Take the road to the left a half mile, then turn right when you see a yellow sign. It will take you down the bluff to the harbor."

She handed me my coffee.

"How'd you know I was looking for the harbor?"

She laughed. Mariana, read the nametag on her shirt.

"You're new here, you're looking for something, and the only new thing in town is the ship towed in yesterday."

"Were you there?"

"There must have been 300 people watching. Television, police, locals. It was something."

I could imagine.

"Thanks."

I received another smile.

My car bounced down the rough narrow road to the harbor. Coming down the hill, I saw the ship's starboard side against the pier, bow facing me. The ship was still smoking above the hold area. The deckhouse was streaked, soot nearly to the pilothouse. The starboard lifeboat station seemed little damaged and the falls hung from the davits, well down. Maybe the lifeboat had gotten away.

The ship listed slightly toward the pier, probably from taking on water. A pipe led from the ship to a tank on the back of a large truck. I could see lights on in the deckhouse, indicating they'd gotten something running for power.

I stopped at the gate and talked to a man inside a guard shack who'd been reading a book.

"Can I help you?"

"I just want to take a look."

"I can't let anyone onto the terminal, I'm afraid."

I had expected this.

"I understand," I said, looking at the guard and noticing his nametag. "Pete, is the tug tied up across the harbor the one which brought the ship in?"

He nodded.

"They're based here. Louise and her brothers own the company. Took over from her father. She lost her husband on the ship coming down, accident. The funeral's in three days."

So abandoning ship had killed 12 souls, not 11.

I drove to the other side of the harbor where the tug company had its offices in a ramshackle building. Two men stood inside.

I recognized Nelson right away. He and a man with badly torn hands and scratched wire-rim glasses worked on a cable.

For a long moment after I walked in Nelson's face remained blank, and I wondered how much I'd aged since I last saw him four or five years earlier.

"Steve Procida. Jesus. Steve." Nelson straightened up. "You look like hell."

"You don't look so good yourself."

"This is Travis. He was on the ship, too."

Travis held out one of his bad hands and we shook. He seemed to ignore whatever pain he must be feeling. He and Nelson looked gaunt, wasted. I could only imagine what their days had been like.

"Steve, I'm sorry about the ship. But I sure am happy to see you, and to see you're all right. Are you all right?"

"Not really, Nelson. There's 11 still missing. It's been eight days, and not good days, either."

"It's never over until it's over, Steve. As you used to tell me."

"You were on the ship when?" asked Travis.

Nelson laughed. "This is the captain, Travis, Steve Procida. Pretty brave, being in Buckhorn territory after what happened. For sure, they're going to try to nail this thing on him." Nelson looked away from Travis to me. "Just before we boarded," said Nelson, "the ship was smoking like a chimney." Nelson nodded toward Travis. "I stayed on the tug, but Travis here went over with Larry to set the tow. He was a damn good man, Larry."

"What happened?" I asked Travis.

"His hand and foot caught between the wire and the side of the chock when we set the cable around the bitts. A wave came under us and pulled the cable tight against the chock, and in a second he'd lost his foot and hand."

I asked them some more questions about the fire and the recovery operation.

Travis said something interesting.

"There was a shitload of stuff in the starboard tunnel, aft. We had a damn hard time passing through when we had to move our stores up after coming aboard."

I was surprised. I had always told my guys to keep those tunnels clear.

"You guys bringing back machinery and tools from Russia?" Travis asked.

I didn't know about any shipments from Russia.

Nelson walked me back to my car.

"If you need to, Steve, call me to testify. I'll confirm the ship was a goner when you were aboard and you had to abandon."

Nelson's a good guy, a friend. He knew what Buckhorn would try to do to me, and he knew my job was on the line.

"You want to go get drunk?" he asked.

"Every second."

December 14, Tuesday

William

During the night Jack had risen to pee and he knocked the ridgepole of the shelter, hard, and part of the shelter collapsed, spilling water, boughs, and the slimy sheet of plastic upon Willie, Kirk and Charlie. Everyone had to get up and make repairs in the rain and the wind, swearing and struggling to work in the dark.

They'd kept the fire going by stretching the plastic out over the flame, above it, tied to trees beyond, and this allowed the fire to continue despite the rain, but not strong enough to heat the more distant parts of the shelter. While they were repairing the plastic and the roof of the shelter the next morning, the rain turned to snow. It was below freezing and growing colder.

"This is good." William was tying a small pole beneath the plastic to keep water from pooling over their heads. He turned his face up to the snow. The flakes were heavy and many.

"Good? Snow is good? We're wet, we can't build up the fire, and it's getting colder. Are you crazy?"

"I meant, Jack, the wind is backing around to the north, which is why the temperature is dropping. This means the storm is passing, and it will clear. It won't stay clear for long but there will be a window to make a try for help." William did his best to sound calm, encouraging, matter of fact. If this snow continued for the entire day they'd have to fight through snow even in the low valleys between ridges. He felt weak. He knew, looking at the others, everyone was weak. They had to leave soon if they were going to try at all. Yet they couldn't leave now, not in this blizzard, for this is what this was becoming, a blizzard.

"More wood, let's go." It was barely daylight. The snow was already covering the sodden ground. Randall was pulling on his boots. "As much as we can find, today. If this snow stops and it gets clear, William is right, it will get damn cold, and then we'll need the heat."

"We need the heat now." Kirk was in his sodden coveralls, lip quivering.

"Finding wood will warm you. Come on, Kirk, follow me." Randall led the way. Everyone except Oleg and Mattiew followed. The two Russians had checked out. There was no food to eat, and the last two days they had been lying in place, not moving.

To get wood now they had to go south, climb 300 feet, and drop into the next valley. Here there was wood, fallen trees, branches, but it was a long distance away. They trudged after Randall, through the falling snow, now over snow covered ground. William brought up the rear. Everyone was moving slowly. Willie was stumbling, walking unsteadily. Jack was lagging behind, parallel to William, hard to see even though only 30 feet away.

The ridge seemed endless. William was breathing hard when he reached the top. The others were worse, most stopping to rest before dropping to the valley below. To the left, east, this ridge rose, rose, to a small summit. William dreaded what he and Anne were going to have to do. He dreaded the coming fight with Kirk over his coveralls for Anne's safety. He dreaded most of all the pain he knew he would feel in his knees, hips. Now he shook his head and followed the others down into the valley.

Randall tried to organize them. He had to shout because the falling snow absorbed all sound. William heard the flakes whispering against his hair, the trees.

It took them an hour to gather wood, another 30 minutes to carry it back to the shelter. All this time it snowed. Each person was carrying an armload, whatever they could hold, some in front, and some on their shoulders. When they came back to the shelter three inches of snow lay on the ground despite the continuing wind. It was colder. William dumped the last load. The pile of wood seemed depressingly small.

"More. We need more." This was Anne, facing the woodpile. In the shelter Oleg and Mattiew watched, mute. Everyone stood around the wood. The fire beneath the plastic sheet was smoking, not casting heat but burning. Now the flakes were not thick and wet, but lighter, fluffier. William realized the sodden collar of his jacket, brushing against his chin, had started to freeze.

"It pisses me off to be breaking my back hauling wood, starving, for god's sake, and then see you lazy Russian bastards just expecting us to bring you heat." Jack was standing before Oleg and Mattiew, a branch in his hand.

"We are hurt." Oleg's voice was muffled beneath his blanket. "Our burns."

William knew many here had burns. He had burns. Jack kicked Oleg's feet.

"Get your sorry ass up. Help us."

Oleg did not move. Randall was now standing next to Jack. Jack started to speak and Randall put his hand on Jack's arm.

"He's right." Randall was speaking to Mattiew. "Get up, help us. We need to make two more trips for wood, at least. This is what we do today. Otherwise we'll freeze to death."

Oleg shook his head.

"I am hurt."

"How's this, then?" Randall pulled the blanket from Oleg and Mattiew. "Either you get wood now or you'll be sleeping somewhere else, not at our shelter."

Everyone was by the pile of wood, watching. Oleg rose and Mattiew followed him. They pulled on their boots. Wind blew snow off the trees. Not everyone had good gloves. Three of them had been wearing survival suits over their clothes when they boarded the lifeboat and now, without the survival suits on, they were underdressed.

"There'll be people getting frostbite," Anne said to Randall. "It isn't like it was the first days, getting wood right here then jumping back in the warm shelter."

"I know." The others were ahead, starting up the slope, following Jim and Charlie. "But if we don't get enough wood everyone will get frostbite."

They were like ghosts, everyone wandering through the snow, feet buried in a carpet, the flakes swirling on gusts of wind. William thought the wind might be dropping, but he wasn't sure. He knew the temperature was dropping.

This time it took them two hours to gather wood and return. It was noontime and they had been working since daylight, though at this latitude the sun rose late.

Now the pile next to the shelter was a pile of wood. William knew, however, all these one and two inch diameter branches would burn fast, leave few coals, be consumed faster than could be imagined.

Everyone was shivering. The snow continued, now eight inches deep. The wind had nearly stopped and William knew now it would become really cold. His collar was frozen. Those without gloves kept their hands in their jacket pockets.

Heather stood like a post next to the woodpile. The snow had dropped on her curled black hair and lay like a halo on her crown. Now her teeth flashed.

"I think we need bigger pieces."

"Shit." Jack groaned. Kirk was standing as close to the small fire as he could.

"We'll keep moving. One more time." Everyone groaned. Randall was steady. "Heather is right. This time everyone needs to find one or two big logs, all they can carry. Let's see. Anne, Jim, Jack, Willie, Kirk, William, Charlie, Heather, Oleg, Mattiew, and me - 11."

"All still here, but Jesus it's cold."

"I know, Kirk. Everyone bring back two logs, and whoever brings back the most wood gets to be closest to the fire."

"Not fair." Anne was not large. She wasn't being serious.

"Life's not fair," Heather pronounced, and she started off.

"We in any danger from bears?" This was Kirk. William could hear him as he started off ahead.

"They're hibernating," William called. Then, because he was tired and hungry, he said, "But now and then they wake up, come out. Then they'll eat anything, Kirk."

After this Kirk maneuvered so he was in the middle of everyone else as they climbed the slope and descended the other side. William found this funny. He was glad he found something funny.

This time when they reached the valley they were all covered with snow, like snowmen. They trudged about, looking for logs, sections of fallen and dead trees which were thicker yet short enough to carry. Heather found two big sections, which she mounted on each shoulder and then started back. Most returned with one log. Anne found two, and they were large, and William was again reminded of Sarah, except Sarah had been carrying rocks for Bob-Bob's grave and here Anne was carrying wood for the fire. Sarah was finishing a ceremony for a life lived, and now Anne was building a fire for lives to save.

They straggled back to the shelter. The snow remained heavy but they had tracks to follow up out of the valley, over the ridge, and down to the shelter. Out in the bay the whales returned, unseen, but heard. William of course brought back the most wood, he was the tallest and largest, and hips and knees aside he had some pride. Heather's load was next, then the others. Anne ended up bringing back more than Randall, Jack, Oleg, Mattiew, or Kirk. Now the pile of wood had some depth to it, some heft.

The snow was lying on the roof of the shelter, thick. It was late afternoon. They removed the plastic sheet which had been covering the small blaze and added wood, which caught and flared. Now there were flames and heat, snowflakes hissing, smoke rising. They added wood and the wood crackled and the heat radiated and everyone hung what they could to dry and stayed as close to the heat as they dared.

There was no food.

"We can't eat heat but my God it's nice." This was Jim, now in position, in place.

It had taken them all day, and several trips, to set aside enough wood for at most two days, maybe two and a half days. William knew after he and Anne left these others would have to go out again, more than once, and each time they would be weaker, hungrier, thinner, and less able.

The day was growing dark. Snow continued to fall.

"We leave tomorrow." William spoke from the back of the shelter. The fire was hot; one of the big logs was blazing. The heat evaporated the falling snow before it could reach the flames. "We must leave. We cannot wait longer."

"Who leaves?" Charlie was making himself comfortable.

"The third. Me and the third."

"Her?" Oleg's eyes were wide.

"Not you, Oleg."

"Yes, but.... she is small."

"I have chosen her."

Anne was next to Heather, calmly working on her gloves. William took a breath.

"Kirk, we'll need your coveralls. They will fit Anne and she needs them."

"What?" Kirk jerked to attention. "Like hell."

"It is Anne who will go for help with me. She needs proper clothing. She needs coveralls to walk through this snow, this cold."

"She can wear someone else's."

"Who else, Kirk? You have the only small pair."

"Why not Charlie? Or the first? Why this green mate?"

"Kirk she may be young but she knows how to navigate, she is strong, and she knows first aid."

"Navigate? What, you going to take a sextant sight out there? Jesus."

"I have the compass from the lifeboat." William had been storing the small compass where he slept. Now he took it out. It was small enough to fit in his hand. "We will use this, to travel east."

Ann rose to her feet and inspected Kirk's coveralls from where they were hanging before the fire. They were still wet. Kirk was scowling.

"You want to go with William, Kirk?" Randall leaned forward, looked down the line of people toward Kirk. "Leave this fire and warmth and walk for, what, William, 15 or 20 miles, in the snow and cold, no idea where you are? You really want to go, Kirk?"

Kirk said nothing. William, hearing Randall, realized his and Anne's quest was nearly hopeless. He realized, also, Randall knew this, and was putting up a good front. Unless someone flew the coast again, once it cleared, they'd never be found.

"Don't forget to scrape off the lifeboat tomorrow," William said, "when we leave, if they fly the coast again."

"We're gonna die." Willie was definite.

"You aren't dead yet." Heather spoke from the other side of Anne. "And if you die then the rest of us will eat you." Willie shut up.

The whales continued to circle the islets before them. It was as if they had taken shelter from the deeper water outside during this snowfall. The islets were white, the water dark. Somewhere William heard a seal bark and he knew the seals were still there, across the inlet, now lying in snow.

"I thought we had global warming. What's this?" Charlie was shivering despite the heat. William could see some frostbite on Charlie's ears. He had been wearing no hat when he went for the wood.

"Yeah, how ironic." Anne was standing, turning the coveralls so the other side would dry. "The whole world in a panic thinking we're going to overheat and instead maybe there's no summer a few years in a row instead."

The clothing furthest from the fire was still frozen. Jim had risen and was turning what he could to catch heat. William remembered a discussion he once had with Alec.

"Alec and Sergei disagreed about global warming. Sergei said it was the CO_2. Alec disagreed, said no way a trace gas like CO_2 could cook the earth. Alec believed we were entering an orbital cycle which would start a new ice age, said the sun is getting cooler. He also said ice cores going back hundreds of thousands of years show times the climate changes 10 degrees in 10 years. Up or down. If we suddenly lost one or two years of harvest, then the world would collapse. Nobody's preparing for cold, yet if it gets suddenly cold, it's over."

"Like here, with us, right?"

"It's not over yet, Jack. Anne and I will find help. A helicopter will see the lifeboat."

"Well, if you're taking off tomorrow tell us what happened, last summer, to you guys in the park after you saw the bear. Did you escape the fire? What happened with the mining?" Charlie's face was flickering red in the fire. Jim finished turning the clothing. Anne had settled down next to Heather. "So she shot two guys with a spear thing? Really?"

"She did, Charlie, and I'm sure if she hadn't Raymond would have shot one of us just as he shot Pete. But then, coming out, we were discouraged. Our cameras had been destroyed. The atlatl had been destroyed. Myra was sure we'd lost any chance to delay the mining, because we had no evidence. Tom was sure he'd never get Sarah's custody because he'd again stolen her into the mountains and this time she'd nearly killed two people. I was sure my body was breaking down, coming apart, and I was afraid I'd collapse before we reached Whiskey Bend. Sergei was afraid he'd be deported as a foreigner and unable to deliver his paper, probably have his career damaged. I thought we were going to be arrested when we emerged from the park, because of Sarah's actions and our support of her."

Beyond the shelter the whales blew. Everyone could hear them as they circled. William rose and added a log to the fire. Now there were two big logs burning. They would burn for hours.

"We'd hoped, by going in there again, and retrieving the thrower as evidence against the mining, it would prove Sarah and we weren't crazy. We could have come out with Sarah and photos of the artifact, and the artifact itself, proof we were more than irresponsible people stealing Sarah. But, in the end, we had nothing."

"You had her story." Anne was sitting up, untying her boots. Then she shook her head. "No. You didn't. I mean, you did have her story, but what would people think, hearing such a story? They'd lock you all up."

"Exactly."

Heather lifted her head. "What I wonder is, how could she shoot those guys with that thing, unless she really knew how to use it?"

"What, you think she learned during that dream she had? Please." Randall was checking his watch. "Pure luck, those shots. What was she, 13? Unbelievable."

"That's what we believed, too, Randall, at first. But after we saw her bear up by the unnamed lake, the bear she drew, the bear Myra said was was extinct, a short face bear, right before our eyes, we could even smell it, even, well, we didn't know what to think."

December 15, Wednesday

William

William and Anne rose before daylight to bitter cold and ten inches of snow. They had gathered their gear the evening before. William had the boat compass secured in a pocket of his big fire jacket. They had matches, a canister of diesel fuel to start a fire, two knives, some rope, and one of the gaff hooks.

The pile of wood next to the still-glowing fire was noticeably smaller. Within a day, the others would have to seek more wood.

William had cut the portion of the chart which showed the islands and placed it, folded, in his pocket. It wasn't much, but maybe when they reached the top of the second ridge, which was higher than the first and further east, they could spot where they were and where the nearest settlement might be.

Both he and Anne wore insulated fire coveralls, the big fire jackets with pockets and hoods. They had gloves as well as pullover woven caps that protect the head under the fire helmet, but would now serve as facemasks and ear covers in the wind. William had earlier fashioned two small backpacks by rigging straps and cloth from the life preservers. They now loaded these with blankets, knives and sundries.

►

While William and Anne were getting ready, Heather announced she would try to kill another seal. Everyone was hungry to the point of desperation.

"Good luck, William." Charlie's voice was faint.

"Waste of time." Jack stayed true to form.

Randall stood before them.

"Anne. Good luck. I know I've been a little hard on you." Anne tightened her belt around her jacket and said nothing. "You're a damn good officer, Anne. I missed it on the ship, but you've done a great job here. You'll go far in this business."

"Only if I go far enough with William to get help. But thanks."

"Wait." Kirk rose up. "You didn't finish, last night, William. What happened? Did you guys get out?"

"I'm here, Kirk. Of course we got out. Took us three days."

"Did Sarah get arrested?" Randall was adjusting Anne's pack.

William, checking his boots, looked up.

"No, not arrested. In the end she got to live with Tom. He's adopting her."

Wind overhead knocked snow off nearby trees. The wind was cold.

"The mining?" Willie was buried beneath blankets and life jackets, but his eyes were wide open.

"No permits yet, or none when I left on the ship." William stood and stretched. "Everyone knows they'll do the mining, though. Matter of time. They held the conference, Sergei even delivered his paper, and his father's. He said nothing to anyone about where we'd been, what we'd seen. Why would he? We had no evidence, not after Roger smashed the thrower."

"Is Sarah doing all right?" This was Heather.

"She's the new kid in school, ninth grade, Port Angeles High. She survives eight days alone in a hole in the ground, comes back, then shoots two people with a spear thrower, dead aim, pins 'em to a tree. She joined the cross-country team. Runs. I think everyone's terrified of her. She's very lonely." William paused, then brightened. "She's taking science courses. Tells Myra she's going to become an archeologist."

"Did Myra get together with Sergei?"

William laughed. "Jack, everybody knows what's going to happen except those two. It's funny." William checked Anne's outfit, her pack, belts, and gloves. Then he checked his own. "Tom's finding being a parent is plenty of work. Sarah's never easy. She is stubborn and they fight a lot. A lot. He's set aside a room in his house for her art studio. She's in there always. But even though they fight I think she likes it there, it's safe, and it's hers and Tom wants her. Tom's also regained his community, I think people saw he wasn't irresponsible, just unlucky, getting crossways with Buckhorn."

Randall checked William's pack.

"It seems port commissioner Fletcher Lynch got the last laugh, though, William," Randall said. "Got Tom fired, got his mining agreement, the center built, his conference."

William pulled on his hat, gloves.

"Really, Randall? He had to announce his retirement, because after what he did to Tom, he'd have lost the election, if he'd run. They held a reception for him, retirement party, after the conference, and only 17 people showed up, this in an Elks hall which can hold 200. The rumor's out he's got a problem with little girls. His precious center will never be named for him."

Randall shook William's hand, saying, "I still think you've told us a fantasy and none of it's true. But you've kept us occupied and there's value in that."

As they left, William took one last look back at the shelter, its low roof covered with snow, clothes and gear hanging from lines, smoke rising from the fire. He saw darkness within the shelter, but pairs of eyes peering out.

They climbed the ridge, to the spine, as they had done before. The snow was deep, the wind cold. Overhead, low clouds raced from the west. William saw other crests, marching north to south between them and the eastern shore where settlements were. Climbing, they were hot in their outfits. Anne followed behind him, step by step. When they stood together on the crest, looking east, William knew she was frightened. He got out the compass.

"There, the next ridge." He pointed. They had to climb down a very steep slope, and then up another, steeper still.

They both worked down the steep slope. William slipped once, sat down, and slid 50 feet before stopping. They came to trees halfway down and struggled through thickets. Near the bottom, Anne tripped on a hidden rock and fell. Snow covered her face and dripped down her head covering.

In the bottom of the valley they crossed a small stream. William used the gaff hook as a staff. Anne used a long stick. They slid as they climbed the next slope, sometimes giving up ground. By the time they got half way up, the snow was two feet deep. In certain steep sections, William had to brace himself against the steepness with his long arms, then crab along sideways until he found a place to go higher. Anne, climbing behind him, kept off to the side, so if he fell he wouldn't take her with him.

When they finally reached the top of the second ridge, the day was half over, the wind stronger, and it had become colder. The sky showed patches of blue as clouds raced past. They faced at least two more ridges ahead.

Again, they started climbing down slowly, step-by-step. By the time they reached the bottom, the afternoon was fading and the sky was becoming dark.

"We have to camp here," William said.

Their plan had been to go as far as they could the first day, camp somewhere, make a shelter and get a fire going. All they had was their gear and some blankets. William believed if they stayed in their jackets and coveralls and were covered in blankets and boughs with a fire going, they'd be fine. He was relieved it was cold, because had it been pouring rain then they'd have been soaked and at risk of hypothermia.

They had no food, but a stream flowed through the valley, so they had water. Anne found a copse of heavy spruce growing so close together the ground beneath their low branches had little snow. Using knives, they cut free as many boughs as they could. While Anne rigged boughs for a shelter, William gathered wood. It was nearly dark by the time they had their place prepared, the shelter covered with boughs, and boughs on the ground for bedding.

William could not start a fire. His hands had become cold cutting boughs and carrying wood, and his big fingers fumbled. Anne took the matches and the canister of fuel. She poured some diesel on the driest branches they had been able to find, protected the flame with her hands and body, and struck matches. It took five matches to start the fuel, but she got the wood burning.

"Glad we have this fuel." Anne closed the canister. They pulled out their blankets and set them next to each other, on the boughs, before the fire. The roof of the lean-to caught the heat and it became much warmer here than outside. "William?" The fire was hot, the shelter warm. William felt his sore legs relax and loosen. Tomorrow would be harder than today, he knew that. "I'm glad you were on the lifeboat with us. I think it was your voice, your story telling, keeping us going, back there."

"This was how we passed the long winters, here, when I

was a boy. We told stories."

"Well, stories make us people, right? Didn't your grandmother say so when you took Myra up here?"

"You remember well, Anne."

"I wish I'd had a grandmother like yours."

"Some day you will be such a grandmother, Anne. You can tell this story, and your part of it, then. You will tell it well."

December 16, Thursday

Myra

Caller ID said, "International."

"Myra? I just got your messages."

I had been wondering if I'd ever again hear Sergei's accent, his low voice, and the way he rolled his vowels.

"Do you know what time it is, Sergei?"

"It is one in the afternoon here."

"Yes, in Kamchatka. But here it's four in the morning. I was asleep."

"I am sorry." He explained he'd been at a conference in Baikal, and they'd lost power and all ways of communicating. He laughed. "I think I am lucky I was able to catch a flight back to Petropavlovsk. When I got here I saw your messages. I called Tom just now, spoke to him. And Sarah. Not 10 minutes ago. Myra, now I'm calling you. I am so sorry to hear about William. The ship."

Sergei was tall, intense, square-jawed. He had dark eyes. I'd never let him know, but I was a little afraid of him. Sergei was a real scientist, a doctorate, published papers, serious. Next to him I felt like a schoolgirl. I didn't even have a Master's

➤

Degree. Sergei was very smart, and, as Sarah once said, "Damn good looking too."

"William has a great spirit, Myra. He is strong."

"Yes. But to be missing for 12 days, in December, is a very long time."

"William was a good friend of mine, Myra. Well, of my father's. Every time his ship came to Petro he would call my father and they would meet, and argue and laugh and drink hot tea. The first time I met him was years ago, when I was not yet 20. He encouraged me to study genetics. He told me to go easy on my father. After my father died, your father helped me in my pain, my grief." Sergei paused. The line whispered. "I have a flight, weather permitting, tomorrow and I will arrive Saturday morning. Tom has kindly offered to pick me up at the airport and give me a room. I have been doing some research you may find interesting, too, if we get a chance to talk. But mainly, Myra, I would like to visit, to help if I can."

"I am sure he is gone, Sergei. I have accepted this."

"Sarah does not. She says he is waiting for you."

"Yes, but in the spirit world." Suddenly I wanted to see Sergei, impossibly difficult Sergei, very much. I couldn't stop smiling. "There's a memorial service in two days, Sergei."

"Before they find what happened to the lifeboat?"

"Not for anyone on the ship. For Larry Hunt. He and his wife owned *Warhorse*, the tug that recovered William's ship. He died a couple of days after a bad injury he received while setting up the tow. The family's taking the tug out to the Strait tomorrow to spread his ashes. The day after, they'll have a public service."

"Be careful, Myra, you don't think this is William's service, too."

"But it will be, Sergei."

"I am looking forward to seeing you, Myra. I have many

points I want to make to show how inaccurate so many of your theories are."

He sounded so serious. I had to laugh.

When Sergei hung up, I tried to do some work on the draft report. Tomorrow we were to have our council discussion and Marcie and I were at total loggerheads about my content. I knew I should be paying more attention to work, but all I could think of was my father, where he might be. Now the broken ship down at the harbor reminded me each day of my loss.

Steve

On the way up to give my deposition to the Coast Guard in the Federal Building, I passed Mark, the first engineer, coming out of the elevator. He'd cut his hair and put on a suit, and I barely recognized him. We had nothing to say to each other.

Greg, the union representative, looked nervous as he waited for the fact-finding deposition to begin. "Be direct and brief, Steve. Don't speculate."

I'd been around this business long enough to know Greg was right.

"You been to the Buckhorn offices yet?" he asked.

"They keep calling, but all I've told them is I want my pay sent to my home address."

We entered the conference room. A recording machine perched on the table, and opposite me sat the Coast Guard investigator, a man younger than Jimmie. He had a lot of gold on his sleeves. We shook hands and he told me where to sit. Another Coast Guard officer, a woman, less gold on her sleeves, held a notebook and pen.

"I will start the recording now," the investigator said, punching a button. "I am Lieutenant Joe Field, Coast Guard, accompanied by Second Lieutenant Linda Wysocki, for the purpose of taking statements about the accident aboard the motor vessel *Seattle Express*."

Before we started, they asked me to sign a form where I vowed to tell the whole truth and nothing but the truth.

Greg had assured me this wasn't a legal proceeding, but this sure felt like one.

"What is your name?"

"Steve Procida, master, unlimited tonnage, license number 83609."

"You were captain of the *Seattle Express* at the time of the incident?"

"Yes."

"How long have you served as captain of this ship?"

"Six years on rotation, and three years before as a fill-in. I also sailed as first mate a year before I served as captain."

"What was your schedule?"

"Schedule?"

"Your work schedule."

"Oh. I worked two trips on, one trip off."

"Where were you on your work schedule at the time of the incident?"

"We were finishing the second round trip."

"You were going to arrive in Seattle and leave the ship?"

"Yes."

"Please describe the voyage."

I had my water-stained notebook. I had always copied the basic notes from the ship's log every day into my notebook, for my own personal record, and this was the notebook I had grabbed when we abandoned ship. Using the notebook for reference, I gave the investigator the details of our route and weather, starting with our departure, delayed two days, from Petropavlovsk on Nov. 27.

"When was the last time your ship had a full inspection?"

"September, in Seattle."

"Were there any concerns you had on this voyage?"

I almost laughed. Concerns about a 30 year old ship? Everything was a concern. Buckhorn wasn't a bad owner, but both my relief captain and I had begged the company for maintenance upgrades, especially to the alarm systems and sensors. They'd always refuse, citing the time and expense.

"Where were you when you heard about the fire?"

"I was in my cabin, sleeping. The fire alarm went off."

"What did you do then?"

"I ran topside. To the wheelhouse. A trace of smoke had already reached the wheelhouse. I had William, the sailor on watch, check all the panels and equipment boxes for an electrical fire in the panels, but he saw none. I sent Anne, the third mate, down through the deckhouse to see if a fire had started in one of the cabins."

"What was the weather, exactly?"

I looked at my notebook. "At midnight we were 42 revolutions into a quartering head sea. The wind was gusting to 63 knots. Seas were eight meters. It was raining and snowing."

"When did you see the fire forward?"

"I got a call from my third engineer, Carlton, on watch in the engine room. They saw a lot of smoke in the port tunnel. At about the same time, we spotted flames by number two hold forward. I took over steering the ship and sent everyone below to their fire stations."

The machine clicked and Joe Field paused the hearing to replace the recording disc.

"Then what happened?"

"I turned the ship before the wind, so the flames wouldn't be fanned by the wind. This also gave us an easier ride to fight the fire. Turning took a while. I heard from our fire captain,

Randall, the first mate, they'd discovered fire in the port tunnel. Some fluids caught fire. The fire also spread to one of the engine room spaces by the port tunnel, on an upper deck. Forward, the fire seemed out of control. Randall sent people into the starboard tunnel and they reported no smoke but heat forward." Everything had happened so quickly. "The second fire crew couldn't get to their gear because of the fire in the tunnel. The fire in the engine room seemed to be spreading. The fire forward was out of control but if I discharged the halon gas there none would be left for the engine spaces aft. I knew if the fire in the engine room continued, then all the oils and materials would go up, along with the main fuel tanks and feeds. We decided to drive Halon into the engine space to starve the fire there. Meanwhile the fire in the port tunnel had now spread into the deckhouse. I went out on the wings and I was sure flames on both sides of the ship would soon engulf the lifeboat stations. We had a big raft forward, but because of the fire forward we couldn't reach it. We had no big life raft aft. We would either remain on the ship, trapped by the fire, or abandon when we could. I sounded the call to abandon ship."

Field took notes. His assistant stared at me. What did she see? Probably a half-bald old man, thick glasses, with a good belly, bandages still on his hands; a man who looked nothing like a ship's captain.

I told Field how my team climbed into the lifeboat and we got away.

"Both sides of the ship were in flames," I said. "I was sure the ship was gone. We all were."

Nobody asked any additional questions. Greg sat, his head lowered, picking at a nail.

"At the hearing next week, bring your notebook, please," said Field.

My deposition complete for now, I left the room. Fred, the

second mate, stood in the waiting room. He must have traveled from his home in Idaho for this.

"How are you, captain?"

"About as well as can be expected, Fred."

"No word?"

"Nothing. More than 12 days, and nothing."

He asked me if I was attending Larry Hunt's memorial service, and I said I was.

"Things go okay in there?" he asked, pointing to the door of the conference room.

"This is just the fact finding stage. The Buckhorn lawyers will jump on this at the hearing and afterwards. That's when things will happen."

"Well, for what it's worth, Steve, I think you did all you could."

William

The next morning was colder. They were slow to rise. William had kept the fire going and they were at least able to get somewhat warm before leaving.

As soon as they started, William knew his left knee was going to be a problem. It had stiffened overnight and now felt rigid. He found himself, like Tom the previous summer, having to swing his leg with each step he took. Behind him, Anne watched him.

They crossed the valley and climbed the next slope. When they reached the crest of the ridge, it took them an hour to find a route where they wouldn't plunge 1,000 feet. Anne finally found the key, a deep gully that seemed impossible but was actually the only way to get under a buttress just beneath the ridge.

On the crest, they had seen one more ridge before them, not as high in elevation as the one they had just climbed. Past the last ridge, far to the east, they could see a glimmer of water, Hecate Strait, east of Graham Island. They saw no roads, no power lines, no sign of people, but William found himself confident that once they came to the top of the next ridge they would be able to see something. The day turned cloudy and

➤

the temperature warmed. William suspected there would be rain.

They were weak with hunger and fatigue. As they descended, sheets of deep snow slid down, pushed by their legs.

Coming down into this next valley, William tripped on a buried branch and fell. He slid on his back, downhill, faster and faster, gaff hook held up with an arm. He struck rocks, then the tops of some small trees buried in the snow, finally coming to a stop in the bottom of the valley. Anne struggled after him, trying not to slide herself. It took her fifteen minutes to reach him. While he lay there, William watched her, trying not to think about what might have happened to his knee. He knew it was very bad.

"You will need to go on, Anne. I cannot." William lay on his back, in the snow, a grimace on his face. "My knee is sprained, at least. I cannot walk."

"I'll get you some shelter," Anne said, dropping her pack. She found a tall tree nearby with some shelter beneath the lower branches.

"Can you move at all, William?"

"I will need your help to move."

Anne dragged William across the snow to the tree. He was a big man and his gear was heavy, but William knew her desperation gave her strength.

She raced to gather wood.

"You should go. If you take too much time, you will not get over this ridge before dark."

Anne piled wood near William.

"William I am third mate and you will do what I say." She smiled at him.

"Randall was right. You will be an excellent officer," said William. His knee throbbed. On the ground, he felt the chill. Anne had cut boughs and then pulled William over onto the boughs. She wrapped him in a blanket and started a fire.

Beneath the branches of the tree, William had shelter. Braced on tree boughs, wrapped in a blanket, he felt almost warm. Anne had piled wood nearby to allow him to easily feed the fire.

He knew his situation was bad, even if Anne did find help. It was hopeless if she did not. He knew she was afraid - the idea of leaving him and striking off alone terrified her. William reached into his coat and passed her the compass.

Anne stood close to the fire.

"You should leave, third."

"I'll be fine, William. It's good if I don't get to the ridge until after dark."

"Then you'll be blind coming down."

"But I'll be able to see lights further east and I can take a bearing."

"Anne, you're not so different from Sarah."

"A great compliment, William."

The wind was blowing. William chuckled, even in his pain. "I am home. I was sent away as a child and now it seems I have come home. This is my land. I belong here."

"We'll find you, William."

"I will wait for you."

Anne looked down at him. He knew what she saw - a man nearly 60, looking 100, huge and loose boned, ugly, almost sure to die here.

"You saw the bear?" Anne asked.

"Myra, Sarah and I saw the bear, Anne. Yes."

"Your story, then, is true? Most of the crew back there didn't believe it, you know."

"I know. And yes, it is true. All of it, Anne."

William saw the day was dying, the light going.

In the gathering darkness, William knew Anne felt a million

miles away from Queens, New York, the maritime academy, the ship, the shelter.

"Your grandmother's story," Anne said. "The oldest legend of all. How we became people."

"Yes. The killer whale and the bear."

William stopped talking. Anne stood for a moment. A tear rolled down her cheek. She clasped William's hand and squeezed. Then she turned and walked away, heading up the ridge.

The wind blew. William watched Anne. By the time she reached the crest of the ridge, it would be completely dark.

December 17, Friday

Louise

Louise looked across the quiet water at the *Express*, which seemed slumped against the pier. Larry loved mornings like this, when the water lay still and only the gulls made any sound. Except this morning, Vince was down in the small kitchen banging pans. Her brother and his wife Peggy and their kids had all moved in to help. All remaining of Larry was in the urn on the little table, and soon his ashes would be gone, too. Her husband, gone. The business, gone. This property soon to be sold and gone.

Two Buckhorn people had showed up the day before. One was the woman, Victoria somebody, smooth as silk, sympathetic, hitting all the right notes. With her was the lawyer. He offered cash for the dock and land, said Buckhorn needed expansion space.

The land had been used for industrial purposes for years: log processing, creosote treatment, ship building and maintenance. The soil was soaked in oil and creosote; a class four contamination, Larry had said. Well, maybe she'd let Buckhorn spend their damned money cleaning everything up.

➤

They had plenty to throw around.

Louise knew she needed to put away her resentment. Today was about Larry. Maybe the service and spreading the ashes would show her a way to let go of some of her anger and hurt. Peggy climbed the stairs and called through the door.

"Louise? People are arriving."

Louise watched cars pull into the lot behind the pier. She'd invited the entire crew, including Dark Cloud and his guys. Jeff drove up in clean work clothes. The wives were as dressed up as they had clothes for, and some carried dishes of food. Jeff looked up and saw Louise at the window. He waved.

She stared at the urn. Goddammit, Larry.

On the way to the tug Louise saw Peggy approaching.

"Louise." Peggy had worked as bookkeeper off and on for the company. She knew how thin their money was. She came forward and placed a hand on Louise's arm. "I'm so sorry. This is so hard for all of us, but for you? What are you going to do?"

"I'm not sure, Peggy. I've asked about a line of credit against the claim for the ship, but I haven't heard back."

People wandered over to the dock and milled around on the rear deck of the tug until Vince showed people the way inside to the galley. Now everyone could sit, but they weren't going far.

"Wait." Louise stopped at the lip of the dock. Travis had not yet arrived. Back at the entrance to their property, a vehicle pulled up and two strangers holding cameras got out and started taking pictures. Then a third person emerged, pudgy, notebook in his hand. How did these reporters have the balls to do this?

Travis finally appeared in his battered VW and parked next to the reporter's car. He caught up with the reporter.

"This is private property, sir. You need to go back."

The reporter stopped for a moment, looked at Travis, then started to push past.

Travis stood in his way.

"Private property. Get lost."

"Who the hell are you?"

The photographers snapped pictures, edging closer to the tug.

"I am a member of the crew," Travis said.

"No you're not. You're the cub reporter for the Peninsula News. I know you."

"Yeah, well, I was on this tug. I was there. You weren't. This is private. Now get lost or get hurt."

Louise walked over and stood next to Travis, facing the florid reporter. "Listen." Louise spoke quietly. "There's a memorial service for my husband tomorrow, open to the public. You're welcome there. But not here. This is private. Now if you don't skedaddle your plump ass outa here, I'm gonna have the tug's crew come over here and let 'em do what they want to you and your car."

The photographers were already heading back to their car. The reporter puffed up for a moment, then deflated and walked away.

"Thanks, Travis," said Louise. "Glad you could come."

The tug's diesel rumbled. Black smoke shot into the sky from the stack. Louise followed Travis down onto the deck after tossing the mooring and spring lines. Then she passed through the deckhouse and climbed to the bridge.

She took the wheel from Jeff. The wheelhouse was crowded. Dark Cloud, Stretch and Billy stood in the back, looking sober for once. She placed the urn in a cup holder and it fit perfectly. Then she put the tug in gear and began steering out to the channel.

A quarter mile away, she could see Buckhorn's security crew watching from the bridge of the ship. Ahead, the Strait lay unruffled by wind, but she could already feel the slow heave of ocean swells.

A small Coast Guard vessel, probably from Port Angeles, motored toward the container ship.

"They could arrest us, probably," said Dark Cloud, "so many people aboard and not enough life jackets." Louise knew he was kidding.

"This time out, I don't think so," said Louise. Out of the harbor, she set a course northwest and handed the wheel to Billy.

"Steer 330. We'll get right out in the middle, away from the cameras."

Down in the galley the tables were covered with dishes of food. People milled around chatting.

Four miles from shore, Louise took the urn and led the way down to the aft deck. Vince took the engine out of gear and the tug began to slow. A bird landed on the roof of the wheelhouse.

"Well," said Louise, looking around "Anyone want to say something?"

Dark Cloud stepped forward.

"Larry and me, hell Louise, you and me, we fought against each other for business all the time, for years. Mostly you beat us out, but we hung in there. Larry was a hell of an operator. He could chase anything. I never knew anyone who could muscle a tow like him." He stepped forward and touched the urn. "Because of Larry we got on the ship and got the tow hooked up. Seemed impossible, but he did it. Larry trusted me and my guys to help, and together we found the *Express* and brought her back."

Dark Cloud stepped back. No one said anything. Then Peggy moved forward.

"I was always afraid of Larry, first few years. He was so intense, but he was kind, too. Gave Vince time off when the kids were born. Made sure everyone got the safety training. Made sure the tug was right. I'm gonna miss him."

Jeff emerged from the deckhouse doorway.

"When Larry married Louise, I was sure he was going to ruin the company. I never understood why my pop let it happen. I figured out later my pop saw what Larry had right away. Larry was useless in the engine room, though." Louise laughed. "He mighta been a good tug handler and a good skipper, but put him near tools and you were asking for disaster. And he was rough on *Warhorse*, too. That's why he needed me and Vince, to keep her running."

Jeff tapped the urn and stepped back. Someone coughed. One of the kids sniffled.

Vince stepped forward, face working, as he tried to speak. Then he waved his hands and shook his head, stepping back.

Louise listened as members of her family spoke. Some told stories, some told lies. People shivered in the open air, but still they all stood on the stern, bearing witness. Larry's third brother, up from Portland, stepped forward. He had brought Larry's ancient mother, who sat beneath blankets.

"Larry was my older brother. I was terrified of him. I'm still terrified of him. But he could get things done. Nobody could get things done like he did. I think only Louise here could have stood up to him, and I think she stood up pretty well. You kept him level, somehow, Louise."

Louise looked at Travis, nodded. She had to nod three times before Travis realized she wanted him to say something.

"Larry hired me when I was 19 and useless. He taught me to splice wire. He might have been a bad mechanic, but he knew wire even if he couldn't splice it well."

Everyone nodded. Larry knew wire.

The wind picked up. Rain fell.

"So damn typical, what happened. All ice and we're trying

to get the wire on the bitts, and who is the guy who goes forward and takes the hardest job? The most dangerous job?" Travis nodded at the urn. "Larry. He made a mistake, which cost him, but even at the very end he was thinking about the tow and asking about Louise. Hard to believe he's gone."

Louise now spoke.

"When I first met him, all I saw was his size and force, his big laugh, his certainty. Even when he was dead wrong, and I told him when he was dead wrong, he maintained that certainty. It carried us through many hard times. He came to our family as the new guy, coming into a family tug operation my pop set up, and he worked for my pop and he worked for me and never complained and always did his work. And when pop died, we all agreed - me, Vince, Jeff—Larry should run things. We all agreed, remember?" Jeff and Vince nodded. "He did pretty good, too."

Louise went over to the side of the tug, downwind from the slight breeze, opened the urn, and scattered the ashes. A white powder, more than she imagined could fit in the urn, fell out and speckled the water. Some flecks drifted in the breeze away from the tug.

"You'll never be far from us, here, Larry, and we won't be far from you. Rest in peace."

The streak of ashes on the water slid astern and slowly sank from sight.

They all crowded back into the galley to escape the increasing wind and rain. Ned brought in fresh coffee.

"Big change," Ned said to Louise as they watched people eat. "What are you going to do?"

"What would Larry want to do, Ned?"

"Keep the company going."

"Exactly. I just don't know how. I can't even pay all you guys right now."

"Don't worry, Louise. We all knew when we signed on we might not get paid. We also know it'll be a long time for the prize. But we trust you, just like we trusted Larry."

"I don't know where I'm going to find the money, Ned. The bank's not telling me anything."

"Look, Louise, let's get you through the next couple of days, the memorial service, then see."

Outside, the water slid past and the tug rolled gently. Well offshore, an APL ship, the three letters huge on the sides of the hull, passed them, outbound.

"He's where he always wanted to be, Louise. On the Strait."

"In it, actually, Ned."

The tug roared.

Travis

Travis hung around the dock after they returned from casting Larry's ashes to see if he could help.

"Go take care of your hands," said Louise. "If they get infected you could lose fingers."

"Yes, mother."

She gave a wan smile and waved him away.

"Go. Get your hands fixed, take a hot shower, go to Port Angeles and buy yourself a thick steak. Hell, have some drinks and find a hot woman."

"Before I do," said Travis, "I wanted to let you know I'd like to keep working here, if you keep the company going."

"You were going to be an award winning reporter. Work from behind a desk like a civilized person."

"I don't like desks and reporting on garden shows and traffic deaths. Besides, I enjoyed it back on *Warhorse*. Plus, when I'm ashore I want to write this story about how we recovered the *Express*, and some stuff about Buckhorn, too. There's a story there, I know it." The mysterious boxes he had seen in the ship tunnel came into his mind. Travis knew the story wasn't yet fully told. He wanted to be around for all of it.

"We can always use a good wire splicer. Let's see how things

➤

work out at the bank. By the way, thanks for coming today." Louise paused. "Thanks for giving blood, too. You and Dark Cloud..."

"Larry would have done the same for me, Louise."

Travis drove out of town, and then changed his mind and drove to the Buckhorn pier. A couple of workers on the ship's main deck were lifting a heavy object using a sling. The reporters had left and all was business down at the pier. The guard stopped him at the gate. Travis remembered the guy from somewhere. His nametag read, "Pete."

"Any chance to get onto the ship?" he asked, knowing what the guard would say. "I have a TWIC card." He pulled out his mariner documentation, which included the security card.

"Okay," said the guard, "but you need more than a TWIC card. This pier is leased by Buckhorn and you'll need their permission to go in."

Travis saw the small crane behind the deckhouse swing out, carrying a lashed pallet. A big, open-bay truck stood on the dock under the crane. The pallet dropped to the bed of the truck. People undid the sling and waved their arms. How could they be unloading materials when the Coast Guard is supposed to quarantine a ship like this until their investigation is complete? The cargo they were unloading looked like the boxes with Russian lettering from the tunnel.

"They're gonna bring in some heavy lift cranes tomorrow, try to get the helicopters out of number six hold," said Pete.

"Helicopters?"

Pete grinned.

"Yeah, I heard this ship was carrying the birds for the mining next summer."

Travis suddenly recognized the guard.

"Hey, you're the guy who got shot out in the woods last summer," said Travis. "I was working for the paper. I remember.

Couple guys pinned by big arrows to a tree. And you got shot, a gun, by another guy working for Buckhorn." Pete had stopped talking. Travis knew he shouldn't have mentioned he worked for the newspaper, but this guy could be a good source of information.

"I was on *Warhorse*," Travis explained. "Used to work on her before joining the paper."

Pete seemed curious. "Were you on the tug or the ship?"

"The ship."

Pete said nothing.

"Hey. Hey." Someone was striding toward the guard shack from the ship, thin, a lantern jaw and sharp eyes. "You got business here, show ID to the guard. If not, get lost. Last thing we need here are gawkers and idiots." Travis recognized him. This was one of the guys who'd been pinned to a tree by that girl the summer before.

"I'm not on your terminal, last I looked."

"I don't care. We've leased this whole place and you're not welcome."

"I was on the tug that saved this ship for you, asshole."

Lantern jaw stopped talking.

Something was fishy here. Travis felt his radar firing off all over the place.

Driving away, he had to smile. Here he was, about to go back to work on the tug again, and yet he still wanted to act the reporter, too. His mother was so right about him. He was scattered and impulsive.

Pete

"You're early today," said Mariana, ringing up another customer.

"Easy, bud," Pete told Sam, pulling his son back from the doughnut display. "I'm the school bus driver the next few days. Sam's at my place for a bit. I'll take two dozen, mixed. Surprise the Buckhorn guys. Can you give Sam a glass of orange juice?"

After his son got the juice, Pete sent him out to wait in the truck.

Mariana helped Pete select the doughnuts. Today he was going to load the Buckhorn guys up on gooey stuff - crème filled, sugar-covered, glazed. He'd have them all on sugar rages down there.

"Buckhorn hired Brad. He and Joyce are moving to Los Angeles. In fact, he's already there," Pete said.

"Can they just do that? Take Sam, I mean?"

"I'm not sure. I'm fighting this. Anyway, last night Joyce shows up at the door and says she and Brad have to go down to look at houses. She asked me to take Sam for the rest of the week."

Mariana stopped picking out doughnuts.

"She says you aren't fit or healthy enough to take him, and then a couple days later she dumps him on you?"

►

"I don't feel dumped on when I get Sam, but yes."

Mariana looked through the front window at Pete's truck, where Sam sat waiting in the passenger's seat.

"How can they just take your kid away? He should at least finish off the school year here."

"I'm going to contest this, if I can find the money. They'll argue I'm unfit."

Mariana laughed.

"Of course, her leaving Sam here argues against her own argument."

"My thought exactly. I was happy to take him."

"What happens after school if you're working?"

"He has a friend, Buddy, on the reservation, whose mother runs a daycare. I'll pick him up there at 4:30."

Mariana gave Pete a look, then hesitated, considering. Then she said, "Pete, what are you doing tomorrow afternoon? You working?"

He unfolded the schedule Roger had given him. "Off at 10 tomorrow, actually." But scanning the schedule, he was also reminded he'd be working the next weekend. And now he had Sam. Damn.

"I run a little catering service on the side." Mariana said. "Most of my customers are retired people in Sequim holding birthday or anniversary parties." Pete hadn't known Mariana had a side business. If he was an old geezer and he knew his caterer looked like Mariana, he'd hire her to celebrate the sun coming up every day. "But this week," Mariana continued, "Louise asked me to cater Larry's memorial service at the Grange Hall. I'm going to need some help, and a truck. Can you help me? I'll pay, of course. Catering is pretty lucrative."

"I won't be much help setting up, Mariana." Pete felt his leg ache. "I can barely move myself around, let alone carry stuff."

"Maybe it's time to start. Really. Can you help me? My van's not working, something about the gas line."

"I was thinking of going to the memorial anyway," Pete said.

"It's going to be a tough afternoon," she said, closing the boxes of doughnuts. "Will you help me?"

Pete nodded. "Of course."

Back in the truck, Sam sat, his feet on the dash.

"Put your feet down, buddy."

"Dad, do you like that lady?"

"She's okay. She just hired me for a little job."

"Will you make enough money so I can stay with you and go to school here?"

"Maybe. We'll see."

Pete stepped on the gas. He wanted to get Sam to school on time.

His leg felt better. He felt better.

Myra

I walked into the council offices, located in the old elementary school, then climbed the stairs up to the second-floor gym where the council chambers were. The facilities were drab compared to the plush, well-outfitted offices of tribes flush with casino money, but I loved the beautiful, undersized basketball court, the long, straight pieces of old growth fir on the floor.

I hadn't seen my report since sending a revised version to Marcie last night. She'd be the one to summarize the reports. Today, I was an observer.

I knew almost everyone in the crowded gym. I'd gone to school with some, including the youngest two council members. Based on what I knew about the audience, the pro-Buckhorn group was on the right side, the anti-Buckhorn camp on the left.

Eldon came over to me.

"How are you?"

"I'm here."

Rose appeared, using a cane. She sat next to me and placed a gnarled hand on my knee.

The session started late, as they always do. I could hear steam hissing through the school's old heating system. The room was

➤

too cold, then too hot. I could see the Buckhorn suits off to the right.

After working through a long list of miscellaneous agenda items, the council finally turned to the Buckhorn project. While most in the tribe wouldn't attend meetings about financing schools or building a sewer system, everyone was interested in the Buckhorn discussion.

As I waited for things to get started, I thought of Sergei and wondered if he would find Tom at the airport, and if they would be back in time for Larry's memorial service tomorrow.

My boss shuffled her papers, then walked over to a projector while someone drew the gym's curtains and dimmed the lights.

"I'll try to be brief," Marcie said, adjusting the focus on the projector. "This concerns the request by Buckhorn Industries for the tribe to support its investment in construction of the Human Dispersal Center on the property down at the harbor. Also, to accept Buckhorn's offer of providing full college scholarships to any tribal member completing high school, B average or better. And finally, they are asking the tribe to not actively oppose Buckhorn's permit application before the National Park Service to conduct limited and non-intrusive mineral extraction from a valid mining claim on a tributary of the Elwha River."

The Buckhorn officials, Victoria Oldsea and someone else, sat up straight, attentive.

I felt Rose's hand tighten on my knee. She took a breath. Eldon, sitting at the council table, scowled.

"The Human Dispersal Center has a budget of $ 2,300,000 and Buckhorn has made a commitment to hire local firms for the work. Buckhorn has asked to retain tribal archeologists to consult on the Center's displays and programs."

This was news to me. Buckhorn had certainly not contacted me about working for them, and last time I looked I was the only archeologist on staff. Maybe they were referring to Marcie, but she was an anthropologist, not an archeologist. Anthro? Archeo? What was the difference to them?

"Buckhorn proposes to conduct one or two seasons of activity in Olympic National Park, at the headwaters of the Elwha River, in the valley of a tributary, Godkin Creek. The area concerned is two to four acres, the slope extending from a tributary creek to Godkin, Bear Creek, to the Godkin Valley. This slope contains erbium, a trace mineral found in a few places around the world, but in the lower 48 states, seemingly only in the Olympic Mountains. Buckhorn proposes removing 6,000 to 10,000 tons of this mineral from the slope. They would then use heavy freight helicopters to move the material to the Sol Duc terminal at the harbor, where the mineral will be transferred to a ship for delivery to Los Angeles." I could see one or two unhappy council members frowning, heads bowed. "In Los Angeles, Buckhorn will replicate the erbium using silicon and other abundant materials such that further mining of erbium may not be required."

I picked up on "may not". There were "may nots" and "shoulds" all through Marcie's report.

"What's erbium good for?" asked Leo. Leo was the youngest council member, hot-headed.

"When erbium is ground into a powder and then added to other materials, the mixture can be injected into the coal-burning process. The erbium, and they hope the synthetic substitute, detoxifies the coal ash and emissions. If the initial tests are successful, Buckhorn will build a facility in Port Angeles or here in Sol Duc to manufacture 1 million tons of the synthetic material per year. The plant will create more than 400 jobs and Buckhorn has made a commitment to hire tribal members for this work to the extent possible."

Despite all the qualifications - "if successful," "to the extent possible" - I could see the tide turning in favor of Buckhorn. Who could reject scholarships and jobs?

"No roads? No power lines? Fly in and fly out?" asked Gabriel, a younger member of the tribe who'd once been a terrific traditional dancer. He'd moved to Seattle, then come back to Sol Duc as a CPA. He now ran the tribe's economic development office. "And they're planning to restore the slope and the landing areas up in the watershed?"

"Yes, to all of your questions," said Marcie. The two Buckhorn executives smiled at each other. Rose let out a skeptical snort. "I've reviewed all the reports, and there have been many," Marcie added. "Reports by Buckhorn, the Elwha Tribe, Myra on my staff, and others. All the reports agree the mining impacts will be limited and not long-lasting."

My heart sank. She was right, the mining methods were not the problem. The potential impact on archeological treasures was the problem. I'd argued we needed a proper survey of the area.

"What do our cousins say?" Eldon asked.

"Well," said Marcie, "the Elwha tribe has recommended this not proceed until more work has been done to assess the danger to cultural artifacts, but Buckhorn's more detailed reports indicate there is no danger. By and large, our staff concurs." Eldon was giving me the sign to keep quiet. I knew the fix was in.

"Isn't it true," said Gabriel, "our archeologist and the Buckhorn surveyors were up in that valley last summer twice, for many days, and they walked over and examined every square inch for many days looking for a lost girl? Did they find anything then? How long would we look? A week? The whole summer? A year or two? Meanwhile we'll lose the scholarships and the plant and the jobs."

I wanted to stand up and scream at them all.

There was more discussion. Much more. It is our way.

In the end, the council moved to support the Human Dispersal Center. The council thanked Buckhorn for the scholarships and remained entirely silent on the mining enterprise. They did not offer support, but they did not stand in opposition. I knew, by remaining silent, they were in effect providing support.

As the audience dispersed, many looked like Gabriel: happy and proud. A smaller group looked sad and disappointed.

Rose turned to me and said, "Are we in the coal business now?"

December 18, Saturday

William

William listened to the wind, felt the warmth of the small fire. William knew the wood would be gone before morning. He was hungry, and he felt empty. His knee ached. Overhead, all he could see were branches, swinging in the wind.

A raven cried and settled on a branch above. It peered at him, eyes black and shining.

William had faith in Anne. He knew he had more faith in her than she did herself. He was in the best of hands, her hands. If anyone could find help, she could.

He remembered the short face bear he had seen in the high basin the previous summer, appearing from nowhere, standing, looking at him, the sun against its coat. It was the most beautiful animal he had ever seen.

Time passed. More time passed.

He might have slept.

He heard, above him, the high sharp cry of an eagle.

Then, it seemed, he woke. He was braced on the thwart of the voyage canoe, steering oar close against his side. They had been without sleep for two days, sailing south, passing the great island and the ice, and he had fallen asleep in place

➤

many times, steering by instinct. Now they had passed the south end of the island and were crossing the great strait toward their homeland. They were very close. He looked forward, at the paddlers moving in unison, chanting, the sail fat, pushing them ahead. The canoe rose and fell in the steady hand of the deep sea. To the left had lain the shore, trees, the coastal mountains, but this day they had been passing the ice, the snout of the great ice bear. Beyond, higher, further east, stood the smoking mountain. Warm, fresh air blew over them. Ahead, past the ice, lay their shore. The sacred river stretched south into distant valleys. The mountains guarding their land stood over their river, fighting the ice bear always.

He leaned on the oar; brought the canoe a bit to the left, saw Tiny Whales blowing ahead.

"Our home." One of the paddlers cried out, his voice high.

The paddler began to sing. Three other paddlers lifted their long heads. They all sang the arrival song.

Steve

Just before I left home to pick up Fred for the memorial service, Bruce called from Buckhorn. I'd been avoiding his calls, but Bruce was an old friend.

"Listen, Steve, Ken just came by. Because you refuse to come in, they want me to draft a letter telling you you've been relieved of your position as one of our captains."

I wasn't surprised. I had union protection for all sorts of things, but the company could dismiss its captains whenever it wanted. Buckhorn had fought for that provision in the last contract. They knew a fired captain could go back to the union hall and find another ship, especially those of us having years of experience.

I asked about David, my reserve captain. "I don't know. Ken did not mention him. I'm sorry, Steve."

"Thanks for giving me the heads up, Bruce. I'm not at all surprised."

"I also heard you showed up at the gate at Sol Duc and spoke to the guard there."

"Yeah, I wanted to see my ship. Some asshole ran over and threw me out."

"Had to be Roger Harrington, head of security." Bruce chuckled.

➤

"Last summer someone shot an arrow into him, pinned him to a tree. He's a piece of work."

Bruce told me they'd called off the search for the lifeboat, but I'd already heard. Two weeks had now gone by.

After I picked up Fred at his sister's place we boarded the ferry in Edmonds. The two of us headed up to the galley where we ran into Jamal the reefer, Carlton the third engineer, and Richard the cook. Most of the guys from my lifeboat were attending Larry Hunt's memorial. We clustered around two tables and caught up on news.

I let everyone know the search for the other lifeboat had been called off.

After a couple of minutes without speaking, Carlton said, "The memorial for this tug guy, kind of going to be a memorial for our guys too."

The ferry's loudspeaker told passengers to return to their cars. As I stood up, my cell phone rang.

"Steve?" Reception was terrible. My phone screen showed 'INT.' International? "Is this Steve Procida?"

"Who's this?"

"You left your phone number, in case anything happened. This is Rex, search and rescue, the co-pilot of the bird. Up on Haida Gwaii?"

I felt short of breath. My pulse began to race.

"Steve. Can you hear me?" Barely. From the phone, in the background I heard the clatter of a helicopter. "I'm at the Sandspit Airport, Steve. We're taking fuel. I was in Prince Rupert an hour ago when some loggers out on Graham Island reported finding a body in the snow..." I waited. Come on, Rex. "We flew out there thinking we'd find a corpse, but the thing is, she's alive."

"She?"

"Yeah, and I think she's one of your crew. She's young, thin and in bad shape. I mean, we got there and I was sure she was frozen to death, but her heart was beating. We brought her to the clinic in Queen Charlotte City. She's unconscious, but she's alive."

"Why do you think she's one of my crew?"

"She's wearing heavy fire gear, stenciled *Seattle Express*."

I grabbed the edge of a nearby booth.

This had to be Anne, my third mate.

"Where was she?"

"South end of Graham Island, on the eastern slope of the coastal range. Listen, I gotta go. The weather's halfway clear for the first time in weeks, and we're going to make another run. We want to slowly check Skidgate Inlet and north of there. Visibility's all right, maybe we'll see something. And when the girl comes out of her coma or whatever, we should know more."

"Call me if you see anything during your flight, all right?"

"I sure will."

In the background, I heard rotors start to whop, whop-whop-whop.

I wasn't surprised they'd found Anne, the youngest, greenest member. She'd been whipcord tough, a thin former runner. When she left to board the other lifeboat not a shadow of fear had crossed her face.

If they found Anne on Graham Island, then her lifeboat must have made the Queen Charlotte coast.

I decided not to say anything to the others, not yet. This still might not be Anne, but worse, we might learn everyone else had died. I should know more from Rex in two or three hours. What the hell was Anne doing in the middle of Graham Island? And where did she walk from?

"You okay, Steve?" asked Fred. "You look pale."

"I'm fine, Fred. This is going to be a long afternoon."

Louise

Vince and Ellie were helping Louise set up chairs in the Grange Hall when Mariana showed up in a truck carrying the food and drinks. Some people were already out in the lot, waiting for the doors to open. Louise recognized townspeople, folks from the tribe, and representatives from several Seattle tug companies. She also saw reporters.

Mariana was getting help from a guy who looked familiar. Louise watched him work for a while, bringing in food, and then pulled Marianna aside. "Couldn't you get someone who can actually work? I mean, he has a good truck, but he can hardly walk. I find it painful to watch him."

"That's Pete Wise. You may have seen him in the coffee shop. He's the guard down at the Buckhorn pier."

"What, you sweet on him? Or just doing him a favor?"

Mariana colored.

"He's got a good truck. I needed a truck to bring all this over, otherwise more than three trips in my little car. Plus, he needed a break from sitting down at the pier."

Jeff hung up some pictures of Larry, and some drawings Larry had done. He hadn't been a bad artist, actually.

Vince turned to Louise.

"How come I have to say something?"

➤

"Hell, Vince, we went through this. You, Jeff, me, we all talk, then let other people talk if they want. Mostly this thing's for people not in the family."

"I hate talking in front of people."

"I know you do. That's why you're so good at it."

Louise went over to help Mariana's friend. She took one of the two boxes he was trying to carry.

"What happened?" she asked.

"I got shot last summer."

Louise had been everywhere but Sol Duc last summer, trying to find *Warhorse* some towing work. She vaguely remembered something about a shooting in the park. "Looks painful."

The man shrugged.

Louise watched the crowd grow. She saw Bill, the banker she was waiting to hear from, and Suzette, the blond she'd thought Larry was screwing. Still thought he might have been screwing. A big SUV pulled up, the Buckhorn logo on its side. Victoria from Buckhorn, and the attorney, and two other suits got out and started talking to people, shaking hands, being good corporate citizens.

The attorney approached her. "I'm Ken Weinhall, Buckhorn VP." He was sort of handsome in a silver fox kind of way. He was still a shark. Victoria and the two suits passed around Ken and entered the hall. "Could I have a moment?" he asked, holding Louise's arm.

"What?"

"We appreciate what you did, out there."

"No you don't." She felt her blood start to boil. "You're gonna tell me, in the nicest possible way, you're going to fight our claim, do anything you can to ruin our company."

Now the attorney blinked.

"Just between the two of us, ma'am, you are astute."

"No, I'm not. You're just so obvious." Louise stepped forward.

Weinhall stepped back. "Christ. Have you no manners at all? Wait. I forgot. You work for Buckhorn."

She turned away from Weinhall and was startled to recognize another new arrival.

"I recognize you," she said, holding out a hand. "I saw you on television when you came back to Seattle. You're the captain, right?"

"Steve Procida. Yes. And these men were on the lifeboat."

"Any word?"

Louise kept holding the captain's hand. She had lost a husband but he had lost 11 men. He looked tired, and old, but there was unexpected energy in his eyes. He shook his head.

"The search was called off."

"Well. I appreciate you coming all the way out here for this. You didn't have to, you know."

"Yes we did."

One of the other crew members, with a heavily tattooed brown face, spoke. "Your Larry spent time on our ship, so he was a crewmember too."

Louise felt her eyes fill.

"That's nice," she said. "Have a seat. There's no real program, just a few words from the family, then the floor's open. I know if anyone here can describe what things were like out there, you can. Means a lot to me, you being here."

Louise took a big breath. They better get started.

Travis

Travis arrived late and had to stand in the back. He saw Sarah Cooley, the girl who had disappeared the summer before and miraculously reappeared. She was studying Larry's drawings, which Travis saw had been mounted on a table. Travis saw Myra and some members of the Sol Duc Tribe. Vince, Jeff and Louise were in front, sitting next to an old woman who must be Larry's mother. Looking around, he recognized Mariana, Pete the gate guard, the ship's captain Steve, and some people in suits representing Buckhorn.

Vince stood.

"Most of you know me. I'm Vince Balon, Louise's brother. Louise told me I had to be the emcee for this and one of these days I'll pay her back." Some people chuckled, and Travis felt the whole place relax. "Yesterday, the family here, we took Larry's ashes out on *Warhorse* and cast 'em into the Strait, where he'd want to be, on the water near his home. Thanks to everyone for coming this afternoon."

"He was a good man," someone called from the crowd. People clapped.

"What we will do here is, me and Jeff and Louise are gonna say a few words, then let anyone else say something. Keep this informal."

➤

"Then talk," said a voice. More people laughed.

"I'll keep my comments short. Our family trusted Larry so much we let him take over the company when our pop died. He was the guy who said 'let's get that ship' and took us out there and snagged her. Even after he got hurt, he made sure we got the ship back to Sol Duc."

Jeff took over.

"When Larry joined the family business, we learned soon enough to keep him away from tools, but I never saw anyone like Larry who knew just how to rig slings, raise gear and secure tow lines. Larry getting hurt was the last thing I ever expected. Must have been all the ice on the deck and the unpredictable sea. I'm gonna miss him."

Jeff sat down and the old woman put an arm across his shoulder. Now Louise rose.

"Larry always said to me 'Louise, if I ever die, throw my ashes in the strait and then have a party. So this is a party. But I want to remind everyone there are other sailors still missing."

She moved over and stood near Myra. "Myra, here, her father William was on the *Express*. He even sailed on *Warhorse* a couple times, years ago. He's a good man. William and 10 others are still out there. I fear for them, and pray for them. Some of the rest of the *Express* crew are here, too." Louise pointed. "I'm honored they came. Thank you all for coming."

Louise paused, gathered herself, then continued.

"Larry was a damn difficult man to work with, let alone be married to."

"Well then he picked a good one in you," yelled someone.

"Maybe he did. I don't know. Some would say we were fools to risk everything going out to salvage that ship, but we did."

The Buckhorn people looked very irritated.

After Louise finished speaking, others began to tell stories about the crazy things Larry had done over the years. People laughed and cried. Travis realized they were all going through a healing process the only way they knew how.

Finally, Eldon LeClair stood to speak. Travis had been told by Louise Eldon had known Larry many years and had always appreciated how Larry never let his tug get tangled in the tribe's fishing gear. Eldon raised his hands, lowered his head, and led people in a prayer:

"Grandmother, watch over Larry Hunt. Make sure he is fed and safe and at peace. Know that we who remain on this side miss him, and we think of him, and wish him well. This we ask of you."

Eldon sat down. After several long seconds, he announced: "Now, we should eat."

Travis knew he better get to the food before everything was gone.

Pete

Pete sat next to Mariana at the back of the hall as people clustered around the tables holding food.

"I should have made more food," she said. The hall was crowded. Local residents, tribal members, tug operators from around the Sound, the crew of the *Seattle Express*, even Buckhorn suits – all had attended.

Pete's injured leg was killing him.

"Hello, Pete."

He looked up. Tom Olsen and Sarah, Tom's granddaughter, stood in front of him. He hadn't seen them since he'd been shot out in the park the previous summer. Next to them was the Russian, Sergei, looking exhausted. He remembered he and Sergei shared a love for tying flies.

"Very good to see you, Pete. Good also to see you are able to work," said Sergei in his distinctive Russian accent.

Myra approached the group.

"Sergei. How was your flight?" she asked, cool.

Myra was pale, tired.

He watched her and Sergei leaning forward, almost in a hug, but then backing off at the last second. Sarah looked at Pete and winked.

➤

"My flight was fine," said Sergei, "but I cannot sleep on airplanes. I think, for me, the time is two in the morning. How are you?"

"I've been better, but thanks for coming," said Myra. "You didn't have to."

"Of course I did. And I could, so I am here."

Pete saw someone come over and shake Myra's hand. He realized he was seeing the same man who'd come by the pier a few days earlier, wanting to see the ship. Now he understood this had been the ship's captain.

"You're William's daughter, aren't you? I remember you from years ago, the time he brought you aboard the ship. You were much younger then. Do you remember?"

Myra looked at Steve and then stepped forward, hugging him.

"So good to see you again, Steve."

A phone rang, and Steve fumbled at his shirt pocket. He looked at the screen on his phone and went rigid.

As Steve put the phone up to his ear, the Buckhorn people started pushing through the crowd.

"Excuse me" said one, practically shouting. He tried to get past Steve, who appeared completely focused on his phone call. "Excuse me, dammit."

Steve ignored him. When he finally put the phone down, he stepped forward and took hold of Myra's forearms.

"After we were rescued, I went up in the Coast Guard helicopter looking for your father's lifeboat. I got to know the pilot, Rex." The whole hall full of people seemed to go quiet. Everyone could hear Steve, but he was speaking only to Myra. "This morning, Rex called me and said they'd found a woman on Graham Island wearing *Express* fire gear. She was in bad shape, and unconscious, but alive. She was my third mate, Anne. They flew another search this afternoon. They found the other lifeboat." Everyone seemed to start talking at once. Steve raised his hand. "The lifeboat was in a tiny cove, damaged. They'd built a shelter, and they're alive, but in bad shape. They flew half of them to Queen Charlotte City and are heading back for the rest, now, before the weather turns." Steve paused. He looked uncomfortable. He spoke directly to Myra. "The survivors told the helicopter crew Anne and William left the camp four days ago to seek help."

Myra lowered her head and closed her eyes.

"And William?" asked Eldon.

"He hasn't been found. Anne's unconscious, deep hypothermia. They'll try to learn more when she comes to. I'm sorry, Myra." Steve spoke softly. Myra had gone limp, as if about to faint.

"No." Sarah grabbed Myra's sleeve. "William knows more about the woods than anyone. If anyone could survive up there, it's him."

"Oh, Sarah," said Tom, reaching out to hug his granddaughter.

"No, dammit. He said he'd be waiting for you, Myra. You heard him."

Myra blinked. Then she nodded. "We've heard nothing for two weeks and we all thought they were dead. Now Anne's alive. And nine others survived. Why not my father? He knows the wilderness. I think Sarah's right. You're right, Sarah."

Tom, spare and thin, nodded, saying, "He might be found."

"And we will find him," added Sarah.

"We gotta move fast, then," said Myra.

"There's flights through Vancouver. Direct to Sandspit on Haida Gwaii," said Sarah. "I already checked."

Could these people be serious? Pete suddenly wished he could join them.

"My crew is up there recovering, and I plan to visit them,"

said Steve. "I'm not much of a woodsman, Myra, but I'll be happy to provide whatever base support you need."

Travis stepped forward, hesitated, then said, "You got a helluva lot to do if you want to get your gear ready to make a flight tomorrow." He paused and his wire rim glasses glinted. "It's the middle of the winter, for God's sake. I'd like to help out. Come along, actually. I was on the ship recovery and I'd like to find William, too."

"Who are you?" Sarah asked Travis, looking surprised.

"Don't you remember?" Myra asked. Myra was laughing. "This is the reporter who interviewed you after you were found last summer. He dressed better then. As he says, he went up on *Warhorse* to retrieve the ship, too."

"Myra, Tom-Tom, Sergei, me, and now you, Travis," said Sarah. She poked Travis in the side. "You better be able to keep up."

"Who said you were going, Sarah?" asked Tom. "This will be a death march through thick snow."

"I want her along," Myra said. "I want her spirit and strength. Come on, Tom. You're almost 70, but you're coming, aren't you?"

"William was my oldest friend."

"We're not going anywhere unless they're flying tomorrow and there's room on the plane," said Myra, pulling out her phone.

Victoria Oldsea, Buckhorn's lead person in Sol Duc, who'd come by the pier once since the ship had appeared, at least when Pete had been down there, barked a short, incredulous laugh.

"You're going 500 miles north from here and God knows how many miles through snow to wherever William is? When you find him, he'll be gone. You'll all die, too."

Myra took the phone away from her ear. "They have six

seats available. We're on the 9:10 tomorrow to Vancouver, then to Sandspit. Not many people go to Haida Gwaii in the middle of December, it seems. Usually the airport's closed, they say."

Steve, the captain, faced the Buckhorn suits. "Ken, Buckhorn Marine fired me this morning. We had to abandon a ship you assholes failed to maintain. As the captain who ordered the ship abandoned, I'm going north to make sure everyone comes home, including William."

Reporters frantically scribbled in their notebooks. Over the commotion, Pete spoke up so Sergei could hear him.

"Bet you didn't think you'd fly all the way here only to head off into the wilderness for Christmas, did you?"

"William was my friend, Pete. How can I do anything else?"

"There's all sorts of gear in our shop," said Vince, who had been listening in. He spoke to Travis. "Even sleeping bags and tents, left over from those times we had to set up stuff in the Aleutians. But you're gonna have to spend some money, too."

"What time are we?" asked Tom.

"Three o'clock." Myra said.

"Then we better get moving," Sarah said.

"Myra, get your gear, meet at my place," Tom said. "Travis, get your stuff, come by my place too."

They left the hall.

Mariana turned to Pete.

"The young girl, the skinny one. She's the girl who shot arrows or spears into your survey pals last summer, isn't she?"

"Not exactly my pals," said Pete. "One of my survey pals, as you call him, Raymond, he was the one who shot me in the knee."

"You need to choose better friends."

Louise

Louise and Jeff helped clean the hall after everyone left. They helped Mariana and Pete load Pete's truck with the casserole dishes, trays, and the small amount of leftover food.

When the hall was clean and the trash piled in the dumpster, Louise wrote Mariana a check.

"Thanks for your help."

Mariana folded the check and looked at Pete. Louise could see Pete was hurting. She knew he still had his kid to pick up at school, and the afternoon was getting late.

"Nice service, Louise." Mariana placed the last of the trays in the back of the truck.

"Now I gotta run back to my place, talk to Travis," said Louise.

"Why?" asked Pete.

"He's nuts to go on such a wild goose chase."

Pete nodded.

"They all are. But now William's the only one still missing. The third mate is the only one who might know where he is, and she's up there in whatever kind of clinic they have, unconscious. If your father were lost up there, wouldn't you go?"

"If the woman they found was nearly dead of exposure," said Louise, "then William will be the same, and she was found

➤

yesterday. Now another day has passed, and it'll probably be at least two more before anyone can find him."

Louise returned home in the dark. Vince and Travis were busy in the workshop, gear spread across the floor.

"Where'd you find this stuff?" she asked.

"Remember we did work for that salmon company up in the Aleutians a couple years ago?" said Vince. "They left all this gear on the tug, so we brought some back. There's a good sleeping bag, a decent pack, and warm coats and rain gear."

"Travis," Louise said. "If anything happens to you up there I'll feel responsible."

"Don't, Louise. I know what I'm doing. And those people know their stuff. I'll be fine. Besides, the cold snap they're having up there is bound to break. I bet we'll be warmer there than down here."

"In the valleys, maybe," said Vince. "Once we took *Warhorse* into Tasu Inlet, on the west coast of the Charlottes. There used to be a copper mine up there. Some of those mountains are more than 4,000 feet high. They'll be covered in snow."

Louise watched Travis stuff the sleeping bag, rain gear, and parka in the pack.

"You have decent boots, Travis?"

"Boots I have. I'll be all right."

"What are you doing for money? I can't pay you yet."

"I have a credit card."

Travis carried the gear to his car and waved to Louise as he drove away. Vince went home a few minutes later.

Louise was suddenly alone. Damn you, Larry. She was still pissed at him.

As she started to lock up, the Buckhorn suits pulled into the parking lot.

"Vultures," she said. "Right on schedule."

"Louise." It was the attorney who'd been at the memorial

service. He wasn't as nice this time.

"What do you want?"

"You know and I know your claim on the *Express* is, at best, weak. Months will pass before a resolution, and in the meantime, it's going to be tough for you financially. You haven't paid your crew. You might be forced to sell the tug, and your property, which won't be easy. The ground is contaminated. The government will require environmental studies costing hundreds of thousands of dollars. The cleanup itself will probably cost millions. It won't be easy to find a buyer for your property, Louise." The son of a bitch was right. "Despite the environmental damage, Buckhorn is interested in this site. It's right across from the pier and our operation there, and we'd like to build a larger complex requiring more land. We understand the potential costs of remediating the contamination, but Buckhorn has a strong interest in the property, and deep pockets."

Louise pointed down the road.

"Get out of here, please. I have no interest in doing business with Buckhorn."

Louise watched the Buckhorn vehicle drive away. Their attorney was right. She couldn't pay the men. The property had been mortgaged twice. She needed something to tide her over until the claim payout. She'd have to go grovel before the banker.

Just as she turned to enter the house another car came down the driveway. A woman was driving. Louise looked closer and recognized Suzette, banker Bill's girlfriend, the woman she still believed might have been Larry's squeeze despite what Vince had said. Suzette parked her car and approached Louise, hand out to shake hands.

"Louise? My name's Suzette. I work with Bill at the bank. That was a beautiful memorial today."

"Why are you here?" Louise did not shake Suzette's hand.

Suzette looked startled. Then she said, "Bill's uncle set up the banking arrangements for your father a long time ago. Larry and Bill both asked me to go through the records to see if there was anything they could use to get the bank's board to advance you further funds." Suzette paused and took a breath. "I'm an admiralty lawyer. Most of my practice concerns loss recovery for owners, or insurance investigations."

"Why was Larry seeing you so much?"

Suzette's eyes widened. Then she smiled as if everything had suddenly become clear.

"I was doing some pro bono work for Larry at Bill's request. Among other things, I found a life insurance policy just after you left to chase the *Express*."

"What?"

"Your father put in a condition years ago, if one of the owners was killed, there would be a life insurance payout."

"There is a life insurance policy on Larry?" Suzette nodded. Louise leaned against the worktable. She took a deep breath. "Are you telling me I am due a payout? Can I ask how much? This is a total surprise."

"I'll tell you in a minute. First, though, I wanted to ask about the car leaving as I was driving in. Were those people from Buckhorn?"

"Bastards. Vultures, picking at the carcass."

"They're fighting your claim, correct?"

Louise nodded.

"And they're probably pressuring you to sell, right?"

Louise nodded again. Shit. She'd been so wrong about Larry. Shit.

"You could probably use some legal help, fighting your case. Am I right?"

Louise looked up. She tried to speak but her lips began

to quiver. She nodded.

Myra

Steve called to say he'd reserved some rooms in a Queen Charlotte City hotel, on the north island. He'd also talked to Randall, up in the hospital there; they were still weak but improving. Unfortunately, Anne was still unconscious.

Tom served us elk stew and then disappeared to go shopping. He was always the cook when he and my dad went fishing. He knew how to use normal, light foods found in regular supermarkets rather than the freeze-dried stuff. The freeze-dried food never stuck to his ribs, he'd say. Instead we had instant pasta, dried meat, sauces, dried vegetables, Thai sauces, oatmeal, and powdered milk. He returned an hour later with full grocery bags.

Travis appeared. He added his pack to the four already lined up against the wall. Tom, Sarah and Sergei assembled and packed the food in heavy plastic freezer bags after marking their contents. Travis brought in some compact, modern snowshoes he told us they'd brought down from Alaska.

"We're crazy," I said. We'd been racing since the memorial service.

"Myra is correct. This is irresponsible," Sergei announced. "You have all acted irresponsibly since I first met you last summer.

Yet, I am here. I am crazy." He flashed his wonderful wide grin.

Travis looked a little stunned. He'd impulsively invited himself along and now, hours later, we were nearly ready to go.

Tom gestured me into the kitchen.

"Myra, I know you and Sergei were joking in there, but I'm worried about this. The people up there are already struggling to find William. We could easily get lost and injured ourselves, which would be no favor to whoever might be searching up there."

"Tom, we know a lot more now than we did a couple of hours ago, based on where Anne was found and where the lifeboat landed. The searchers will need all the help they can get."

The boat had come ashore between Rennell Sound and Skidgate Inlet, against the southern coast of Graham Island and separated from the interior by four ridges of high mountains. Anne had been found, as the crow flies, 5 miles from the coast, but 5 miles of wilderness: peaks, cliffs, and valleys. My father was somewhere along that line.

"I know my dad, Tom. If anyone knows how to hunker down in snow or rain, he does. I realize the search will be difficult."

Tom glanced at Sarah, who was helping Travis re-roll his sleeping bag.

"She's not yet 14, Myra, and she's small and thin, so the cold will be harder on her. And of course she'll be missing school." He gestured toward Travis. "And he's an unknown quantity."

"Travis was out there in the woods on his own last fall, Tom. He went up toward Bear Creek before he did that short story about our trip in the local paper, remember? He's not helpless."

"Are you sure about this, Myra?"

"I had a vision in the sweat lodge, Tom. Dad said he'll wait for me. I know this is going to be tough, I know the chances are poor, and I know, if we do find him, he'll be frozen to death, but what else can I do?"

"Travis, we're leaving really early," said Tom. "Stay here tonight. You need anything back at your place?"

"Uh, not really."

"Good. It's settled. You'll be in the downstairs bedroom, Sergei in the other bed."

I was tired, but Sergei looked ready to collapse. He had jet lag, and here he was about to fly again. I opened the door to go home to my place when Sarah followed me out.

"Remember the bear," she said. "And what William told you in the lodge." I nodded my head. "He's waiting for us, Myra."

I longed for her youthful optimism. Despite the trouble she'd had in life, Sarah carried a faith stronger than steel.

I envied her.

December 19, Sunday

Steve

While we waited at the gate for the flight to Vancouver, I called Laureen at Willow Run.

"You were going to call me yesterday, Mr. Procida."

"I was, but the searchers found some of my crew and I had to spend the day preparing to fly back north." I heard Laureen shuffling some papers.

"I notice we haven't received payment for the next quarter. I understand your schedule makes it difficult sometimes to meet our deadlines, and we have always done our best to accommodate you, but Jimmie's bill falls due in less than two weeks."

Buckhorn still hadn't paid me for my last trip. They claimed they were delayed because of the ship's accident.

"You'll get paid," I told her. "I'll bring the payment when I come up next week. How's Jimmie?"

"He got into an argument with one of the staff. Again."

"Ritchie?"

"How did you know it was Ritchie?"

"Jimmie mentioned him. Did you know Ritchie, according to Jimmie, flicks patient's ears as he walks past them? The patients he doesn't like? Have you heard this?"

"You can't believe everything you hear from our patients."

"I believe what my son tells me."

If Laureen found out I'd been fired as a Buckhorn captain, she would immediately move to give Jimmie's room to someone else who could pay. He'd literally be out in the cold. It wasn't much, but his room at Willow Run was his home. After his many years in an institution, he hated change.

"Laureen, please do something about Ritchie. I've been hearing this from Jimmie for a year now." I heard Laureen talking to someone else. The loudspeaker at the airport kept making announcements.

"I think, Mr. Procida, when you arrive up here next week we need to have a discussion about Jimmie's future at Willow Run."

Jimmie disliked this woman. I disliked this woman. Yet I felt helpless, because she was the gatekeeper to Jimmie having a place to live day to day, where he could receive proper care.

"I'm looking forward to our talk, Laureen. And I will have a check for you as well."

I realized Laureen had ended the call. Sarah came up to me, dressed in a big parka covered by a rain jacket. She also wore a hat and boots. Like the others, she wore the clothes she'd go searching in. They'd already checked their packs. The Russian, Sergei, was inspecting four hand-held radios, checking their batteries. Sarah pulled out a small sketchpad and began drawing.

"You think we're all crazy," Myra said softly to me.

"I think your father's a lucky man, to have so many people willing to drop everything to look for him," I said. "I'm not surprised, of course. He was a great sailor, and a good man. He was very proud of you, you know." Myra lowered her eyes. Sarah was explaining to Travis how she drew shadows. "I was captain when Sergei made passage back to Seattle from Petropavlovsk last summer. He and William had spirited arguments about the origins of modern humans. I don't think I've learned so much on the bridge, ever, about a subject I hardly knew existed."

"Don't start arguing against Sergei, captain," Myra said. "Hopeless."

"Steve, please."

"OK. Steve. An argument with Sergei Dujin, you cannot win."

I observed the group. Sergei and Myra were obviously very interested in each other, but working hard to hide their interest from each other.

"Disgusting," Sarah said to me, following my gaze.

"What?" I grinned at her.

"You know what." Sarah crossed her eyes.

On the flight to Vancouver, I sat next to Sergei. The weather flying north was fine, but a new system was headed south from the Gulf of Alaska. We'd be lucky to reach Sandspit before they closed the airport. In the meantime, I enjoyed my view of the snowy mountains to the east.

In Vancouver, we passed through customs and walked to the gate for the flight to the Charlottes. We'd be flying on a turboprop commuter plane holding 30 or 40 passengers. I watched the handlers load suitcases, then backpacks, into the back of the plane.

Sarah passed her sketchpad to me and showed me the portrait she'd drawn. It was perfect. I am not a handsome man. My eyes are too lidded and round, my chin weak. I am half bald, and my thick glasses make me look like a chipmunk. Sarah was a terrific artist. She caught every detail perfectly.

Travis looked over my shoulder, taking in the drawing.

The flight took two and a half hours. Flying at a little over

10,000 feet, we were in cloud most of the trip. The plane jerked and bumped and someone behind us was sick. When the stewardess came by pushing the coffee and drinks cart, the cups all went flying and soda spilled on the floor. Sergei slept the entire flight.

"Didn't he say he couldn't sleep on planes?" I asked Tom.

"That's what I thought, too, but he's exhausted."

We listened to Sergei snore as the plane bounced.

When the plane dropped out of the clouds to Sandspit we passed dozens of green islets among whitecaps on an angry ocean. I was looking forward to seeing my crew. I knew many of them disliked me, my direct manner and tendency to get loud when I'm frustrated. Still, I cared about them all. I was particularly concerned about Heather, the steward. She was diabetic, and I was sure she hadn't carried enough insulin for the two weeks they were missing. I'd find out soon, about her and the others. And about Anne. In fact, we'd all agreed to check on her before going to the hotel.

Finding William all started with Anne.

West, beyond the relatively flat plain of Sandspit, rose the snow-covered crags of the Charlotte's coastal range. My heart dropped as the plane fell into an air pocket.

"Damn rugged country," I said to Myra.

"Sure is."

She looked pale.

Travis

Travis sat near the backpacks while Steve and Myra talked to the taxi service. The airport was tiny - a couple of small runways, a minimal tower, and a terminal building more like a couple of double-wides.

Sarah came over and sat next to Travis.

"What time is it?"

"Three-thirty," Travis said.

"It's almost completely dark outside."

"We're at 53 degrees north latitude."

"Smart-ass."

"Well, we're 500 miles north of Sol Duc. Days are shorter here."

Sergei had pulled a pair of snowshoes from a sixth backpack we had brought. He was trying them on.

"Day after tomorrow is the winter solstice. December 21," Sergei said. "The shortest day of the year." Lights inside the terminal building cast patterns on the ground outside. Travis scratched his neck. "Sun won't rise until almost nine. Sets at three. Six hours of light is all we'll have each day for searching."

Myra and Steve walked back from the taxi counter.

"They have a van," said Myra. "They'll take us. Turns out

there's a ferry in half an hour to Graham Island and Queen Charlotte City."

From behind the small taxi building, a battered white van appeared. Travis understood that during the summer this place probably had its share of tourist traffic, but in the winter not much happened. He wondered how often this ferry ran.

At the ferry landing, the ferry was nowhere in sight. Across the dark water, Travis saw lights he supposed were from the town. Then some other lights, moving. The ferry.

"What's your plan?" asked Steve.

"Find out where Anne was found," said Myra, "and start there. Then backtrack."

"How will you get to where she was found?"

"When we get to the hotel, I'll make some calls. My dad's from here, originally. That should mean something."

Sergei traced a finger against condensation on the van window by his seat, saying, "Whoever is in charge of the search for William here will not be happy to see us."

Sarah reached forward and tapped Sergei on the shoulder.

"Sergei. You're from Siberia, right?"

"Kamchatka. I am Koryak."

"Whatever. Is the snow deep there? You know how to camp in the snow?"

Sergei turned around to face Sarah.

"I have camped in the snow, yes. I know how to use snowshoes."

"Good. Means one of us knows what to do."

"But Siberia, Sarah, is not this Haida Gwaii. There, we have cold. Sometimes 50 below zero. The snow is light, and frozen, and packed, staying cold for months. This is different. There is snow on the mountains here, and even in the lowlands, but we are near the much warmer ocean and we will have rain, and often. The danger here is not the icy cold, but the wet cold.

Staying dry."

"We have rain gear."

"We will be wet, Sarah. I am sure. That is why we tried to bring wool clothing, wool keeps us warmer if wet. Cold water can suck heat from a body fast."

"William, wherever he is, knows how to stay warm and dry," said Sarah.

They drove on to the ferry. The ferry crossed the narrow channel.

"Take us straight to the general hospital, OK?" Steve said to the van driver once they docked.

"Anne ought to be awake by now," said Tom.

"Maybe," said Myra. "Hypothermia has different effects on different people. Some die quickly but others can live for days in a coma. Anne and William were probably starving when they started, and who knows how much food they carried. That must have been extremely difficult terrain they walked across. She may never wake up again."

Travis listened to Myra and Tom and Sergei and wondered if he should be here. Why had he forced himself along, anyway? Right now this seemed like a bad decision.

Myra

To me, Steve had seemed rumpled, sort of scholarly-looking, but not impressive. When the van reached the hospital, however, he became a different person. He strode to the door, erect and intent.

The hospital was a large wooden building attached to a cement building three stories high. With a winter population of fewer than 4,000 people across all of Haida Gwaii, I was surprised they even had a hospital. They were raising funds to build a replacement, according to a sign near the front doorway. We followed Steve inside.

He strode up to the counter and said, "My name's Steve Procida. My crew members are here, I believe."

"We've been expecting you," said one of the women behind the counter. "We had a call from someone at the Buckhorn Corporation, Bruce somebody, telling us you were coming up here to see to your people."

"How are they? Where are they?"

"All of them are at dinner except the woman suffering from hypothermia. The dining room is down that corridor and then to the left. They don't know you're coming. We just got the call an hour ago, and I called Herb, here."

Two men stood by the counter. One wore a badge and

➤

a gun. The other looked like he could be my dad's brother or cousin.

The man wearing the badge held out his hand to Steve.

"I'm Herb Wakinshaw. I'm in charge of the search up here."

"Who found Anne?" Steve said.

"Surveyors from the logging company. They were running one of the roads off the main road to Rennell Inlet when they found her, a total stroke of luck. She was half-buried in the snow, as if she'd been trying to make a snow cave. They radioed in and I went out and brought her back in my all-wheel rig."

"Where is she?"

"In her own hospital room. We took hours yesterday to warm her up. She came to for a few minutes - opened her eyes, asked for something to drink - but then she went out again. She's been in and out since, but not talking."

"We've been giving her food intravenously," one of the nurses said.

Herb took off his hat. His jet-black hair was cut short, close to his skull.

"When we found her, we thought she'd been out there alone. It wasn't until the chopper got to the rest of the crew we learned she had a companion. That was late yesterday, too late for a search. We went out all day today looking for him but the weather over there on the coast was bad." Herb studied Sergei's boots. He sized up Travis and Sarah. Sized up me. "We can draw a line from the lifeboat to where Anne was found, but until we talk to her, we don't know the exact route they took. That's tough country out there."

I stepped forward and shook Herb's hand and the hand of his tall companion.

"Thanks for trying," I said.

A nurse accompanied Steve as he made his way to Anne's room. The rest of us followed.

"You can't all come," said the nurse. Her nametag said Rachel.

"Why not?" asked Sarah. "We'll be quiet. If she's asleep, she won't know. If she wakes up, it will be good for her to see all of us."

Steve, up ahead, swung open the doors of the last room on the right at the end of the hall. Rachel ran to catch him. The rest of us followed. In the small room, a slight woman lay propped up in the bed, two IVs in her arm. Her face was gaunt and chapped, frostbit. The lids of her closed eyes fluttered.

"She was almost still a cadet," Steve said, softly. "This was Anne's first real assignment. She'd made one full trip out and back. This was her second. She's barely 23." Anne looked 50.

"She was a runner," continued Steve. "The night the ship burned, she ran below and checked the decks for fire. We didn't know where the smoke was coming from. I saw her again for a second when the other boat crew mustered, and then she was gone."

Steve' shoulders shook. Tom placed a hand on the captain's shoulder. Sergei stared at the screen showing Anne's heartbeat.

Rachel scowled, but didn't shoo us out.

"When she came in here her body temperature was below 88," said Rachel. "She should have been dead. Her heartbeat had slowed to only 31 beats a minute, almost as if she was hibernating."

Sergei spoke to Rachel.

"Some people argue humans may once have had that ability. If humans become cold very fast they can survive without breathing for a long time. There are stories of people lost in icy lakes for hours who then recover and have no apparent brain damage."

Rachel adjusted Anne's IV.

"I don't know about hibernation, " she said, "but this young woman nearly died. If she had been out there another few hours she would have died. She may recover fully, and she may not. She has to wake up, and stay awake."

We all looked at Anne.

Steve found a chair along one wall and sat down, his head close to Anne's.

"Anne. This is Steve, Anne. Wake up."

"Please, sir, she needs to rest," said Rachel.

"You just said she needs to wake up," said Steve. "And we need her to wake up, to tell us where to look for William."

Rachel shook her head.

"Wherever this William is, he is surely dead."

Steve stared at Rachel. Then he pointed at me.

"Rachel, this is William's daughter. Her name is Myra. Watch what you say."

Rachel stared at Steve, and then turned to face me. "It's the truth, miss. I'm sorry. Up here, cold and wet like this, we lose people all the time. The cold icy water sucks the heat from their souls. You've come an awful long way, I'm afraid, for nothing."

"I came up here to find him, dead or alive," I said. Sarah quivered at the end of the bed. Sergei had his arm around her shoulders. Travis looked back and forth among all of us. "And this we will do," I added.

Steve returned his attention to Anne.

"Wake up. This isn't a dream, Anne. You made it out, and you were found, and we found the others. They're all here, in this building, eating dinner at the end of the other hall. Wake up, Anne."

She remained unresponsive. Steve watched her. Then he stood, bent over Anne, and slapped her face, hard.

"Sir!" shouted Rachel, moving toward Steve. Steve slapped Anne's face again, even harder.

Anne jerked, gasping for air. Her cheek flushed red and she

coughed, then coughed again. Rachel grabbed Steve's arm.

"This is outrageous. I don't know who you people are but you are no longer welcome here. You must leave." Rachel was furious.

Anne suddenly opened her eyes and struggled for breath. Her mouth opened and she reached for her red cheek. She looked up, unfocused, unseeing. Then Steve bent over and put his face into her line of vision. She blinked.

Rachel called out, "Herb. Herb."

"Ahhhh. Ahhhhh." Anne struggled to speak, her eyes wide open. Steve bent close to her.

"Anne you're awake and you're on the Queen Charlottes in a hospital. We need to talk to you to find out where you last saw William."

Herb rushed into the room and caught himself short when he saw Anne was awake. Anne raised her head, then fell back, eyes still wide.

"Oh, thank God," said Steve, gently grasping Anne's hand. "Stay awake, if you can. Can you speak?"

Anne's eyes moved over Steve, slowly. She turned her head and examined the IV tube, then the screen displaying the beat of her racing heart. She looked at the rest of us.

"Who are these people?" she asked in a thin and scratchy voice. Steve' face lit up. His glasses flashed.

"Anne do you know where you are?"

Anne shook her head. She swallowed. Sarah handed her a glass of water, which Anne drank, greedily. Some of the water spilled off her chin onto her chest. She held out the glass for more.

Now Anne looked at Steve again. Her eyes widened.

"Captain? What are you doing here? Where am I?"

"What do you remember, Anne? Please. This is important."

Anne stared back at Steve. Then she examined the rest of

us, one by one. She drank more water.

"Who are you? You weren't on the ship."

Steve pointed to each of us as he spoke.

"This is Myra, William's daughter. This is Sergei, William's Russian friend. This is Tom, William's oldest friend. And this is Sarah, Tom's granddaughter. Finally, this is Travis. He worked on the rescue tug that recovered our ship."

Anne looked at each of us, then nodded. Then, to my astonishment, she laughed.

"I feel I know you all. Well, not you, Travis. William told us a story when we were marooned. About all of you. His story kept us sane. A story about last summer, ancient weapons, and an ancient land. William's last words to me, before I left him, were, the story was true."

Sarah beamed.

I spoke carefully. "Where did you leave him, Anne, and how was he?"

Anne drank more water. Then she hitched herself a little higher on the bed. Rachel and Herb stood in the rear. "You came up here to find him, didn't you?"

I nodded. I saw tears fill Anne's eyes. I dreaded what she was going to say. I could tell we all did.

"We left the camp, William and I, and we crossed one ridge and camped. The second day we crossed the second high ridge, but coming down was steep, lots of snow. William fell and hurt his knee. I helped him get to shelter under some low, tight trees, and I gathered wood and set the tarp over him so he would be out of the rain and snow. Nearby, I placed some water. He was in a lot of pain but he had a little food and he was warm enough. But he was badly hurt. He told me to keep going."

"Where were you going?"

"We didn't know where we were, but once we got up on the second ridge William recognized Rennell Sound and we headed for the road at the southern end of the sound. Or I did, once I got on top of the third ridge after I left him. I did not want to leave him."

"Did you follow a compass course?"

"Yes. We went at 88 degrees east from the lifeboat and cove and then I changed to 63 degrees east to reach the base of Rennell Sound once off the third ridge. I got lost on the logging roads, I think. But I kept trying to go 63 degrees. "

Sarah pulled out a map of the islands I didn't know she had and began looking for Rennell Sound.

Sergei touched my arm.

"We can take this information, plot where Anne was found, which Herb here can tell us, and draw a line back to their camp, follow that."

"Damn rough country, mister." Herb shook his head. "Thick brush, steep ridges, snow, and landslides. Rough."

"Well, if this girl here was able to walk out after a week lacking food, we can certainly try," said Tom.

"And, looking at you, I know you'll go whether I give you permission or not."

"True, Herb," said Tom. "Will you help us?"

"You want to start tomorrow, don't you? Going to be a bad one, tomorrow."

"Each day goes by, it gets shakier."

"You think he's still alive?" Herb asked.

Sarah stood before him wearing a fierce expression.

"If anyone can survive, William can."

"I'm tired," said Anne, her eyes drooping. "Nice to see you, captain."

"Everyone out of here. Let the poor woman sleep," ordered Rachel.

"How old are you, miss?" Herb asked Sarah.

"What do you care?"

"Are you even 14?"

"I'm 13 and I'm old enough."

"And how old are you?" Herb asked Tom.

"I'm 69."

Herb started to mutter.

"A 13-year-old. A guy nearly 70. A Russian. Greenhorns, perhaps, all of you. If I have to come out there to rescue the five of you I'm going to be very angry."

"I can understand," I said. "But you'll help us? Show us on the map where Anne was found? Tell us what you can about the country out there?"

"I'll do better. I'll come along, and so will Buster."

"Buster?"

"The big scary looking guy I was with. Don't worry, his looks are a lot worse than his bite."

I laughed.

"He sounds like he's one of my dad's cousins. My dad's looks were a lot worse than his bite, too."

Herb looked at all of us.

"We don't have to backtrack to where Anne went, exactly. They followed 88 degrees east from their camp, and she said William was hurt in the second valley. She kept on at 88 degrees then turned to 63 degrees when she saw the base of Rennell Sound. But I know that country. We might be able to get a little further on logging roads south of the sound and get to their original line a little easier than backtracking Anne. A little easier and shorter."

"Wouldn't it be simpler just to send a helicopter?" asked Travis.

Herb shook his head.

"Socked in. Could be days. You think I want to go walking out there? I don't. But this woman here wants to find her father and if we want to start searching now, we can't use a helicopter. Hopefully, if we find him, a chopper can pick him up."

Steve was already heading toward the dining room to see his crew. In the lobby, the van driver was talking to one of the nurses. Outside, heavy rain fell.

Other people had filled the hospital waiting area while we had been in Anne's room. Most were Haida, dressed in rough clothing and heavy woolen capes. They watched us, quiet.

"Be more than me and Buster out there tomorrow," Herb said to me.

Buster had been knotting and unknotting a rawhide thong. Now he looked up.

"William's grandmother was my great grandfather's sister."

I blinked. He was my cousin. He was about 10 years older than me.

"William came back here once, 17 years ago, when his grandmother was still alive," said Buster. "Had his daughter. I remember you." He looked at me.

I searched my memory. I'd been 12, far from home in a strange land. I remembered a scary ancient great-grandmother telling stories, the room crowded and filled, people young and old, smoking and laughing. Had Buster been there?

"We will find him," Buster said. "He will be found."

People standing along the wall nodded in agreement.

Sarah watched Buster tie the thong. When he was finished, he handed Sarah the thong and she unfastened the knot before retying the thong quickly and perfectly. Buster nodded. Sergei had wandered over toward the people standing near the wall, where he looked over one of the woolen capes. The man removed his cape and draped it over Sergei's shoulders. Now Sergei looked like my cousin, too.

I felt myself relax, reassured being here surrounded by my dad's friends and relations. My relations.

When we got back in the van rain pounded the roof.

December 20, Monday

Travis

Travis rode next to Sarah in the back of an extended cab pickup. The pickup was following a jeep. Two other vehicles were behind the truck. The convoy drove through thick fog in the early morning dark. The rain had changed to snow overnight, covering the roads. Now rain fell again.

They'd soon left Queen Charlotte City and any signs of human settlement. It was pitch black, before sunrise. They traveled over rolling hills, passing dripping firs, spruces and cedars. After a while, Travis saw scattered piles of brush and debris, signs of recent logging. They turned left onto a gravel road and the hills became steeper. Soon they were dipping into valleys and coming over exposed ridges, where the snow was deep and four-wheel-drive a necessity.

Herb drove the truck, Tom next to him. They'd risen at five, grabbed some breakfast in the hotel dining room, and checked their gear a final time before loading everything in the truck and Buster's Jeep. Myra and Sergei were riding in the jeep. Besides Herb and Buster, six others had joined the search. Tom poured coffee from Herb's thermos and passed two cups back to Travis and Sarah.

➤

"What's out this road?" Sarah asked.

"This is the only road to the west coast," said Herb. "Rennell Sound comes 20 miles deep into the island and this road gets to the east end. Two smaller roads then run the north and south shore for a few miles, and we'll take the south road. But the roads end soon enough. Then, nothing."

"But what's out here? What's done here?" Sarah persisted.

"In the summer, people come out here to camp and fish. And there's logging. But this time of year, nothing happens out here."

The vehicles climbed over ever-taller ridges, where snow fell at the top and rain fell in the valleys.

Sipping the bitter coffee, Travis now saw a hint of color on the trees edging the road. The fog remained white and thick, The Jeep slewed through mud in front of them.

"Did anyone ever live out here?" asked Sarah, looking forward out the windshield.

"Maybe in the past. Not now. The coast is too steep, too exposed."

"Weren't there villages along the outer coast once?" asked Travis. He'd been reading some brochures, and learned that much of the south island was a national park, sacred, containing ancient villages.

"Yes. There were villages in Tasu Sound, on Moresby Island, and at the mouth of Skidgate Inlet, which separates Moresby and Graham Islands. There were a few villages up on Rennell Sound, too. Long gone, though. " Herb tapped the top of the steering wheel. "The lifeboat came ashore between the mouth of Rennell Sound, ahead, and Skidgate Inlet about 20 miles south. Between Rennell and Skidgate it's steep, exposed, a few inlets and bays, but mostly it's cliffs, mountains. The lifeboat drifted into the one little place anywhere along a stretch of nearly 20 miles where a boat can come ashore without being smashed. If they hadn't been seen day before yesterday they'd have been there at least until May, when someone might have seen them, flying over. They'd have starved to death."

"Did they know where they were?" Sarah was resting her chin on the seat ahead of her, near Tom's shoulder.

"Not really. I think they had to climb through the coastal range to see where they were. Not sure how they did it. Few go into those places in the summer, let alone December. They're too steep and remote."

"Anne and William went into those places," Sarah said.

"They had no choice." Herb tapped the steering wheel.

They drove and drove. They were slow, taking time to work over the tops of the ridges. Finally, they came down a long, steep, curving slope, past thick trees, where the road reached a T. Ahead, even deep in the protected sound, was crashing surf. They turned left and began following the south shore, stopping where another narrow road branched left again. The jeep stopped and Buster got out to talk to Herb. Rain battered his wide, felt hat.

"This one, right?" asked Buster.

Herb read his map.

"Yeah." He turned to Tom. "We found her four miles up this road. Lucky we saw her at all, the snow was so deep."

The branch road was narrow and pitted, trees growing close to the sides. Fallen branches littered the road, and exposed rocks stuck out from the gravel surface. Herb held up the map so Tom, Travis and Sarah could see it.

"Here's where we are, see?"

He pointed to a place on the map along the south shore of Rennell Sound.

"The lifeboat was here."

Herb pointed to a tiny indentation on the coast, halfway between the mouth of Rennell Sound and Skidgate Inlet.

"Anne said they walked at 88 degrees from there."

Herb followed a penciled line on the map. The track crossed a high ridge near the coast and then dropped into a valley. It rose and fell twice more before striking a dotted-line to the east.

"I think she kept going at 88 until she got to the last ridge, here, and then she could see the foot of Rennell Sound from the high point. She might have even made out the logging roads. She was found here."

Herb pointed east of the last ridge, to where the dotted track intersected the road they were on.

"If we backtrack her, we'll have to climb back over that third ridge," said Herb.

Travis could tell by the close-together contour lines on the map the climb would be extremely steep.

"On the other hand, we could follow this shore road to the end, about two miles away. We can start the climb there and angle into the second valley, avoiding the third ridge. Won't be as steep as the other way."

"How far," asked Travis, "from where the road ends to where William is supposed to be?"

"About 10 miles?" said Buster. "A damn long 10 miles."

Buster returned to his jeep. Herb turned in his seat and looked back at Travis and Sarah.

"Main thing to do, out here, is stay as dry as we can."

That looked impossible. Travis wondered how an old man like William could possibly survive without food and heat.

They bounced and slid along the steadily deteriorating road. It ended abruptly.

Travis pulled on his wide hat and stepped outside. His boots squelched in the mud. The trees beyond the road seemed thick, dark, and sinister. At least, down here, there wasn't snow, but the brush looked soaked.

Myra and Sergei pulled packs, rain covers tied tight, from the back of the jeep and helped each other put their packs on. Travis lifted Sarah's pack for her, then his own. He helped Tom into his pack. Some of the others, the men from the tribe, had bulky packs. They all used tumplines, bands attached to the packs, which came forward around their foreheads.

Herb led the way, followed by two of the local men. Myra, Tom, Sergei, Sarah, and Travis followed. Buster and four others brought up the rear.

They followed a rough trail through the fog and mud, winding among rocks and fallen trees. Travis could hear surf breaking on the south shore of Rennell Sound, well below him. Rain-soaked boughs had turned the trail into a dripping tunnel. They passed through slowly, in single file.

Sarah, though small, strode ahead easily. She broke a dead branch from a tree for use as a walking stick. After 15 minutes, Travis did the same. Within 20 minutes the line of hikers had spread out. Sarah was so far ahead Travis couldn't see her. All he had was a faint trail and her muddy footprints to guide him.

When he looked up again, Sarah and the others stood bunched up, dripping in the rain.

"We'll stay close together." Herb was out of sight but his voice carried. "When we get to the top of this long rise we'll leave the trail and start inland. It's going to go up quickly. Keep the person ahead of you in sight and let them know if they get too far ahead."

Travis was sweating and his pack dug into his shoulders. His hands throbbed, still sore from his work on the ship. Water dripped off his hat.

Too late now to back out. What the hell had he been thinking? First he quits a job and joins a tug and willingly gets on a dead ship, and then he invites himself along on a desperate search. What was the matter with him? Was any possible story worth this, or was he just running from something?

Travis was damned if he was going to be the one who slowed everyone down, but here he was, breathing hard and sweating, his shoulders aching. Yet, when they stopped, he was soon chilled from standing around. During breaks, he just kept his pack on since he could find no dry place to set it down. The rain was now half snow, big, heavy flakes. Through the fog, he could make out ancient, blasted trees.

"We get up to where the trail ends, we'll have some soup," said Buster. The others stood near him and smoked, the tumplines up against their heads.

How far had they come, Travis wondered. A mile? He was wet, overheated and in pain, yet there was little Sarah, walking easily, whistling tunelessly, swinging her stick. Did she ever complain? Did anyone?

If he ever wrote a story about this search, maybe he would submit it to a medical journal.

"What's the joke?" Sarah asked.

Travis shook his head. Had he been smiling?

Myra

At about 11:30, after two hours of hiking, Herb stopped. We set up a rain tarp and somehow started a fire, then heated water for instant soup. The hot soup burned my tongue, but the warmth felt wonderful. The fire hissed and smoked, and rain kept splattering the coals, but we managed to sit beneath the tarp in turns to drink soup and warm up. We were high on a long ridge, about to start into the snow.

I asked Tom about his leg. He'd had trouble during our long trip last summer, but he waved a hand, indicating I shouldn't worry.

All too soon, we packed up and started off again. We had two hours left of daylight at the most. Herb told us we needed to get over the ridge ahead and down into the valley to camp.

We crunched through snow. More came swirling from the clouds. We'd left the trail an hour ago. We were forced to push branches aside and step over fallen logs as we worked our way around or through blow downs. The higher we climbed, the deeper the snow. Finally the shoulder of the ridge flattened and we began to descend.

As we came down, the fog began to lift, until we could see the narrow valley floor spread out before us spotted with snow and clumps of trees. About a mile across the valley, we saw the next ridge we had to climb. I tried to imagine Anne, alone, further south where the ridges were higher and steeper, struggling across this unfamiliar territory.

Of the five of us who had come on this ridiculous journey, Sarah seemed the most comfortable, striding intently, swinging her walking stick. Sergei glided along effortlessly on his long legs. Tom now had a hitch in his step. We'd have to stop soon to let him rest. I didn't feel so great, either. I could feel a blister rising on the sole of my left foot.

As we angled down the slope, the snow thinned, and soon we were hiking among thick trees, many of them twisted and bent from past avalanches. Pools of water covered the sodden earth of the valley floor. We'd dropped down from a world of white and gray to dark green firs and black-gray rock. Herb led us to a small knoll by a stream where an earlier avalanche, maybe five years before, had flattened the trees.

"We camp here," he said, dropping his pack.

Near a clump of uprooted trees, Sarah and I found a fairly level place to pitch our tent. We put down a ground cloth, and then set up our tent beneath another light tarp strung over for further protection from the rain, which was now falling harder than ever. Not yet even 3 p.m., daylight was already fading.

Herb and Buster created a wide lean-to by slinging a long branch between two trees, leaning branches against it, then hanging a tarp over the leaning branches. The men created a big fireplace using rocks. Then they gathered wood.

Sarah watched the men dump armloads of wood next to the fire pit.

"I think their lean-to will be warmer than our tent."

Herb had chosen our campsite carefully. Elevated above the nearby stream, we had plenty of wood because of so many dead trees nearby. Soon, he had a fire blazing. The underside of the lean-to glowed in reflected light.

We all crowded under the shelter. Tom fired up a stove and Buster pulled a big pot from his huge pack and slung the pot over the fire on a notched branch. After we ate, Buster and I washed our dishes in the stream.

"Thanks for coming," I said.

"No thanks needed, Myra. I am on the rescue crew here. This is my job."

"What, going on a hike in December into the coastal range? I don't think so."

Buster laughed.

"This is my home. We do not come here often, and never in the winter, but this is where William is. He is my cousin."

"Uncle, more like. I am your cousin. Still, thanks for coming. We'd have been lost, without you and Herb."

"I am not sure. You and the Russian, Sarah, her grandfather, Travis, you all seem comfortable out here. Even in this weather. You would have been fine."

I wasn't sure he was right. The whole day had seemed a march into a dream-like tunnel of fog. We could have been walking anywhere.

Later, the heat inside the lean-to warmed my damp clothes. Tom was next to me, arms across his knees.

"You OK, Tom?"

He nodded.

"I'm fine now."

My legs relaxed in the soothing heat. Sarah kept retying the leather thong from Buster, practicing knots. Sergei's leg felt good, resting against mine.

"I'm sorry, Sergei. Whenever you come to visit us we drag you off on these ridiculous trips."

Sergei laughed softly.

"I find this interesting, this ancient land, Haida Gwaii. I'm honored to be walking these ancient valleys, to have such knowledgeable guides." Sergei nodded to Buster, Herb, and the other men. "This country is very different from my Kamchatka. Kamchatka is birch and aspen, and some firs, but here you have spruce, firs, and cedar. "

"Will we reach this place tomorrow?" Travis asked.

Herb nodded.

"Yes. We'll cross the ridge ahead into the next valley. Maybe five miles, about the same distance we hiked today."

We sat beneath the lean-to for hours. It was the night before the winter solstice, the longest night of the year. The fire burned, rain fell, and wind coursed up the valley.

Later, after Sarah fell asleep, I heard snoring from the lean-to. As always, I worried about my father. Anne had been found three days ago, and she'd left my father about three days earlier. Anne said he'd been resting under trees in warm clothing, a tarp over him for shelter. He had water nearby, and some wood to keep a fire going. But his knee was injured and he was surely starving.

Could Sarah be right? Could my dad still be alive?

December 21, Tuesday

Travis

By the time Travis woke, and had rolled up his sleeping bag, a big fire blazed in front of the lean-to. It was almost seven and still fully dark. Tom boiled water on his stove for oatmeal, while Buster made some kind of gruel for Herb and the others in the big pot.

Travis could see that his companions from Haida Gwaii were old-school, from a simpler time before specialized cook stoves and Gortex gear. Travis watched them efficiently roll and pack their gear in big sacks. He envied their capes, which shed water and provided warmth, yet allowed them to move freely. He also envied their speed, and the way they seemed to know what needed to be done without a word being spoken. He felt as if he'd gone back in time, to the days of canvas lean-tos, open-fire cooking, one pot, simple woolen clothing, minimal gear.

The overcast had lifted. The air was colder. Buster stripped off the tarps and packed them, but left the cross-bar from the lean-to in place.

"Look," said Tom, pointing south. The overcast was lifting. They could see more of the slopes on both sides of the valley.

The slope they still had to climb looked nearly vertical. How had Anne crossed that?

Travis wondered if they were mistaken about Anne's route and they were searching the wrong area. Maybe they'd hike for two days and find nothing.

Crossing the stream, Travis slipped and nearly fell in. Water rose above the lip of his left boot and soaked his sock.

"You OK?" asked Sarah.

"Yeah." Travis was not OK but he would never admit this to a 13-year-old.

Sarah studied the sky. She turned to Travis.

"Today is the shortest day of the year. That's what Myra told me last night. The winter solstice." Sarah waved an arm. "After today every day gets longer as the light comes back."

"It's an ancient pagan holiday, Sarah."

"I know," Sarah said. "This is the day. I know it. The day we find William."

Crossing the valley, they worked around avalanche paths, tangled broken trees, and piled brush. The slope, once they started up, seemed less steep than he'd thought. The climb was still difficult.

Herb had the group angling south, but then he turned and switched back the other way. They worked up the slope, going one way, then the other, in long traverses. When the snow reached a depth of two feet, Myra asked Herb to call a break. Myra, Sarah, Travis, Tom and Sergei put on their snowshoes. Herb, Buster and the others just kept going in their hiking boots, seemingly impervious to the snow. The snowshoes made walking easier, once Travis got the hang of it.

"A sign," said Sarah, pointing at an eagle, circling.

Before reaching the top of the slope, they passed back into clouds. The people walking in front of Travis seemed to vanish—Herb, Myra, finally Sarah. They passed below some tall stone cliffs, and Herb had them turn again. Travis realized they were now above those same cliffs. He imagined himself sliding in the snow over the edge.

"We need to keep going," said Herb. "We need to get over this."

Herb stopped to let stragglers catch up. Standing still, Travis felt the cold. Watching the Haida men climb so easily, Travis felt totally inadequate. This island was their home, and had been for thousands of years. Surely their people had walked in these valleys since time began.

To their left, the slope was steeper yet, but Herb angled them right, to the north, where the gradient became gentler as they reached the crest of the ridge. Travis could now see the valley beyond. The valley looked the same as the one they'd camped in. It too had a stream down the middle.

Herb examined his map, then said, "About a mile."

Travis noticed Tom, behind Myra, limping.

"You all right, Tom?"

"Been better. But we're close, now."

Myra, adjusting her pack, looked pale. Her father had been alone for almost a week, maybe in this very valley, starving and badly hurt. Tom pointed ahead.

"Look for a place which might provide shelter, a clump of tight trees and debris, not far from water, where there might be firewood within reach. Maybe an old avalanche chute."

"What do you mean, Tom?" asked Travis.

"William explained to me his survival strategy if he was ever hurt out in the woods. I'm just repeating what he said."

Travis saw many clumps of trees.

"According to the map," said Herb, "A course of 88 degrees had them coming over the ridge ahead, there."

A large band of ledges stood below the ridgeline to the west. It would have been easy to tumble over those ledges if they'd crossed there. Maybe that's where William fell.

Everyone moved ahead along the valley floor. But now, instead of walking single file, they walked abreast, 15 feet apart, a band of people sweeping the terrain in a wide line. Travis walked between Sarah and Tom.

Ahead, they saw three clumps of trees, the biggest clump closest to the stream.

When they reached the thicket, the trees grew so close together Travis had to drop his pack to enter. Tom was to his left, 20 feet away. Sarah, to his right, was the same distance in the other direction, next to the stream.

Once he got through the smaller trees at the edge of the clump, Travis found himself able to move around more easily. Overhead, branches were woven together in a thick mass. He might have missed it but for the sheen of plastic under the scattered snow. What he had seen as the ground, covered in needles, was, he suddenly realized, a debris-covered poncho or tarp, tied with dark brown line to small trees. The tarp shook as Travis approached.

"Here," Travis called, his voice hoarse.

He saw many things all at the same time - a small fire ring filled with needles and old ash, the greasy, tan fabric of coveralls and a jacket, an arm lying across a chest, a hood pulled down over where the head and face might be. "Here," he called again, in a louder voice.

Travis lifted the edge of the tarp and waited for the smell of decay. He lifted the hood, gently.

A desiccated face emerged; utterly still, a huge nose and sunken, closed eyes, mouth half open. So this is what death in the wilderness looks like. Not so different than Larry, after dying on the ship.

Steve

"You're a terror," said Bruce.

The crew and I had just landed in a charter plane at Boeing Field. When I met the crew at the small hospital in Sandspit, I knew right away they needed better care. Heather, suffering from diabetes, was listless and sick. Randall's burns were worse than I'd thought. None of them had any idea how they'd get back to Seattle or what their futures held. I called Buckhorn and argued until they agreed to pay for a charter.

"They needed better care, Bruce. It's the least Buckhorn could do."

"Well, they're still not going to pay you for flying back up there in the first place."

I'd heard nothing from Myra or the others about their search, but I hadn't really expected to. I knew they were probably still out wherever they were. Now, back in Seattle, the crew climbed into a waiting van. Bruce handed me my paycheck.

"When's the hearing?" I asked.

"Postponed, of course. Two weeks from today."

"Good. Right now, I want to see my kid."

"You'll be fine at the hearing, Steve." Bruce threw my little carry-on bag into his car. "You won't lose your license."

➤

"We'll see. It helps that most of the guys were found. Still, two guys dead: Larry, the tug owner, and William. Could have been a lot worse, I suppose."

"That's right. You'll find work. You're senior. It's just Buckhorn you can't work for."

The paycheck in my hand meant I had the funds to carry Jimmie at Willow Run for another quarter.

After Bruce dropped me at my home in Green Lake, I quickly threw some clothing in a suitcase, deposited the check at my bank, and headed north.

I felt displaced. Only a few hours ago, I'd been up on the Queen Charlottes running around getting a charter flight organized. In the end, Anne had stayed behind, partly because she was still too weak to travel, but mostly because she wanted to be there when they found William. I could tell the two of them had formed a tight bond, traveling together across those mountains in the snow. She had been forced to leave him behind, with a damaged leg, in order to find help. She wanted to be there when his body was found.

When I got to Willow Run, Laureen looked as snide and angry as ever. We met in the common room of Jimmie's building. She told me he'd join us soon.

"James has been disruptive this week," she said, her eyes focused on my hands, as if the check she wanted might magically appear. "I think perhaps he needs to find other lodgings."

"Might take time," I said.

"You have the payment?"

Jimmie approached in his wheelchair from down the hall. Head lowered, he pushed using one hand, then the other.

"Don't worry, Laureen. I've got the money."

She visibly brightened.

Jimmie rolled into the room, barely glancing at Laureen.

"Hey, dad. Did you finish that stuff you had to do?"

"I did. Yesterday at this time I was up on the Queen Charlotte Islands. I met the crew, well, everyone but William. Then we all flew down here today, except for Anne, who stayed behind."

"They moved me. Changed my room. It's smaller. I hate it here."

Laureen excused herself. She walked away, her back stiff.

Jimmie seemed happy to see me, but he looked a little wary. I knew he expected me to say, as I had done so many times, I had to cut my visit short. I leaned forward and took his hand.

"How's the accounting work coming?" I asked.

"OK. I have the online test next week."

During the trip up here, I'd been thinking about Jimmie's losses, the ship's losses, and my losses. What bothered me most was the worry I'd lost my son.

I had a proposal for Jimmie, but I didn't know how he'd react.

"I'm done sailing, Jimmie. I'm almost 63. Buckhorn fired me, and if I start again at a new company, my schedule will be crazy and I'll never see you. My house is all paid up, and if I pull my Social Security and pension, I think we can survive, you and me. You become an accountant and work from the house, and I'll cook. It won't be easy, and a big adjustment, but that's what I'd like us to do, if you're agreeable. You willing to give me a try?"

I was being optimistic. My Social Security was next to nothing and my pension not much better. But this way, my son would have a room of his own in a house of his own.

Jimmie stared at me.

He nodded.

Louise

"What's the deal, Louise?" Jeff asked. "Why are we here?"

Vince and Peggy sat together on a bench. Dark Cloud, Billy and Stretch, looking hung over, slumped in three old chairs. Across the harbor, the blackened *Seattle Express* lay against the pier, a yellow oil boom snaking around her waterline. Yesterday, Louise had seen people scurrying about and the bright arc of a welding torch aft of the deckhouse. This morning all was quiet on the Buckhorn dock.

Louise reached into one of the deep pockets on the front of her jacket and pulled out some envelopes. She passed them around.

"Christmas cards, Louise?" said Dark Cloud cynically. "You shouldn't have."

"Not a card," she said. "Your pay."

Vince tore open his envelope and looked at the check.

"You rob a bank?"

"No, Vince. Turns out Larry had been working on Suzette, Bill's girlfriend, trying to get more credit from the bank. While examining some old records, they found a life insurance provision in pop's original contract. Larry never knew and I only learned two days ago." A tear rolled down her cheek. "He had $300,000 in life insurance. The money was transferred yesterday." Everyone looked down at their check and then at Louise. "I paid you guys for the time we worked plus I added another two week's pay in hopes you'll stay on the payroll. There's a possible tow right after Christmas to reposition some Alaska oil equipment going from Portland to Seattle. I put a bid in." Louise looked at Dark Cloud. "Cloud, I know your tug got seized by the bank last week. You and your guys, you're welcome here. I need a mate anyway, someone in the wheelhouse to help Nelson."

Nelson kept turning his check over as if it wasn't real.

"We're not selling the tug?" he asked.

Louise shook her head. "Not this place, either. Those Buckhorn suits can pound sand."

Someone whistled.

"Hey, Louise," said Vince, "Have you heard anything from Travis since he went up north?"

"He called a couple days ago. Said they were at the hotel, ready to head out the next day. The woman they found in the snow, the one traveling cross country, gave some information about where they might find William." From across the harbor, gulls cried. "Now, how about we all go up to the coffee shop? Splurge and celebrate our good fortune. Cloud is buying."

Pete

Pete locked up his cabin as Sam ran ahead and jumped in the truck. School was out for Christmas vacation, so they decided to have a doughnut at the coffee shop. Joyce had called to say her house-hunting trip in California was extended.

"Seat belt on, buddy," said Pete, starting the truck.

"Don't forget the mail, dad."

He didn't regularly check the mailbox at the end of his driveway. It hurt to cross the road to reach the box. He hobbled over and pulled out a small stack of junk mail and one damp letter, official looking, probably a bill. Pete tossed the letter and the junk mail on the seat next to Sam. Sam put the mail in his lap.

"Hey, dad," said Sam, "you didn't howl when you climbed into the truck this time. And you didn't limp so much getting the mail, either."

Pete realized Sam was right. He was so used to the constant pain he'd found a way to ignore it. Surprisingly, his leg wasn't hurting right now. And what's this? He could bend the knee without pain, too.

At the coffee shop, Pete waved at the *Warhorse* people, sitting in a booth, the table in front of them piled high with doughnuts and steaming cups of coffee. He chose another

➤

booth, and Sam sat across from him, holding the mail.

Mariana came by.

"Thanks for your help the other day, Pete."

"You're a helluva caterer. Thanks for asking me. I was sure my leg was going to fall off from the pain, but the last couple days it's been a lot better. See? I can even bend the knee a little."

Sam passed the damp letter across the table. It was from the National Park Service. Pete wondered how long it had been in the mailbox.

"Are you going to open that, or just stare?" asked Mariana.

"I don't dare."

He'd given up ever hearing from the park people. He'd filed his application after being shot, many months ago. This looked like a form letter, an acknowledgement he had applied but no, thanks.

Sam took the letter and tore it open.

"Dear Mr. Wise, we are de...delighted to inform you of your selection for the position of Ranger, GS level 8, for the Olympic National Park. Please contact the address below to schedule an intake app...app...appointment." Sam looked across at his father. "Dad? This is good, isn't it? Isn't it?"

A steady job, benefits, regular hours. They'd put him at the visitor center, at least until his knee got better. He wouldn't have to listen to Roger ever again. In fact, if Travis decided to write a story about the ship rescue, or even this whole thing with Buckhorn and Sarah and her adventures, maybe Pete could give him some great background information. He had been up there in that valley, too, getting shot, hadn't he?

And, now he had a job offer, there was no way he'd be found to be an unfit caretaker. He'd be able to keep Sam. Sam would be able to go to school here.

Pete felt Mariana's warm hand on his shoulder.

"Yeah, Sam, this is good. Very good."

Myra

was approaching the clump of trees ahead of me when I heard Travis cry out.

Sarah and I both moved quickly in his direction.

By the time I pushed through the branches and small trees, Sarah was on her knees near Travis, looking down at something. I saw dirty canvas coveralls, boots, and a debris-covered tarp.

I pushed ahead.

My father's face looked up at the trees and sky. Fir needles rested on his hollow cheeks. He had become unbelievably thin compared to the man I'd known, and as Sarah gently pushed back his hood, I saw half his left ear had been torn off and was now partially healed. I wondered how long he'd been dead.

My father's long hair, hanging on the side of his face, was darker than I remembered.

Travis clutched my right arm. Sergei appeared on my left.

Sarah placed her head against my dad's chest, ear to his heart, one hand covering her ear on the other side. At the same time, Sergei bent down and took my dad's wrist to check for a pulse. My father's knee was bent at a strange angle.

A weak shaft of sunlight pierced the trees and struck my dad's face.

➤

I tried to imagine him lying here, abandoned and lost, without food, waiting for the end. I hoped his spirit had found some peace before departing this world.

"We will bury him here," I said. "This is his home, and here he will remain."

Sarah spoke from her position on his chest.

"His heart's beating, I think. It's beating!"

Sergei, holding my dad's left wrist, nodded in agreement, just as Herb appeared from between two trees.

"If he's alive," Herb said, "we need to gently move him, make him comfortable, get him warm. He needs fluids, and food. Let's get a big fire going and set up another lean-to."

I leaned down next to Sarah. My dad looked long dead. Sarah's eyes shone. I swallowed, then spoke.

"Dad, we're here. We found you." Could he even hear us, I wondered.

Buster, somewhere beyond the trees, was speaking into his handheld radio.

"William. We're here," said Sarah. "You're safe, now. We found you."

High overhead, I heard an eagle cry, twice.

"The chopper can be here in the morning," called Buster.

I looked down at my father, wasted from hunger and cold, appearing dead but somehow alive.

I started to cry.

~ The End ~

ABOUT THE AUTHOR

Charlie and a replica of a Short-face bear at the Royal Museum, Victoria, British Columbia.

Charlie Sheldon studied at Yale University and the University of Massachusetts, where he received a Master's Degree in Wildlife Biology and Resource Management. He then went to sea as a commercial fisherman off New England, fishing for cod, haddock, hake, lobster, red crab, squid, and swordfish. Active in the fight for the 200-mile Fisheries Conservation Zone, he later worked as a consultant for Fishery Management Councils, developing fishery management plans and then engaging in gear development projects to develop more selective fisheries. He spent 28 years working for seaports (New York, Seattle, and Bellingham, WA) as a project and construction manager and later as an executive, including habitat cleanup projects and working with Puget Sound Tribes to reduce tribal fishing conflicts. Later he returned to sea, shipping out with the Sailor's Union of the Pacific as an Ordinary Seaman, Able Bodied Seaman, and Bosun. His last gig was as bosun aboard USNS *Shughart*, New Orleans to New York, in 2016.

Always a writer, Charlie published *Fat Chance* with Felony and Mayhem Press in 2005 and *Strong Heart* with Iron Twine Press in 2017. After finishing work on *Strong Heart* in 2013, he realized there was more to the story. *Adrift* is the second tale in the Strong Heart series.

These days Charlie lives in Tacoma, hikes in the Olympics whenever he can, and continues to spin yarns.

CPSIA information can be obtained
at www.ICGtesting.com
Printed in the USA
FSHW01n1546090918
51919FS